NOT LIKE THE MOVIES

Center Point
Large Print

Also by Kerry Winfrey and available from Center Point Large Print:

Waiting for Tom Hanks

This Large Print Book carries the Seal of Approval of N.A.V.H.

Kerry Winfrey

CENTER POINT LARGE PRINT
THORNDIKE, MAINE

This Center Point Large Print edition
is published in the year 2020 by arrangement with
Berkley, an imprint of Penguin Publishing Group,
a division of Penguin Random House LLC.

The text of this Large Print edition is unabridged.
In other aspects, this book may vary
from the original edition.
Printed in the United States of America
on permanent paper.
Set in 16-point Times New Roman type.

ISBN: 978-1-64358-706-6

The Library of Congress has cataloged this record
under Library of Congress Control Number: 2020942113

For Hollis.
You're so much better than the movies.

Chapter One

I can tell what's going on by the way the customer looks at me. The concentrated stare as I pour her coffee, the anticipatory smile as I put the lid on. This isn't someone who's only here for the caffeine hit. No, this is something different.

"Have a great—" I start as I hand her the drink, but she cuts me off.

"It's you, right?" she asks, breathless, eyes wide. "From the movie?"

I'm always friendly—some might say *too* friendly—to our customers here at Nick's coffee shop. It's kind of my thing. I don't even mind gruff patrons or rude comments; not because I'm a doormat, but because I'm genuinely not bothered by them. People have hard days, and while they definitely shouldn't take them out on their baristas, I know it's not about me.

But this . . . this is different. This couldn't be more about me.

"Um, yeah," I say, trying to keep my voice down. "It's me."

"There's an article about you on People.com," she says, the excitement palpable in her rushed words. "With . . . pictures."

I see her eyes dart toward my boss, Nick, who's tending to the espresso machine behind me. I wince before I can stop myself.

"Oh, is there?" I say, and before she can complete her nod, I smile brightly and say, "You know, I would love to chat more, but this is our afternoon rush and, whew, we're swamped!"

She smiles and walks away, so starstruck she doesn't notice that there's no one else in line. I let out a long sigh, then pull up People.com on my phone.

There it is. "The Real-Life Love Story Behind the New Film, *Coffee Girl*!"

There's a picture of me, one that I don't remember taking and certainly didn't give to *People* magazine, and there are a couple of pictures of Nick and me here, at work, behind the counter. The saving grace is that I was wearing an especially cute cardigan that day, one with little embroidered flowers and bees, so at least I look good, but that doesn't take away the strangeness inherent in seeing a picture of yourself that you didn't even know someone took.

But why am I, Chloe Sanderson, resident of Columbus, Ohio, and no one all that special, gracing the pages of People.com?

Because my best friend wrote a movie about me.

Okay, so Annie maintains that the movie isn't *about* me so much as *inspired* by me, and she's right. But anyone who knows me and sees the trailer can see the similarities. The movie's lead character, Zoe (come on, Annie), has a stubbornly, almost annoyingly positive attitude, even in the face of rude customers or family tragedy. She works in a coffee shop. She takes care of her sick father, although Zoe's father has cancer, while mine has Alzheimer's.

But there are a few key differences between Zoe and Chloe. Zoe is at least four inches shorter than me, with hair that has clearly been professionally styled. She has a team of stylists picking out her artfully vintage clothing, whereas I stick to the Anthropologie sale rack, where all the truly bonkers stuff lives. Oh, and Zoe makes out, and falls in love, with her boss, Rick.

The names, Annie. You couldn't have changed those names?

"Put your phone away. You're working."

Nick is so close I can feel his breath on my face. He smells, as usual, like coffee and this aftershave I've never smelled anywhere else, something that feels old-fashioned (like a grandpa) but kinda hot (not like a grandpa).

I jump, startled by his proximity, and shove my phone in my apron pocket. Nick and I do *not* talk about the movie; it's like the elephant in the room, if that elephant were making out with one of its elephant coworkers.

There are a few people clustered around tables,

9

but still no one in line. "Ah, yes, things are bustling," I say, gesturing at the nonexistent line. "I wouldn't want to ignore anyone."

"It's the principle of the thing," he says, staring at me for what seems like a beat too long. Or maybe it isn't.

The thing is, this ridiculous movie my best friend wrote (wow, that sentence will never stop sounding weird) has really screwed up a lot of things for me. Things I never thought about before, like whether Nick is sexy or whether his smile *means* something or what his perpetual five o'clock shadow would feel like on my cheek . . . all of a sudden those thoughts are in my head, and I don't like it. I'm just trying to work over here, you know? This is my job, and I need this to make money for the business classes I'm moving through at a glacial pace.

A new song starts playing: "Steal Away" by Robbie Dupree.

"Chloe," Nick says, his voice a low growl.

I straighten an already straight stack of cups to avoid looking at him. Why is he so close to me? Why does his voice naturally sound like that? My mind jumps automatically to the listicle I read on Buzzfeed yesterday: "Ten Reasons Why Rick from *Coffee Girl* is #relationshipgoals." Since the movie's not out yet, it's based entirely on the trailer, which I've watched approximately 9,756 times (give or take a few), mostly late at night

10

when I'm trying to sleep and I feel like punishing myself. *Reason #6: His voice sounds like he wants to argue with you and rip your clothes off. Maybe at the same time.*

The stack of cups goes crashing to the ground.

Nick and I bend down at the same time to pick up the cups, our faces way, way too close to each other. He seems unaffected by my presence; maybe he hasn't been reading the same Buzzfeed lists.

"Didn't I explicitly ban your yacht rock playlist?" he asks. "Didn't I tell you that if you played Robbie Dupree in this shop *one more time,* I wouldn't be responsible for what I'd do?"

I stand up, and so does he. "I don't remember any of those conversations. I only remember the vague sense of dread that overcomes me as I'm forced to reckon with my own mortality every time you play the depressing music you like."

I smile at him, back in my element: making fun of him for his god-awful taste.

Nick sighs, then gives me another one of those looks. It's kind of a smile but kind of a frown at the same time, which is a face he's really good at. I widen my eyes back at him.

This is the fun part, the part I love about work. I like arguing with Nick because it's not serious (I mean, I seriously do hate the music he listens to, but I don't actually care that much), but we both treat it like it's life and death. I don't even know if I'd like yacht rock half as much if I didn't have to defend it to him every day.

To Annie, a born-and-bred rom-comaholic, our playful banter means we're destined to be together. Because that's what happens in rom-coms, right? Two people who can't stand each other are actually hiding deep wells of passion, and eventually all those pent-up feelings will explode in one of those make-out scenes where shelves get knocked over and limbs are flying and people are panting.

But listen, I get angry with Siri when she willfully misunderstands me, and that doesn't mean I should marry my phone. Sometimes people just argue and don't want to make out with each other, because life isn't a rom-com (unless you're Annie and you're marrying a literal movie star).

Nick shakes his head and points toward the back of the store. "I'll be in my office. Think you can handle it up here?"

I gesture once more toward the mostly empty shop. Business isn't due to pick up for another hour. "Somehow, I'll manage."

I lean over the counter and pull my phone out again, but between you and me . . . yes, I do look up to watch Nick walk to his office. It's like that old saying, "I hate to see you go, but I love to watch you leave," except that it's, like, "I hate the depressing AF music you play, but I love to watch you leave because *fire emoji*."

Although it pains me to admit it, Nick Velez is objectively good-looking. He's tall and thin, with light brown skin, dark hair that's not too long or too short, and the aforementioned persistent scruff on his face. I don't think I've ever seen Nick clean-shaven, and I regularly see him at 5 A.M. That's just how his face looks, apparently.

But, unlike my romance-obsessed BFF, I am not someone who gets carried away by fantasies of love. Sure, Nick is hot, and okay, maybe I've had a couple of daydreams where he pins me against the brick wall of the coffee shop and rubs my face raw with his stubble, but there are lots of hot people in the world who aren't my boss. And since I kind of need this job, and I really need to keep my personal life as drama-free as possible, I think I'll stick to dating people who aren't intertwined in any other area of my life. Because taking care of my dad is messy enough, and I don't really need anyone else's feelings to worry about.

If only I could stop being so damn awkward around him.

My phone buzzes. It's Tracey Liu, the receptionist at my dad's care facility.

"Do you think you could check in for a minute when you get a chance? Your dad's having an episode."

Chapter Two

I find Nick in his office and tell him I'm going. Another reason why Nick is a great boss, despite his abysmal taste in music: he's always okay with me leaving, on no notice, to take care of my dad.

"Let me know how it goes, okay?" he says, concern in his deep brown eyes as he places a hand on my arm. I jerk my arm back so fast that I bump into the shelf behind me and knock an entire box of pencils onto the floor.

"Um, I . . ." I stammer, trying my best to get my bearings. I was fine until Nick touched me, that jerk. *Reason #8: Have you even* seen *the way he grabs Zoe before he kisses her in the rain?*

"I'll get them—you just get out of here," he says, and I exit his office with a wave.

I don't drive to work since Nick's is just a couple of blocks from my place, so I briskly walk down the brick sidewalks of German Village. This is why I usually wear flats or brightly colored sneakers—brick sidewalks are death traps if you're wearing heels. The early spring air is just slightly chilly, but the sun is hidden behind the perpetually cloudy Ohio skies, making it feel colder than it is. I wrap my mustard yellow pea coat more tightly around myself as I walk past the beautiful homes and businesses.

A short drive later, I buzz the door at Dad's facility and wait to be let in. The potential bad mood is coming over me, so I take a deep breath. Inhale positivity. Exhale stress. I smile along with my exhale, willing myself to be Good Mood Chloe for my dad, regardless of what greets me on the other side of the door.

Because no matter what I find—no matter what condition my dad is in—this is my responsibility. It's not my twin brother Milo's, because he lives in Brooklyn in an apartment I've never visited, on account of I can't fathom leaving my dad that long. And it sure as hell isn't my mom's, considering that she bounced right out of our lives when she left us for some dude she met on the Internet when Milo and I were ten.

It was the week before the fourth-grade Christmas pageant, aka the biggest event on my calendar at the time. Milo wasn't involved, because even back then he was too cool for earnest performances, but I was an angel narrator who delivered a lengthy speech about the importance of the baby Jesus's birth. (In retrospect, a public elementary school probably shouldn't have put on such an explicitly religious production, but what can I say? It was the '90s in Ohio, and anything went.) Mom was a fantastic seamstress who made most of her own clothing, and she promised to make me a costume that would leave all those donkeys and wise men in the dust, meaning that everyone in the audience would be unable to focus on anything but me, instead of the birth of our Lord and savior. Mom might not have said it that way, but that's the way I interpreted it.

But then she left with some dude named Phil, and I wasn't about to bother Dad or Milo by telling them I needed a costume. Dad was shell-shocked, staring at the TV for hours, and Milo was alternating between preteen anger and sobs. The worst part was that online dating as we know it didn't even *exist* back then, which meant that her leaving us for a guy she met online was Super Bizarre and basically a schoolwide scandal. Everyone, even my teachers, looked at me with pity.

So I got shit done. I tore the white bedsheets off my bed and, using the most rudimentary of sewing skills, fashioned them into a sort-of-toga, sort-of-angel-robe. I'm not saying it was the best angel costume the elementary school had ever seen, but it worked, and it was the first time I realized two things: I can only count on myself if I want to get something done, and I'm capable of doing pretty much anything.

I'm still smiling and deep-breathing as the door clicks unlocked and I walk through, right to the reception desk where Tracey's waiting for me.

"Everything's *okay,*" she says, hands out to calm me. "But I thought you might want to come see him."

Tracey covers the front desk at Brookwood Memory Care, but she's more than any old employee. She's sort of my ex—we went on a few dates, years ago, before it quickly became apparent that she was looking for a relationship and I was . . . well, not. But we stayed friends, and she was able to get my dad into Brookwood, which is a huge step up from his previous facility.

"What happened?" I ask, tugging on my tangled blond braid. When it comes to my dad, an "episode" can mean almost anything. There was the time he was convinced that the entire facility was being taken over by "the Amish" and wouldn't stop yelling about it. Or the time he slapped another resident because he was certain he'd broken his television. Or the time he claimed to be "starving," despite the fact that he'd eaten dinner half an hour before, and went on an hours-long rant about how "this hellhole" wasn't feeding him.

Tracey sighs, clearly not wanting to be the one to break this news to me. But I'm glad she is; I'm glad I can count on her to give me the full story.

"He says someone stole his watch," Tracey says. "He can't find it anywhere."

"And do you think someone really stole it?" I ask, even though I know the answer.

17

She shakes her head. "If you want to file a report, you can, but you know the drill. We'd have to involve the authorities, and—"

I hold up a hand. "No. I'll go talk to him. Thanks, Tracey."

I try to give her a look that says, *I value your friendship and appreciate you breaking this to me gently but also, man, this really sucks.*

I'm grateful for my friendship with Tracey, because here's the thing: sure, we didn't date for long, but we transitioned fairly seamlessly from "two people who might make out at any moment" to "two people who talk about feelings and get lunch sometimes and call each other for emotional support." I mean, I was there when she married her wife last year. But I've never—*never*—stayed friends with any man I've hooked up with. A week ago, a guy who took me out on two uneventful dates two years ago walked into the coffee shop, saw me, and turned right back around, and left.

I resent that, because I'm a wonderful friend. Attentive, loyal, helpful, ready to drop everything and get pizza at a moment's notice if you need to have a lengthy, emotional chat over a slice of pepperoni. But apparently dudes can't realize that . . . which is, of course, yet another reason I only date people who aren't involved in my personal life. I can't assume I'm going to meet another amazing friend like Tracey.

The TV blares through my dad's shut door. I

knock three times, right on the name tag. *Daniel Sanderson.*

When he doesn't answer, I slowly push the door open. "Dad?"

There's no telling what I'll find when I open his door. I'm not expecting full-scale catastrophe, of course, because the entire reason he's here at Brookwood is so a team of nurses and other trained professionals can care for him around the clock. But I don't know what his mood will be, how agitated he'll get, until I see him.

Bracing for the worst, I find him sitting in his recliner, remote in hand. He looks up.

"Hi, sweetheart!" His smile is so big it just about breaks my heart, because it's *him*. There he is. This is a good day, or at least a good moment.

"Hey, Dad," I say, leaning over to give him a hug. "How's it going?"

He gestures toward the TV, which is playing a rerun of *Three's Company*. He can't recall what he had for breakfast or whether I called him this morning, but he definitely remembers how much he loves *Three's Company*.

"Catching up on TV. You ever see this show?"

"Uh, yeah, Dad," I say, sitting down on the love seat as Jack Tripper concocts another sitcom scheme onscreen. "Listen, I talked to Tracey . . ."

He pauses, thinking.

"She works at the front desk," I say gently, willing him to remember.

"I know that," he says, an edge in his voice.

"She told me you think someone stole your watch." I observe his face.

He looks up and meets my eyes, instantly angry. "I don't *think* that, I *know* it. You're treating me like I'm a child, Chloe, like I don't know where my own stuff is. The people here are taking my things and I—"

I stand up and cut him off. "How about I look for it, okay?"

He makes a big show of shrugging. "You aren't going to find anything in here. I looked already and I can tell you, it's not in this room. Someone took it."

I suppress a sigh and look under the bed. Behind the toilet. In the shower. All places his things have "mysteriously" ended up before. Finally, I check the fridge, and behind the half gallon of 2% milk, there it is.

I hold up the watch. "Found it."

Dad squares his shoulders. "I did *not* put that there. Someone else must have snuck in here and—"

"Dad!" I nearly shout, before I can stop myself. "Why would someone do that? Why would one of the residents or one of the nurses come in here, find your watch, and hide it in the fridge? What kind of sense does that make?"

Dad looks away from me, toward his lap, and the expression that comes over his face is instantly familiar to me. Eyes cloudy, unfocused. "I don't know," he mutters, staring at his hands.

I'm well aware that my frustration doesn't help him—in fact, it makes it harder for him to communicate with me. Asking him questions and putting him on the spot only makes him more agitated and confused, and I know that. But when I'm dealing with the same problem again and again, it's hard to remember.

"Hey." I cross the tiny room in three steps. "I'm sorry for shouting. I didn't mean it, okay?"

He shakes his head. "I'm sorry, Chloe. I'm sorry this is happening and I'm . . . I'm sorry I'm such a burden."

This is the worst part, the part when he realizes what's happening. The part when he knows he has a disease, knows that his brain tissue is shrinking and his cells are degenerating, even if he can't say it in those words. I bite my lip and hold out an arm.

"You aren't a burden," I say with force, as if that will make my words stick in his brain. And I believe that. This is hard and it sucks, but if I have the choice between seeing this shitty glass as half-full or half-empty, then I'm gonna pick half-full every time. Because my dad may be different, but he's still my dad. Our relationship may not be what I wish it were, but at least we have one.

"Come on over to the love seat," I say. "I've

21

got some free time; let's find out what kind of zany hijinks Jack and the girls get into, okay?"

He smiles weakly and lets me guide him into the love seat, and I sit down next to him. We sit there, my head on his shoulder, and watch three entire episodes of *Three's Company* (I guess this basic cable channel is having a marathon), and I try my best to keep the sadness at bay and take this moment in. Because as bad as this is—as frustrated as I get, as worried as I am—it's only going to get worse. Barring some sort of miraculous overnight medical discovery, he isn't going to get better. He's going to forget my name, then he's going to forget my face, and then he's going to forget everything.

A fourth episode of *Three's Company* starts, that iconic theme song playing, and Dad leans into me. "This is the longest episode of *Three's Company* I've ever seen," he says, and even though I feel like crying, I can't help but laugh.

Chapter Three

If you're an outwardly optimistic person—someone who dresses in bright colors, who listens to pop music, who looks on the bright side and sees the silver lining and all those other refrigerator magnet clichés—people tend to think you're, well, kind of dim. Like maybe you don't know how to read, so you haven't seen those news articles about the unbearable atrocities happening all over the place every single day. That you're unaware of the real world, or worse, that you don't care that people are suffering constantly.

But I'd argue that it's the opposite. I *need* my optimism to get me through the day, because if I'm not listening to Christopher Cross sing a smooth jam about sailing, or wearing a heart-printed blouse, or creating some adorable llama-shaped sugar cookies with colorful royal icing, then I might stop to think for a second about what's actually happening in my life. That my dad is sick, that he's not going to get better, that my brother left me, that my mom is MIA, that my best friend's career is blowing up while mine is stalled, that I'm always going to be here while she jets off to New York or Los Angeles.

And that's, like, the tip of the suffering iceberg. For as bad as I have it, millions of other people have it so much worse. If I stop to think about all that, what am I supposed to do? Curl up in bed and never, ever get out?

No thanks. I'd much rather put on some yacht rock and get on with things.

Which is why, as I drive home from my dad's facility in the rapidly darkening evening, I'm loudly harmonizing with the Doobie Brothers, even as the weight of stress sits so heavy on my chest that I can barely breathe. I'm just so *tired*. Before I left Dad's place, I texted Nick that I wouldn't be back in to finish off my shift, which he characteristically accepted, promising to call in my well-meaning but incompetent young coworker, Tobin. Now I have to force all thoughts of Dad's decline out of my head and take a quiz for my online business class about . . . ugh, who even knows what?

And then there's the constant cloud of guilt that follows me around, hanging over my head and reminding me that I put my dad in an assisted living facility instead of keeping him home to take care of him myself.

I tried that, back when things with Dad were just starting to get bad, back when I assumed I could handle it all alone. I went to his house every morning and every night, and then, when I realized he was doing things like turning on the oven and forgetting about it, I started checking in during the day, too. When things got worse, I would come over to find him sitting in the yard, wondering how he got there, or staring into the pantry, completely forgetting what he came into the kitchen to do, or wandering around his garden in only his boxers and socks.

One day I went to check on him and found the front door wide open. I walked through the house, calling his name, trying not to panic and telling myself he was in the backyard. But he wasn't. He wasn't anywhere. It was a gray, rainy day, and as I stood there in the backyard figuring out what to do, I had one thought: *I lost him. I screwed up and I wasn't here and now the worst possible thing is going to happen.*

I called the police, keeping my voice steady as I told them what happened. I tried not to think about the horror stories I'd heard, about people with Alzheimer's who wandered off and got hurt or worse. And I hated myself for letting this happen.

The police found him a couple of harrowing hours later, wandering through a grocery store with a basket full of frozen food and insisting that he was just shopping for dinner. Outwardly, he seemed annoyed that I'd gone to all this fuss to hunt him down, but I saw the fear and confusion in his eyes.

Dad needed supervision 24/7, and the only way I could keep taking care of him myself was if I quit my job and moved in with him. I considered it. But while I might be patient and while I love my dad more than anything, I'm not a medical professional, and also I couldn't afford to be jobless.

Cobbling together Dad's social security, his veteran's benefits, his savings (which I had to put in a trust so that he could qualify for veteran's benefits, because this entire process *has* to be super confusing and time consuming), and my salary, I managed to afford a place with around-the-clock care where I know he's safe and secure. This is the one thing in my life I had to outsource, and even knowing that he's in the best place for him doesn't ease my guilt. There's still that little voice in my head, whispering, *You should be taking care of him yourself.*

I turn into the narrow driveway for my apartment (which is actually the carriage house behind the house where Annie lives with her uncle Don), debating what kind of pie I'm going to procrasti-bake tonight, when my headlights flash across a person. Two people. I slam on the brakes and scream, because this is it. This is the beginning of my murder story, the one that will eventually be told on the true-crime podcast about my death. Clearly whoever this is has been methodically stalking me for weeks—no, years!—and has finally come here to finish the deed, while Annie's out of town and Uncle Don's preoccupied with D&D and no one will hear me scream and—

Oh. I blink as I realize that one of the people is my brother.

I step out of the car and slam the door. "What are you doing standing in the middle of the driveway, you maniac?" I ask.

"Blasting the Doobs, huh?" He squints at me through his giant glasses (the kind that are in style but sort of make him look like a serial killer from the '80s), and that's when I remember that he's not alone. He's standing next to a tall, attractive, almost impossibly fit black man who I'm certain I've never seen before in my life. Trust me. I'd remember a man who looks this good.

I paste a smile on my face, using my years of customer service training. "I mean . . . um . . . to what do I owe this pleasure, brother?"

Milo steps toward me with his arms outstretched, his dirty-blond hair rumpled and his T-shirt wrinkled, and even though I've barely seen him for the past few years, I let myself sink into his hug. For one second, I bask in this familial embrace, but then I take a step back and smack him on the arm with my purse.

"What the hell, dude? I haven't seen you for, what, an entire year, and you show up in my driveway with no warning and a beautiful man?"

Milo gives the other man a smile, one of those *Sorry, this lady's crazy* smiles that I hate so much. The other man steps forward, offering me his hand.

"Fred," he says.

"It's so nice to meet you, Fred," I say sweetly, then turn back to Milo and hit him with my purse again. "I texted you last week about changing Dad's medication and you didn't even bother responding. You don't think you could've been, like, 'Okay, thanks for handling one hundred percent of our father's medical care and PS, I think I'm going to be back in Ohio next week'?"

Milo groans. "Chloe. This is exactly why I didn't tell you I was coming back."

"Great. Put it all on me."

Milo looks me in the eyes and then, there it is. My own smile mirrored back at me. "Hey. Can't you be glad to see your other half?"

The traitorous corners of my mouth start to twitch up in a smile. That's what Milo and I used to call each other when we were little: *my other half.* Back then, when we'd only been given an incomplete birds-and-the-bees lesson from a VHS tape my dad borrowed from the library that left a lot to the imagination, we thought that being twins meant we were actually two halves of the same person. And then Dad told us that "other half" was more typically used to refer to romantic partners and not so much fraternal

28

twins, but we didn't care because the description felt true. He's the irresponsible half, and I'm the responsible half. He's the half with his head in the clouds, I'm the half with her feet on the ground. Together we make one complete person, and knowing that he's been out there floating around Brooklyn for the past few years has made me feel, well . . . not whole.

"Damn it," I mutter, smiling, as I let him hug me again. I catch Fred's eye and he shrugs, signaling that he's already well aware of Milo's charm. "Just come inside," I say into Milo's shoulder.

"So how long has it been since you've been home?" I ask as Milo and Fred settle into the couch. My apartment, which is a glorified room above a garage, is tiny; one room with my bed, a couch, and a small, round kitchen table, with a sloping ceiling that means you can only stand up straight if you're directly in the middle of the room. At the back is the kitchen, separated from the rest of the apartment with a half wall, and only big enough for two people to squeeze in.

Milo shifts on the couch. "It's been . . . a while. Things have been busy."

"But now you're back," I say slowly, waiting for him to explain what he's here for.

"Now I'm back," he says, staring at me. A long silence hangs between us.

29

"This coconut cream pie is divine," Fred says, holding up the slice I gave him from the pie I had chilling in the fridge.

"Thank you, Fred." I smile. Frankly, Fred seems great. He's polite, he never abandoned me while I was taking care of my father, and he likes my coconut pie; what more could I want in a person? But right now, I'm a little more concerned with what my brother's doing here.

"Listen, I want to be here for Dad, all right? I know I missed a lot—"

I snort-cough.

"But I'm here now, okay?" Milo leans forward and looks at me with those big blue eyes that are also my big blue eyes and we're back to being seven years old, to me giving him all the cheese from my Lunchable because he asked nicely. I've never been able to resist him.

"Why are you really here, Milo?" I ask quietly.

"To see Dad," he insists. I look at Fred for help, but he's curiously focused on his pie.

"Is that the only reason?" I ask, familiar with Milo's belief that lies of omission don't count.

He shrugs and rolls his eyes. "I mean, I don't know, maybe the lease on our place was also up so it seemed like good timing. Among other reasons."

I stare at him. "You're not here for Dad. You're here because you need a place to live."

"Can't it be both?" Milo says, charming smile aimed in my direction.

"You can't stay here," I say, standing up and grabbing their empty plates. Milo follows me into the kitchen.

"I know. I know. I forgot that your place was so small."

"At least I have a place," I say icily, turning on the water and rinsing off the plates.

"Touché." Milo sighs. "I think we can stay with Mikey Danger. Remember him?"

I eye Milo. "How could I forget a high school classmate who tried to convince everyone his last name was *Danger?*"

"Well, he's no longer seventeen and he legally changed his last name to Danger. He's a delivery driver now but from what I've heard, he can still land a pretty sick ollie."

He trails off and gives me a wry look, and that's it. I can't help laughing. This is the allure of Milo, the reason I can't be mad at him even though he left me alone here to care for Dad, the reason I've *never* been able to be mad at him no matter what crap he pulls. The time he took my junior-year prom dress, the one I was saving because I loved it so much, and used it for a zombie bride costume. The time he ended up leaving that same junior prom with *my* prom date. All the times he was either too clueless or self-absorbed to notice anyone but himself—I've forgiven it all.

"Milo." I look at him until he looks me in the eye. "What's the deal with Fred?"

"We've been together for a few months," Milo says. "He's great, right?"

"I mean . . ." I peer over the half wall at Fred, who's on the sofa, scrolling through his phone. "Yeah. What does he do? Like, for work, if you guys work at all . . . ?"

"We work," Milo says, an edge to his voice. "Fred's a model."

"Oh," I say, still staring at Fred. "That makes sense."

"And I work—well, worked—in an upscale men's boutique. We met because Fred was a customer."

I frown. Milo says "upscale men's boutique" the way a server at a pretentious restaurant says "house-made artisanal sausage" when everyone knows it's just meat stuffed in a tube.

"And he's kind, and he's funny, and, I don't know. This feels . . . different than all the other guys I've dated."

"So you're settling down with Fred?"

He pokes my shoulder. "Settling down isn't so bad. You should try it."

I've never known Milo in a relationship, and not just because he's been living in another state for the past several years. He just never seemed all that interested in dating, but the way he's looking at Fred is something I've never seen on him before.

"Also, the man can put together a puzzle."

"Um," I say. "Is that some kind of euphemism?" Milo shoots me a look of disgust and pokes me in the shoulder again. "No, you perv. That's what we do for fun—puzzles. You really get to know someone when you're putting together a thousand-piecer of hot air balloons. Puzzles take patience. Attention to detail. Stamina."

I shake my head. "So what are you guys gonna do for work while you're here?"

Milo shrugs. "I'll get a job at a store."

I'd question his nonchalance, but he's right— this is the way it always works for Milo. Retail is where he shines, probably because he can talk to anyone and, after five minutes, know the name of their first pet *and* convince them to buy $500 worth of merchandise.

"And there's catalog work here. Fred can get a job anywhere. Look at him."

Fred looks up at us. "Fred can hear you, you know. Fred is about three feet away from the kitchen."

"Right." I nod.

"Small apartment," Milo says, but he's smiling at Fred, not caring even a little that Fred overheard him say that he plans on settling down. Fred smiles back at him and I get the distinct feeling that they no longer know I'm here.

I frown. "Maybe you two lovebirds should go make out at Mikey Danger's now. I feel like a third wheel in my own place."

Milo wraps me up in a hug again. "It's good to be back, you know? I missed home."

I don't know how Milo can be so Milo about this—so nonchalant about being technically homeless and jobless. I've spent my entire life pedaling at warp speed to avoid that exact situation, but he willingly put himself into it. He's the personification of those motivational posters that say, *Jump, and the net will appear,* whereas my motivational poster would say something like, *There is no net, so maybe reconsider jumping and just find a ladder or something?*

But he's here now. Milo. My other half. I look at his silly glasses and his messy hair and the blue T-shirt that I know he's wearing to make his eyes look bluer, because we have the same eyes and I do the same thing.

And even though I have a million and one reasons to be annoyed at him, I say, "I'm glad you're here," because it's the truth.

Chapter Four

If you'd told me when I graduated from high school that I'd be working in a coffee shop down the street from Annie's house when I was almost thirty, I probably wouldn't have believed you. But then again, I might have, because at eighteen part of me still sort of thought I'd become a mermaid when I grew up.

When Annie and I started college at OSU, she majored in film studies without giving it a second thought, while I went for the beloved major of aimless students everywhere: undecided.

College was a financial stretch for me, and instead of moving into the dorms, I moved into Annie and Don's carriage house. Don asked me to; he worried about Annie, he said, since her mom recently died of a heart attack. If she couldn't have her mom around during such a big transition, then maybe at least she could have a friend who felt like family. It was an easy decision, because I knew the feeling. Although my mom hadn't died, I'd accepted that she was dead to me and I would never see her again.

Don tried to get me to live there rent-free, but my Chloe Sanderson sense of pride wouldn't let me accept that offer. Instead, we agreed on a rent payment so low that it was almost embarrassing, but at least I was paying my way.

But college was harder than I expected. Not the classes themselves, but everything else in my life, like how my dad was starting to need my help more and more often. With Milo and me out of the house, I chalked up his frequent confused calls as the activity of a man who suddenly had way too much free time on his hands, but eventually I had to admit that something was wrong. Add that to the fact that I had no real career direction and very little money and, well, dropping out wasn't such a hard decision.

Over the next several years, as Annie graduated and pursued her writing dreams, I took a slew of jobs to support myself. None of them were glamorous and most of them were awful. Right around the time I realized I had to find an assisted living facility for my dad, I was fired from my crappy call center job (it turns out most employers do *not* like it when you routinely bail on your shift because you're having a family crisis).

In my state of financial despair and panic, I saw a sign. I mean, a literal sign, in the window of Nick's cozy, brick-walled coffee shop: *Now Hiring.* So I walked in, applied, and told him up front that I had to leave anytime my dad needed me. And whether it was desperation or something else that made him hire me, he said okay.

That was years ago and I've been here ever since, turning Nick's into not only my place of employment but also my home away from home. Eventually I started taking online classes to finally finish my degree. The only difference is that now I have enough direction to know what I really want to do—I want to own my own business, a place like Nick's but really *mine*. One where I can decide the menu, spruce up the boring walls, and create a homey café that makes everyone comfortable. A place where I can take care of people but, you know, get paid for it.

Until then, Nick's is where I shine. And now, as I'm sitting here with Annie at her usual table, I'm focusing on another venue where I can showcase my strengths: her wedding.

"I'm envisioning a pom wall," I say, spreading my hands in front of me.

Annie stares blankly from her seat across the table.

I sigh. "Have you never been on Pinterest, Annie?"

She shakes her head. "Only for writing mood boards."

"Wasn't your break over . . . oh, about ten minutes ago?" Nick asks from behind the counter.

"We're in a lull, Nick," I shout, not looking at him because I do *not* have time for the awkward jitters I get whenever his eyes are on me (*Reason*

#3: When you google the phrase bedroom eyes, *his picture comes up).*

I pull up a picture on my phone. "As I was saying. Pom wall. See, like this."

Annie and her fiancé, Drew, are getting married here in Columbus—down the street from Nick's, actually. It turns out Nick knows the guy who owns the building, and he has this loft space no one ever uses that will be perfect for a small wedding. It's big and open and the paint is peeling in that artfully decrepit way that makes for great Instagram photos. I'm thankful they're not getting married in some faraway city, like New York or LA or Shreveport, where Drew's from. I didn't even want to leave my dad for the premiere of Annie's movie (thankfully, she pulled some strings and worked out a Columbus premiere, which everyone is super excited about), so there's no way I'd feel comfortable jetting across the country for a celebration while God knows what happened in my absence.

"I just think it will add a nice pop of color to the whole 'abandoned warehouse' vibe," I say.

"It doesn't look like an abandoned warehouse," Annie says. "And you know I wanted to get married in the park, but it's spring, and no one else wants to stand out there if it's cold."

"True," I say. "I'm glad you're keeping this wedding super small, but I wish Drew would invite more celebrities. Especially hot ones. Brie Larson seems nice."

Annie presses her lips into a thin line, but I can tell she's amused. "I don't even know Brie Larson. I told you, we're keeping this small. And *secret*."

"I suppose that makes sense. But the pom wall. Think about it."

Annie wrinkles her nose, then takes a sip of coffee. "I don't know. That looks like a lot of work."

I throw up my hands. "Exactly! It's one of the most romantic things you can do with tissue paper!"

"And how many romantic things can you do with tissue paper?" she asks, eyebrows raised.

"If you have to ask, you don't want to know," Gary, one of our regular customers, says from his table, where he's clearly been listening to our entire conversation.

"Let me take care of the pom wall, okay?" I ask, getting up from the table.

"Are you sure?" Annie asks. "I mean, you have a lot on your plate . . ."

"Well, let's add a side dish of folded tissue paper, because mama's hungry," I say. Annie stares at me until I add, "This is why you're the writer, not me."

I tie my ruffled apron around my waist and leave Annie to her laptop. Back behind the counter, I salute Nick. "Reporting for duty."

He snorts. "It's a good thing you're not in the military. You'd be a god-awful soldier."

I place my hand over my heart. "Excuse me? I'd be a great soldier. I'd keep morale up and, you know, I'm sure all the other soldiers would appreciate a piece of lemon cream pie."

Everything feels so normal that I think the curse of the movie may be broken; maybe we're back to our typical banter and I can forget that the entire rom-com-loving Internet thinks we're meant to be.

But then Nick turns to look at me and stares. Again, longer than is necessary. I count one breath, two breaths, and we're still looking at each other, like this is a thing regular people do. It's like we're communicating with our eyeballs but I have no idea what we're saying and I need to do something fast to end this silence so—

"I mean, unless they were lactose intolerant. In which case I'd make them a dairy-free lemon cream pie, which I know sounds impossible because it's, y'know, in the name. Lemon *cream*. But I bet with a little bit of online research I could figure out a suitable substitute and oh look! A customer!"

I shake my head quickly and paste on my customer service smile, taking an order for a butterscotch latte from a regular. I don't let myself turn around to look at Nick, because I'm afraid he'll still be there, looking at me, letting me stammer on for minutes about the possibility of dairy-free pies.

The customer pays and Annie catches my eye. *What was that?* she mouths, and I shake my head. I finally look over my shoulder and practically slump with relief when I see that Nick isn't standing there anymore; he must've gone into the kitchen. Now I don't have to think about his hot face or his expressive eyes or that stupid scruff on his chin that should not even be this much of a turn-on.

I don't get awkward. I don't stammer. I certainly don't ramble about desserts.

But something about this ridiculous movie is making everything go haywire.

Chapter Five

As usual, I have about ten million things to do, but when Milo asks me to help him move into Mikey Danger's guest room, I say yes. This is how it's always been. Milo says jump, I say how high. Or, more accurately, Milo whines at me to jump and I bitch at him for a few minutes and then do it anyway, because family comes first.

Blessedly, Milo and Fred crammed very few personal belongings into the tiny rental car they drove from wherever they lived in Brooklyn (I know it's not accurate, but after watching so many sitcoms I imagine everyone in Brooklyn lives in a giant loft), so we borrow Nick's truck and load their boxes into the back. Of course, the Ohio skies pick this day to release a torrential downpour, so we secure an ugly bright blue tarp to protect everything.

"Damn," Milo says, crammed behind me in the back seat of the truck's cab. "Your boss has a nice truck."

"I didn't know you cared about trucks," I say.

"I don't, but I can appreciate a quality ride when I see it," Milo says, sounding offended. He continues muttering to himself as I drive slowly, trying to avoid harming Nick's spotless truck. "It's positively *roomy* back here."

I tear my eyes away from the road long enough to shoot an eyebrows-raised glance at Fred in the passenger seat, and he smiles back at me.

"Is his name really . . . Mikey Danger?" Fred asks in a low voice.

"It wasn't the name his parents gave him," I say, "but if he's anything like he was ten years ago, I think you'll agree with me that he's always been Mikey Danger at heart."

Mikey lives right by Ohio State University on a street full of duplexes inhabited by constantly inebriated college students. I suspect the reason Mikey, a man who is almost in his thirties, chooses to live among twenty-one-year-olds is that he has the soul of a twenty-one-year-old.

The three of us ring the doorbell and huddle on Mikey's front steps as raindrops pelt our one umbrella. I kick a crumpled can of Bud Light off the steps, then feel bad and pick it up. I look out over the yard full of overgrown weeds and say, "Milo, there has *got* to be somewhere else you guys can live."

"Where else are we supposed to go?" Milo asks. "We spent last night on your floor and I would be *happy* to stay there, but honestly you didn't project a welcoming spirit toward us."

"We don't want to sleep on your floor," Fred reassures me.

"It's just nice to be asked," Milo mutters.

"I appreciate that," I say. "But I think—"

The door swings open to reveal Mikey Danger, in the flesh. A lot of flesh. He's wearing shorts and no shirt, despite the fact that the sky is currently spitting cold rain. He smells like weed and he looks like a less-good-looking version of Jake Gyllenhaal. Like, if Jake Gyllenhaal were making a surprising cameo in an indie comedy as a hilarious stoner? That's Mikey Danger's look.

He squints at all three of us in turn, then shoves a twenty at us.

"I'm sorry?" I ask.

"Keep the change," he reassures me as he starts to shut the door. He stops, opens it again, shakes his head. "Oh. Duh. I didn't even get my food."

"Mikey," Milo says patiently, adjusting his glasses. "We're not delivery people. It's me, Milo. My boyfriend and I are staying with you?"

Mikey's eyes widen as the realization dawns. "Oh! This makes so much more sense. I was like, 'When did restaurants start sending three delivery people?'"

"It's raining," I state, and Mikey nods before moving aside so we can enter.

With all of us crammed into the dirty kitchen, Milo introduces Fred and points to me. "And you remember Chloe."

Mikey looks me up and down. "Chloe. Yeah. I remember Chloe."

"Hi, Mikey," I say. I don't know what he's remembering, since the extent of our interaction was working together on a Revolutionary War project in ninth grade that involved me doing all the work. However, I am unfortunately forced to admit that "less-good-looking Jake Gyllenhaal" is a vibe that I'm into.

This kitchen, though? Not so much. There's an overwhelming amount of stuff in such a small space; Milo attempts to lean against a counter and knocks over several empty soda bottles. He leans over to pick them up and Mikey murmurs, "Don't worry about it."

"This is great, Mikey," Milo says with bravado. He's trying to save face, trying to convince me that this is really a great idea and that living with Mikey Danger is going to be nonstop fun, because he's always been unable to admit when he's wrong. Milo looks at me and flashes a giant smile, and I roll my eyes.

I help them carry in the rest of their few boxes, wading through a messy living room that boasts a futon, a TV, and nothing on the walls. The guest room is similarly bare—a bed and one tiny window that overlooks the patchy grass outside.

"Home sweet home," Milo says with a contented sigh, and then he leans in to give me a hug. "Thanks for helping us. I mean it."

"Um . . . you're welcome," I say, unexpectedly touched. Fred gives me a quick hug, too, and then both of them walk me to the door. Mikey Danger is now cooking something unspecified at the stove.

"See ya, Chloe," he says, raising his spatula. "Gimme a call sometime if you ever want to . . . gimme a call."

"I probably won't do that, Mikey."

He nods, accepting this.

As I step out the door and Milo and Mikey are in conversation about something, Fred grabs my arm, his eyes wide, looking like Tyra Banks just asked him to do *abject fear at the idea of living in a nightmare garbage dump, but make it fashion.* "Take me with you," he whisper-hisses.

"You'll be out of here so soon," I promise, then step on another beer can that somehow materialized on the front steps. I think about asking him why he's with my brother—why he even agreed to come all the way to Ohio—but it's still raining, hard, so I pull my hood over my head and run toward Nick's truck.

"Sorry, sorry, sorry," I say, rushing through the coffee shop and into Nick's office. I slide out of my coat, spraying water everywhere. "I know I'm late. It took way longer than I expected because of the rain and—"

"It's okay." Nick looks up from his computer, where I presume he's balancing the books. Or reading fan fiction about Canadian ice dancers.

Nick's a private man, so who knows. Perhaps the greatest part of the Nick Velez allure—I mean, not that he has an allure to me, but if he did—is the mysteriousness. What does he do when he's not working? What goes on inside that head?

"Ugh," I say, wiping my bangs off my forehead. There's no mirror in Nick's office because it's Nick's office, but I can tell my sopping wet hair isn't exactly a great look. "I'm disgusting. Customers are going to be like, 'Who let a soaking wet golden retriever become a barista?'"

Nick stops what he's doing and focuses on me. "You look good, Chloe. You always look good."

He doesn't say it dismissively, like he wants me to shut up and stop complaining. He says it matter-of-fact, like it's so obvious, and the way he's staring at me makes me feel hot and tingly. I can feel my skin growing pink under his gaze.

"Uh, okay, well," I say, bumping into a shelf. "Better go help Tobin. God knows what he's getting into up there."

I make my way behind the counter and exhale loudly. Good Lord. This is Nick. I need to be professional, and I need to focus on my job and school and my dad and *not* the unbridled lust that is currently running rampant through my entire body.

Tobin stares at me, not moving.

"What's wrong, Tobin?" I snap, then feel bad

because it isn't his fault I have an uncomfortable amount of sexual tension with Nick. "I mean, why are you staring at me?"

"I heard this story, on NPR," he says slowly, which isn't unusual, because Tobin says everything slowly, "about how measles are making a comeback. You know, because people don't vaccinate their kids or whatever?"

"Right," I say, wondering what this has to do with me. "Wait, you listen to NPR?"

"And, like, no offense? But you look hella sick right now."

I stare at him.

"Not sick in the good way, like, 'Your new tat is sick.' Like, you're really red."

"Ugh." I rub my hands over my face. "I promise I don't have measles, okay?"

"Actions speak louder than words when it comes to infectious diseases," says Gary, who's standing at the front of the line, waiting for a refill on his usual black coffee.

"Do you want me to cough on you so we can watch you *not* get measles?"

Tobin shakes his head. "Nah. Nick says we're not supposed to cough on customers."

Gary waves a hand at me. "Psh. Cough on me all you want, Chloe. I can take it."

Maybe it's all the infectious-disease talk, or maybe it's the Radiohead that Nick is playing, but I'm feeling much less turned on now. "Hand me your cup, Gary," I say, and I finish the rest of my shift in a state of blissful distraction.

That is, until I have to close.

Tobin departs to go do whatever it is Tobin does when he's not at work and leaves me alone with our quiet weeknight crowd . . . and Nick. The rain means there are even fewer people than usual in the shop, and since Nick's still in his office, I turn off his Bill Callahan tunes and take the liberty of putting on some yacht rock. Yacht rock, in case you're not familiar, is the smoothest, chillest music of the late '70s and early '80s (although the yacht rock spirit, if you ask me, can belong to music of any era). It's music that always sounds upbeat, that makes copious references to sailing, that is best enjoyed while sipping a tropical drink with one of those little paper umbrellas. And it's my genre of choice, because it's fun and the lyrics never make me pause and think about the realities of my life. Unlike Nick's music, which seems expressly designed to make a person reflect on regrets and losses, yacht rock will never let you down. It will never make you sad. It will always be there, with a buoyant beat and a smooth male vocal (there aren't a lot of ladies in yacht rock).

When our last customer leaves (Gary; it's always Gary), I flip the *Closed* sign over. For a moment, I peer into the dark night at the rain that's coming down even harder than it was earlier. My walk home is short, but it's much more pleasant when it doesn't involve getting soaked. And it's not like I want to ask Nick for a ride home because, well, the last thing I need to do is put myself in a confined space, like a pickup truck, with him. I might be unable to avoid flinging myself at him, which would at best cause some awkwardness and at worst cause a car accident.

But I can't pretend that my respect for vehicular safety is the only reason I'm reluctant to give in to our physical connection. The truth is, I have enough responsibilities already without having to manage another person's feelings. And while Nick may act all quiet and mysterious, the sad male indie rock playlists I've had to listen to let me know the truth. Somewhere underneath that gruff exterior, Nick Velez has feelings, and I sure don't want him spraying any of them in my general direction.

I pop behind the counter to crank up the music, then put the chairs up on the tables. As I grab the broom to sweep up the empty sugar packets and napkins that cover the floor, "Steal Away" starts playing.

"Take me away, Robbie Dupree," I whisper to myself as I sweep the floor with a little more bravado than usual. The rain is pouring down outside and I spent my day helping my brother move into a hellhole and I didn't visit my dad tonight which makes me possibly the worst daughter in the world, but for now, it's just me and the smooth, smooth music. I shake my shoulders, let my hips wiggle, do a slight body roll. When the song gets to its breakdown, I belt the lyrics into the broom handle/microphone and spin around to see Nick standing three feet away from me, arms crossed.

I shriek and throw the broom at him.

He catches it, his eyes wide. "What the hell?"

"I didn't know you were there," I shout. "Way to sneak up on me."

"I work here," he says, starting to sweep where I left off. "In case you forgot."

Lightning flashes and the power flickers. "Well, so do I, and *I'm* sweeping." I grab the broom out of his hands, my fingers brushing against his.

"You are . . . *tense* today," Nick says, leaning against the counter and shoving his hands in his pockets.

My shoulders are near my ears as the power flickers again. A crack of thunder booms as I flash him my trademark Chloe Sanderson smile, the one that charms customers and elderly people. "I have a lot going on."

"Want to . . . talk about it?" Nick's voice is tentative, and for good reason. We don't normally "talk about" anything, unless we're talking about how much the other person's musical selections annoy us. Sure, I tell him when I have to leave to take care of my dad . . . but the other stuff? Feelings? Personal lives? The movie? It's all off limits. But then again, the two of us are usually surrounded by people, and it's hard to have a serious conversation when Gary's around.

"There's nothing to talk about," I say, my tone as brisk as my efficient broom sweeps. "Everything's gravy."

"Gravy?" Nick says from behind me, sounding disgusted. "Is that supposed to be good?"

"Duh," I say. "Everyone loves gravy."

"Well, they wouldn't love it if *everything* was gravy. I can tell you that much for free," Nick mutters.

"Okay, grandpa." I think about how he smells like a sexy grandpa and I remind myself not to get close enough to find out if he smells like that right now.

I hum along with the music, aware of Nick watching me. It's not like I can sweep the floor in a suggestive manner (not that I even want to), so I try to be competent. But then he says, so quietly I almost can't hear him, "You don't have to take everything on by yourself, you know."

I stop, broom in midair, then spin around. "What?"

The lights turn off for one second. Two seconds. We stare at the ceiling, as if the answers to something are up there, until they

52

flicker back on. Nick looks at me again. His face is even scruffier than usual at this time of night. "I said, you don't have to do everything all by yourself."

I snort and grip the broom handle tighter. "Okay. Uh, thanks for the advice." I know he's only offering me a platitude that's meant to make me feel better, but it pisses me off. Like he knows. Like he even knows *half* of what I'm carrying on my shoulders.

"Seriously," he says. "I can finish up here. Go home and go to bed."

Bed. The thought of sinking into my mattress, listening to the rain fall on the sloped roof of the carriage house as I'm tucked under the orange, white, and yellow quilt I found at a yard sale, sounds so good that I almost melt into a puddle right there on the floor. The mere idea of sleeping *all by myself* is almost sensual. But I have some busywork assignment for one of my online classes that needs to be finished by tomorrow, and if I'm up then I might as well make a pie because I have the crust chilling in the fridge, and I can see the way this night is gonna go. It's not going to involve bed in any way, shape, or form until at least 3 A.M.

"You sure you don't wanna talk about it?" Nick asks, his voice uncertain and low. And I don't know what it is. If it's the fact that rain has always made me feel safe, or the fact that everything's built up so much that it has to explode, or that I'm so tired. At least if I'm talking about my shitshow of a life, then I'm not thinking about how Nick's ass looks in his jeans, which is obviously *not* an appropriate place for my mind to wander.

I don't know why Nick is asking me, what's making him push his way into the uncharted waters of my personal life, but I don't even hesitate before I unload it all on him.

I lean against the broom handle, one hand on a hip like I'm about to start a stand-up set. "Well, my dad's been accusing the staff members at his facility of stealing from him, which is a real bummer because they definitely aren't and so he's worked up and they keep calling me and it's all a big mess. Since no one else is around to take care of him, it's kind of my problem. And, as you know, Milo's back in town, but he hasn't given me an apology or anything for leaving me here to care for our father. He did, however, expect me to help him move into a terrible duplex that, oh yeah, is owned by a grown-ass man who chooses to call himself Mikey Danger. Also I have business school homework. And I need pie but pie doesn't currently exist."

I take a deep breath. "Oh, and my back hurts. I've been standing all day."

Nick walks toward me, closing the gap between us in a couple of long-legged steps. I stop breathing when he's in front of me, the way you do when you step outside into freezing weather; his nearness is a shock to my system.

He puts a hand on my arm; that's all it is. A hand on an arm, but it feels like more than that. "That sucks, Chloe," he says.

"Why are you being so nice to me?" I ask, desperately trying to avoid the small fire burning under his hand. "Shouldn't you be making fun of me or something? Or complaining about how I'm not working hard enough?"

Nick gives me a half smile, one eyebrow raised. "I think we both know how hard you work."

I swallow hard as "Steal Away" ends. And then, as we stand there staring at each other in the empty coffee shop, broom forgotten, the opening notes of "Steal Away" start to play. Again.

"Chloe," Nick says, and I really wish he would stop saying my name, because every time he does I imagine him saying it in other contexts and in other places, like against my lips or in my ear. "Didn't we already have a conversation about the song 'Steal Away'?"

"Perhaps," I whisper.

"And what song is playing on repeat right now?"

I take a breath. The words come out shaky. " 'Steal Away' by Robbie Dupree."

He still smells like a sexy grandpa, and I hate that this is turning me on.

The lights go off again, and this time, they

don't come back on after two seconds. We stand there in silence and darkness, except for a lightning flash that illuminates Nick's face. He is too close to me, and his hand is entirely *too* on my arm. I can barely see him, but I can feel him, the warmth and Nick-ness of him right in front of me, the heat from his chest radiating toward me like he's a portable space heater. I want to hold out my hands in front of his chest to warm them.

I should take a step back, away from his hand. I should go find my coat, walk home, let the rain function as a cold shower, and then go to bed, where he can haunt my erotic dreams and nightmares. That would be the logical thing to do.

But I'm not always a logical person.

"The last time I played Robbie Dupree . . ." I say in a low voice. He leans in closer to hear me. "You said you wouldn't be responsible for what you'd do."

My eyes adjust to him in the glowing red light of the *EXIT* sign. I may be imagining it, but I think I see the outline of his Adam's apple bob as he swallows. "I did say that."

Reason #9: You know that grumpy demeanor is just hiding secret wells of passion.

"Well, Nick," I say, attempting to sound more confident than I feel. I'm poking at him, needling him, pushing him with the typical banter we always use, but even I know that this feels

56

dangerous. This feels like I'm going too far. "What are you going to do?"

Without replaying security footage, I'll never know the exact order of events, whether Nick grabs my hips or whether I grab his shoulders first. All I know is that we smack into each other like high-powered magnets, locking so tight that no one could pry us apart. Every second of built-up tension that's occurred during all of our ridiculous arguments explodes here, now, as his mouth covers mine. I'm so out of my mind that I wonder if we're going to have sex right here on one of the café tables, which seems unsanitary, but also maybe like a good idea. My hands run up and down his body, which I've admired but never been able to touch. There's just so much of him, and I want to get my hands on every single inch of it.

He's not built like a bodybuilder, and I'm not tiny, but he effortlessly spins me around and pushes me up against the brick wall, pinning me there with his mouth and his hands. I'm making noises I didn't even know I was capable of making, and listen, I've made some noises before, okay? His hands are rough on my neck and I think I'm going to die if I don't feel them all over my body tonight. His tongue in my mouth makes me forget about everything—my dad, Milo, school. This is Nick Velez, and he's kissing me up against a brick wall like he's been training his entire life for this.

Wait.

This is *Nick Velez*. As in, the guy I have to work with day in, day out. The guy I'm going to have to continue seeing in a professional context, even though I now know exactly how his tongue feels against mine.

"Ack!" I shout, pushing him off me.

He shouts back.

"What are you shouting at?" I ask, wiping my mouth.

"I don't know!" He throws his hands in the air, his breathing ragged. "You startled me!"

"This," I say, pointing back and forth between us even though it's dark and he probably can't see the gesture I'm making. "This is not a good idea, Nick."

"Maybe I'm misreading some context clues, but it seemed like we both thought it was a good idea thirty seconds ago." Nick crosses his arms.

"Well, we were wrong!" I say, waving my arms wildly. "We were under the spell of the rain and the music and the power outage. Everyone knows power outages are extremely sexy."

Even in the dark I can tell he's smiling, that infuriating Nick Velez half grin, the one that means he finds me funny even when I'm not trying to be. "*Does* everyone know that?"

"Weather phenomenons are sexy!" I shriek. "I can't help it that a thunderstorm is affecting my libido. This was . . . not smart. We work together."

Nick rubs his hands over his face. "Shit. Right. You're right. I'm your boss and I came on to you. That was . . . God, that was not okay."

"Oh, give me a break," I say, getting angry. "You're my boss in name only. I practically run this place half the time. You didn't bully me into sticking my tongue down your throat, okay? I have some agency here. I came on to *you*."

"Even if you came on to me, it's not—"

"We both," I say slowly, "need to stop saying the word *came*."

The lights flicker, then come back on. "Great timing," I say to the ceiling.

I hazard a glance at Nick. He's looking straight at me. I can still feel the scratch of his stubble against my cheek, the way his hands grabbed my ass, the feel of his—

Well. There are a lot of things I'm going to have to excise from my memory.

"This was a mistake," I say, my voice firm. "Both of us have been acting weird ever since stuff with Annie's movie started ramping up—"

"You think this happened because of the movie?"

"And the Buzzfeed lists."

"What the hell is a Buzzfeed?"

"Why are you a million years old?" I shout.

"Wait. Forget it. I don't have time to explain the concept of websites to you. We have to remember that Annie's movie is fictional. It's about characters, not about the real us, the people who should absolutely, under no circumstances be making out in their place of work. We just . . . need to forget about this."

"Chloe."

"Stop saying my name."

Nick scowls. "Fine. Valued Employee . . . I think this is going to be a little hard to forget about."

"Well, try," I say, taking off my apron and tossing it over the counter. "Put the memories in the ol' spank bank and throw away the key, dude."

Nick screws up his face into a look of horror. "You are *disgusting,* you know that?"

"All the more reason to pretend this never happened," I say. "You good with cleaning up the rest of this?"

He takes a step toward me. "At least let me give you a ride home. It's pouring."

"Nope." I walk into his office and emerge with my coat. "Let the rain baptize me and wash away this evening."

"Stop being dramatic and listen to me. You're right, okay? We shouldn't have done . . . what we did. We work together, and this will make things awkward, and . . . I'm sorry, okay?"

I stop in my tracks. Obviously I wanted Nick to agree with me, to concur that this was all one big mistake and that we, as coworkers who see each other every day, shouldn't be involved in any sort of physical manner. So why does hearing him say those words out loud make me . . .

Disappointed?

I turn around and pull my hood over my head. "Yep."

He takes a step toward me, and then another. My heartbeat quickens as his heavy boots step across the creaky wood floor, and I know I should move. I should go home. But I can't, because I don't know what's going to happen, or what I want to happen . . .

He holds out a hand, pinky crooked.

"Um . . ." I say.

"Pinky swear," he says, so seriously you'd never know he's uttering words primarily used by junior high school students.

I hold out my pinky and hook it in his.

"Nothing happened," he says, holding my gaze, not blinking.

I stare right into his brown eyes. "Nothing happened," I whisper.

And then I let go and bolt out of the shop. The rain has let up to a light drizzle, so I take my hood off and let my head get wet. With the power restored, the glow from the neighborhood businesses and homes makes the wet sidewalks shine, lighting my way home.

Nothing happened, I remind myself as I touch the tip of my pinky finger to my mouth, pretending that it's Nick's mouth instead.

Chapter Six

It all started when I made a bad pie.

The dough seemed fine when I rolled it out. It was sturdy, smooth, and flecked with butter. My filling, a peach, whiskey, and ginger mixture, was sweet and spicy and just the right amount of boozy. I crimped the hell out of that crust, stuck it in the oven, and prepared to have a beautiful, delicious dessert when the timer went off.

Only that's not what happened. When I pulled my pie out of the oven, the crust was shrunken and warped, burned in places and almost raw in others. When it finally cooled enough for me to cut into it, the filling oozed out, far too liquidy. And that once-beautiful crust had, as the judges on *The Great British Bake Off* are all too fond of saying, a soggy bottom.

In other words, it was a pie disaster of epic proportions, and I took it personally. How could I have screwed this up so monumentally? I mean, isn't the saying "easy as pie" supposed to mean something? How is it that I can make a baked Alaska, turn out a perfect tray of macarons, and decorate a layer cake in my sleep but I can't master pastry dough?

And so Project Pie began. I started experimenting with different fats—lard, butter, shortening, a mixture of butter and shortening. I added vinegar. I added buttermilk. I added vodka. I used a pastry cutter, a food processor, my bare hands. I tried every thickener out there for my fruit fillings: flour, cornstarch, tapioca, arrowroot powder. I made lattice crusts, cut decorations out of dough, tried egg washes, milk washes, cream washes, you name it.

It worked—I made some good pies. Some great pies, even. But have I hit upon that mythical perfect pie, the one with a flaky-yet-flavorful crust and a filling that sets up and tastes so good that I can't stop eating it? No. And so my quest continues.

Tonight, after I read some article for class and write a quick reaction paper, I pull my pie dough out of the fridge. That's the first secret of good pie: just as in yacht rock, everything needs to be very chill.

After covering the counter in plenty of flour, it's time for my favorite part: rolling out the dough. At first, this was the part of pie making that scared me. What if I tore a hole in the dough? What if it got stuck? What if it . . . sucked?

But a few pies in, the practice of rolling out the dough became truly therapeutic. In my tiny kitchen, it's me and the dough, working out our annoyances. Sure, maybe I'm bringing an unhealthy amount of sexual frustration to this pie-making session, but the dough can keep a secret. It isn't going to tell anyone that I want to jump my boss's bones and totally have sex in his office.

I pause and blow my bangs off my forehead. Not that I've imagined that scene, or anything.

Once my dough is securely in the pan, back in the fridge it goes (remember: the dough must be more chill) as I get my filling all mixed up. Tonight it's an apple-cinnamon-ginger mixture—perfect for a rainy and cold night, not that I'll be eating it tonight. Perhaps one of the biggest pie mistakes is cutting into it immediately after it comes out of the oven. I mean, is it warm and delicious and kinda irresistible? Yes. But resist it you must, because if you cut into it now, all will be lost. Your filling will gush out and leave your pie one big, deflated mess.

Patience is a virtue when it comes to pie. By tomorrow morning, when the pie is cooled and I've slept at least a few hours, I'll have a (hopefully) delicious pie ready for breakfast, and the fact that I threw myself at Nick tonight will be nothing but a distant memory.

But first, I need to talk about it with someone.

Hey. I tap out a quick text to Annie. Are you home, or are you in LA at Drew's love nest?

In approximately five seconds, I hear Annie's feet clomp up the stairs before the door swings open. "It's his house, not a love nest," she says. "And I'm here. I don't leave until tomorrow morning."

My entire body relaxes as soon as I see her. Of course, I know she'd still talk through my Dark Night of Sexual Frustration even if she were out of town, but FaceTime has its limitations. Annie might be a truly hopeless romantic who thinks every part of my life story is merely a beat in a rom-com script, but she's still my best friend. The one who knows everything about me, better than anyone else.

But keeping up with her schedule these days would be difficult even if I didn't have a million things on my mind. Sometimes she's home, staying in her old bedroom and planning stuff for her wedding and her movie premiere. Sometimes she's in LA, doing whatever it is she has to do to get a movie made (I space out during those parts of the conversation, honestly) or hanging out with Drew when he's on breaks from the sitcom he's starring in. And sometimes she's in New York, doing even more things I don't understand.

And listen, it's not like I want her life to go back to the way it was when she lived with Uncle Don full time and she was an Internet content writer who wrote listicles about, like, snack foods and home repairs and celebrity hairstyles. But there was a comfort in knowing she was always next door, hunched over her laptop on the couch or in her twin bed, typing away into the night as she wrote her articles or her screenplay. I'm happy that she's finally pursuing her dream and kicking ass at it—I mean, she has a real, big-time job, like an almost-thirty-year-old should. But part of me can't help but feel a little left behind.

"Um, it smells amazing in here," she says, kicking off her shoes and sitting down on my bed, moving some of my approximately one hundred throw pillows out of the way. "What did you make?"

"An apple-ginger pie," I say, sitting down beside her and laying my head on her shoulder. "It won't be ready until tomorrow. By the way, I made out with Nick."

Annie slides her shoulder out from under my head and looks me straight in the eyes, her mouth hanging open. "Is this a joke?"

I shake my head, thinking about the way his hands gripped my body. "This isn't a joking matter."

"Oh, wow." Annie puts a hand over her heart. "Did I . . . write this into existence?"

"Annie."

"I mean, I always knew you and Nick had a thing for each other, but for this to happen now, right before the movie comes out . . . I feel so powerful."

"Annie. Stop." I roll my eyes. "Yes, we made out, and yes, I blame you, but not because we're, like, meant to be or whatever. You know I only believe in that kind of thing for sentimental freaks like you and Drew."

She smiles smugly.

"That kind of thing doesn't exist for us mere mortals. But your movie put all kinds of ideas into my head. Think about how you would feel if there were frequent listicles online about all the reasons why your boss was super hot and why the upcoming movie about your life was, and I quote, 'relationship goals.' "

Annie leans back against my pillows. "There are a lot of articles about how my fiancé is the Internet's boyfriend, in case you forgot. And that list where he was named the second-sexiest celebrity named Drew."

"True." Sometimes, I forget that Annie's betrothed is a literal movie star, and that she met and fell in love with him in a positively rom-com-esque series of misunderstandings and tropes. Although now I know him as my BFF's future husband, he was, for a while, known for being in a movie where he was shirtless and covered in grease/jumping out of exploding helicopters/ having sex with former models who were trying their hands at acting.

"I still think it's wrong that the Property Brother beat him," she continues. "Drew isn't even the hot Property Brother. Everyone knows that's Jonathan."

"Annie," I say. "I think you're taking a random Internet list a little too seriously. And anyway, it's not the same. You and Drew were already bonkers for each other by the time gossip websites even cared who you were. No offense."

"Absolutely none taken."

"You don't have to deal with the stress of people writing about something that isn't even happening."

Annie raises her eyebrows. "It *did* happen. Tonight." She leans forward. "Can you please describe the entire event in detail?"

"No!" I look at her in horror. "You'd probably write it into a movie."

She shrugs.

I sigh and lean against the wall. "I'm sorry I made you come over here—I'm sure you're busy with work and planning a wedding. Although you'd be less busy if you took your time with wedding planning, like most people. Like, have it next year or something."

"Nah." She inspects the stitches on my quilt. "We don't want to wait that long."

"But why are you insisting on planning an entire wedding in one month? I barely have enough time to make a sufficient quantity of poms!"

Anne sits up straight, eyes wide. "I told you not to worry about the poms!"

I hold out my hands. "That wasn't a complaint.

I'm living for this pom wall. All I'm saying is, I don't get why you're rushing this. You and Drew are the real thing and . . . Wait, are you guys, like, waiting?"

She looks at me and blinks a few times.

"You know. Are you waiting until you get married to have sex?"

"Chloe!" Annie's mouth drops open. "Do you not remember that I texted you after the first time Drew and I slept together?"

"Oh, yeah." I cross my arms. "With details about his penis."

"Which is why, frankly, I think you owe me details about your after-hours make-out sesh with Nick."

"I only *felt* his penis through multiple layers of fabric, so I have very little to offer," I say, then stand up. "I'm gonna open a bottle of wine. You want a glass?"

She waves a hand, back to inspecting the quilt. "Um, no. I'm good."

"But . . . drinking wine and talking about my hookups is one of your favorite activities," I say. She still doesn't look at me, and the realization washes over me slowly.

"Wait," I say, sitting down so close to her that I'm practically on her lap. "Are you . . . pregnant?"

She presses her lips together but can't stop them from spreading into the hugest of grins. She nods quickly.

70

"YOU'RE CARRYING DREW DANFORTH'S PRESUMABLY HOT OFFSPRING?" I screech. "How pregnant are you?"

"Eight weeks."

"Eight weeks? And you're just now telling me? You bitch!" I smack her on the arm, then recoil.

"Oh, God. Oh, I'm so sorry. Did I hurt the baby?"

Annie laughs. "Uh, my womb isn't located in my upper arm, so no. We're good."

I cover my mouth. "And I shouldn't have called you a bitch. The baby can hear me, right? I don't want to teach them that sort of language until they can understand context."

Annie scrunches her nose. "I'm not sure my eight-week-old fetus has a very developed sense of hearing. I mean, maybe. But either way, your light cursing is probably not going to traumatize it."

I shake my head. "Whatever. The point is, you should've told me as soon as you felt a twinge of nausea. As that pee was drying on the stick. I should've known before Drew knew. You should've been texting me every time you had sex so I'd know there was a *possibility* you could conceive. Does the BFF designation mean nothing to you?"

"I didn't feel sick! I mostly feel fine, but tired. I had my first doctor's appointment this week to confirm, and I didn't want to say anything until I really *knew*."

71

She exhales a little shakily. "So . . . that's why we're getting married so soon. I want to have the wedding before the baby comes, because we're probably going to be so busy after it comes that we'd never get around to it and . . . and I don't know, I want to be married to Drew as soon as I can."

"Ugh. You two make me want to barf."

"We're sickening." She shrugs.

"And about to be parents." I throw an extremely soft pillow at her, so as not to cause further damage to her developing baby. "I can't believe this."

"It feels like a dream," Annie whispers, and I reach over and hug her. Because this really is her dream—after losing both of her parents (her dad when she was just a baby, and her mom when she was in high school) all Annie's ever wanted is a big family with a million kids and a dog and probably not a white picket fence because she's a writer and she'd find that detail too clichéd. But now, with her wedding coming up and her baby on the way, she's living her dream. Everything's going according to script.

"I'm so happy for you, babe," I say, and I am. I really am. But there's still a part of me that feels like I'm stuck here, sinking in quicksand while everyone else moves on.

It's late when Annie leaves, but I'm wide awake. I need to sleep if I want to be functional at work tomorrow (have you ever messed up someone's coffee order? Let me tell you, caffeine-hungry customers don't care about your fatigue!), but I find myself lying in bed, staring at the sloped ceiling, my mind scrolling through the events of today like they're an endless Instagram feed of frustrations.

Nick and I promised we'd pretend like that kiss didn't happen, and that's exactly what I intend to do. But just because my mind and pinky agreed doesn't mean that the rest of my body can forget; I'm keyed up and jittery, waiting for some kind of payoff.

I pull my phone off my nightstand and text Nick. Our texting history isn't robust—it's mostly about work, saying I'm going to be late (me) or asking if I want to pick up a shift (him)— and I'm sure he's asleep right now, but I go ahead and text him anyway.

> Hey. I thought texting might be a safer medium for us, on account of there's no physical contact and nothing inappropriate can happen. Unless you send me dick pics or something, which doesn't sound like you, but I don't know your texting habits.

He doesn't respond.

> Anyway, do you want me to bring you a piece of pie tomorrow/today?

73

I wait for a second, then text again.

> That sounded sexual, but I mean it
> literally. And it's an apple pie, so it's not
> one of the more sexual pies (cherry and
> peach, if you're wondering).

> Except wait. Wasn't the pie in American
> Pie, the ultimate pie-sex cultural
> touchstone, apple? Ugh.

> Do you want a piece of
> nonmetaphorical, nonsexual pie?

There's no way Nick's awake right now, so I don't expect a text back. I only sent these because . . . well, who knows? I don't want a relationship or an anything-ship with Nick, but the weak, impatient part of me can't stop myself from poking. As long as I keep it to a text format, it will be fine.

I let my mind wander as I consider what Nick might be doing if he isn't sleeping. Maybe he's watching a boring documentary. Maybe he's reading a book. Maybe he's in bed with someone.

I sit bolt upright, horrified by the thought, as my phone buzzes.

> Bring me a piece of pie tomorrow.

I flop back down. And that's it. No acknowledgment of anything else I said, of my rambling, of my analysis of the most sexual pies. No clarification of whether he's being metaphorical or literal. One sentence. It's all very . . . Nick.

I can't sleep, so I check my email on my phone. Yes, I know a phone's glowing screen and constant distraction is a terrible thing for sleep and blah blah blah blue light, but I never said I made good decisions. Clearly.

I have an email from—ugh—a gossip website. They're trying to put together a piece related to Annie's movie and this dude wants to know: *Are you and Rick really a thing? Is there any truth to the story behind the movie?*

This guy obviously hasn't done any sort of research, or else he'd know that Rick is only Nick's name in the movie, not in real life. The grossest thing is, this isn't even the first time a website or magazine has contacted me. They always want something—a comment, a picture, any sort of "exclusive"—and I never, ever respond. I get that they're only doing their jobs so I'm not going to be an asshole about it, but I'm also not going to open up my personal life to score a website a few clicks.

But tonight . . . well, tonight is different. I'm reeling from that kiss and my conversation with Annie and I would love to tell the world (or the

75

Internet, which might as well be the world) the truth.

So I reply.

> Hi. Thanks so much for your email.
> There is actually nothing between Nick
> and me—we're coworkers, and that's
> it. We've never been in a relationship
> and we're never going to be in a
> relationship. End of story.

I click send, then quickly type out another reply.

> Oh, and also stop emailing me.

I place my phone on my nightstand and roll over, but it takes me forever to get to sleep.

Chapter Seven

Nick stays in his office the next morning. In between customers, I steal glances back there at his barely cracked-open door, wondering what's going on. Is he replaying our kiss in his head, pinky promise be damned? Is he hoping for a round two? Because that would be a very bad idea. A very, very bad but also tempting idea. I lean on the baked goods case, thinking about all the things we could get up to in that office. We could definitely move that grungy old desk across the floor. Knock some filing cabinets over.

Tobin taps me on the shoulder. "Hey. Uh, are you saving that pie for something?"

"What pie?" I stand up so quickly I almost lose my balance and topple over.

Tobin points to the slice that's on the back counter, loosely covered in a clean dish towel. "Uh, the literal one slice of pie on the counter right now?"

"I don't appreciate your attitude, young man," I say, pouring a black coffee and handing it to a regular who doesn't need to order at this point. "And that pie is for Nick."

"Then, like, could you take it back to him? Because Gary keeps asking if he can have it."

"Gary!" I call out. "Hands off this apple pie. You know I'll make you any pie you ask for, any time."

"Have you ever made a Concord grape pie?" Gary asks from his table near the corner.

I blink a few times. "How does that even work, Gary?"

"You have to peel about a hundred and fifty grapes—" he starts, but I cut him off.

"Dude. You know I love you. You're my favorite customer," I say, mouthing *No offense* to the regular who's still standing beside us, listening to this conversation, "but I will not peel a hundred and fifty grapes for you. I don't think I would peel a hundred and fifty grapes for a member of my own family."

"But what about the slogan? 'When you're here, you're family'?"

"We don't have a slogan. That's the Olive Garden, Gary," I say. "Do you see endless soup, salad, and breadsticks? No. That's because you're a treasured friend and customer but you're not family and you're not getting a Concord grape pie and—why am I talking about this? I've gotta get this pie to Nick."

I grab the slice of pie and stomp back to Nick's office, where he's staring intently at his computer.

"What is it?" he asks without looking away

from the screen. "Do you and Tobin need backup?"

I frown, a little annoyed that he seems to find it very easy to forget about yesterday. I mean, yes, that's what I wanted, but also . . . well, doesn't everyone want their make-out prowess to be unforgettable?

I set the plate on top of a pile of papers on his desk. "Here. I saved your pie from Gary's clutches."

He finally looks up and meets my eyes. "Thanks."

I trace a circle on the floor with one of my flats, for some reason unable to move from this office. I remember the way we smacked together like magnets yesterday; like I can't make myself move, even though I want to.

"Try it," I say.

"What?"

"The pie." I point to it. "Try it. I need to know if it's good enough to bake for the shop."

He sighs.

"Oh, yes, poor you," I say. "Here I am, forcing you to eat delicious baked goods."

He sighs again, louder, but reaches for the pie this time. His fork slices off a perfect triangle at the end and he puts it in his mouth, staring straight at me as he chews. Watching someone's jaw move shouldn't feel like this, should it? It shouldn't.

"Tell me it's good," I say, too loudly, trying to stop my train of thought.

"It's good," he says.

"I would've accepted a little more enthusiasm, but okay."

Nick takes another bite, and then another. I watch him chew as I bite my bottom lip.

He stops chewing. "Why are you looking at me like that?"

"I'm not looking at you in any particular way," I say lightly, but let's be real, I know that I am. I'm giving Nick intense *I'm going to rip your clothes off* vibes right now and even though he's under the spell of an amazing pie, he'd have to be a fool not to notice.

"So that's all you have to say, huh? Not, like, 'Wow, this is the literal best pie I've ever had and I'm now ruined for other pies'?"

Nick puts down his fork. "Stop needling me."

"That's not what you said last night," I mutter, waggling my eyebrows in an exaggerated manner.

"That doesn't even make sense," Nick says with an eye roll. "And I don't know what you're talking about. It didn't happen, right?"

We stare at each other a moment, the air heavy, until I say, "Whatever. I'm out of here."

"Yes, please. Get out of here and go do the job I pay you for."

"You mean you don't pay me to stand around and make inaccurate sexual innuendo?"

Nick leans back in his chair, and I have to stop myself from having a physical reaction to the sight of his chest straining against the fabric of his flannel shirt. "Chloe. I don't even have enough money to pay you for that."

"I have been working overtime in that regard," I say, then flee the room.

After work, I head over to my dad's. It's a perfect spring night, the kind where the trees are starting to bud and the air is cold but promising warmth and you can kind of forget that you just endured several long months of Ohio winter and seasonal depression. But part of being the type of person who sees a silver lining in every spring cloud means that I'm determined to appreciate this brief and mercurial season. I'm wearing an extremely cute denim jacket over my favorite butterfly dress, plus a thick pair of black tights because while I may be an optimist, it's not exactly sundress weather yet.

As soon as I'm buzzed in, I head to the front desk to see Tracey, who tells me all about the trip she and her wife are taking to Punta Cana for their first anniversary.

"We're going to do nothing but sit around and eat. Oh, and I plan to drink about one daiquiri for every hour that we're there."

I grimace. "Well, I guess it was nice knowing you, because you're definitely going to die of alcohol poisoning."

She waves me off. "Whatever. Vacation is for indulging. When's the last time you took one?"

"It's been a while," I say as I drum my nails on the counter, but the truth is, it's been more than a while. The last time I took a vacation, Milo and I were crammed into the back seat of our family car as the four of us drove to Myrtle Beach. And it's not like I didn't have a good time, but I have a feeling the highlight of an adult vacation isn't a trip to Ripley's Believe It or Not.

I let her get back to work and head to Dad's room. He's in good spirits today, and since the weather's somewhat nice, we go out to the courtyard to sit. That's the thing about Ohio— winter drags on so long that once mid-March hits, if it's above forty degrees everyone's wearing shorts and T-shirts and dining on patios.

"So where's that boyfriend of yours been?" he asks as we sit down on the wicker furniture.

"What boyfriend, Dad?" I ask patiently.

"You know." He stares off into space for a moment, then looks at me again. "Dave Whatshisface."

I bite my lip to avoid wincing. Dave was my last "serious" relationship, way back in high school. We were together for an entire year, or seven years in Chloe time (which is basically measured like dog years).

This isn't the first time Dad has brought Dave up. I don't know if it's because he hasn't really met anyone I've dated since Dave (well, he's met Tracey, although he doesn't know we dated) or if it's his brain snagging on a memory, but for some reason he thinks Dave and I are still together.

"Dad," I say, putting a hand on his arm. "Dave and I aren't together."

He sighs. "I wish you could settle down with a nice boy."

"Dad," I say again. "You know I date boys *and* girls."

"Men and women" would be more accurate, but when my dad looks at me, I can tell he's seeing me as I looked when I was in high school.

He shakes his head a few times. "I know that. I'm old but I can remember some things."

"I know you can," I say with a small smile.

He looks at me and his eyes, so often unfocused these days, look crystal clear. "I'm worried I'm never gonna be able to walk you down the aisle, Chloe. I want to know that someone's gonna take care of you after I'm gone. You deserve someone who will look after you."

I blink a few times. I will not cry in front of him. "I can take care of myself, you know."

He looks at me for a few more seconds and smiles, then asks, "Nice day, huh?"

"Yeah," I say, leaning back, the wicker poking through my tights. I'm glad the awkward moment has passed. "It's—"

"So where's that boyfriend of yours been?" he asks again.

I change the subject, asking him about the trip to a buffet everyone took last week. I try to listen as he responds, but all I can think about is how I'm letting him down. How all he wants is a normal daughter, one who wants to put on a white dress and walk down the aisle, and I can't even give him that because that's not who I am. And even if I were that person, it would never happen because he's sick. It's all a sad fantasy, one that I can't bear to think about for too long.

Tracey's in conversation with another employee as I leave, so I shoot her a look that I hope communicates, *Well, that went as well as could reasonably be expected and also, good night,* and then I head out to my car. I get in, cue up "Escape (The Piña Colada Song)," and start to drive home.

But I'm literally one line into this smooth banger about a guy getting tired of his lady when the tears flood my eyes so quickly and absolutely that I have to pull over onto a side street. I slide to a stop in front of a split-level house and turn off the car. Without Rupert Holmes's voice singing about tropical drinks and attempting to cheat on his wife, the car is so, so quiet, and I decide this is the perfect time for one of my Five-Minute Cries.

Even someone like me, someone who stead-fastly refuses to engage in pessimism or the dark side, someone who takes every possible chance to walk on the sunny side of the street, feels bad sometimes. It's like every bad aspect of my life is a drop in the bucket, and eventually, the bucket is so heavy that I have no choice but to pour it all out in one slightly terrifying but brief cry session. It was my need for compartmentalization that led me to develop the revolutionary Five-Minute Cry system; sometimes, I pretend I'm on an infomercial describing it. There are several black-and-white shots of people attempting to go through their day-to-day duties, like working and school and baking, but unable to do anything because they can't stop thinking about the overwhelming sadness in their lives. And then, we cut to me, on a stage in front of a live studio audience.

"Do you suffer from Unexpected Crying Jags Due to Shitty Life Circumstances?"

(The crowd applauds; there's a close-up of a woman in the audience nodding at her friend.)

"I did, too, until I discovered the power of . . . the Five-Minute Cry!"

(Audience "oooohs.")

"With this simple, patented system, you can get through almost your entire day, week, or even month without breaking down in tears! All you have to do is box up everything that upsets you, shove it into a corner of your mind, then open that box right back up when you have five minutes to spare. And then . . . you let it all out, baby. Sob, scream, ugly-cry your heart out, wherever you are. Maybe you're at home. Maybe you're in the shower. Maybe you're parked in front of a nicely maintained split-level near your father's assisted living facility. Wherever you are, let yourself feel it, but here's the catch: only for five minutes."

(The audience murmurs their approval and begins clapping. I take a bow in front of my adoring subjects.)

It's a good system, one that has saved me a lot of heartbreak and pain. All I do is push down my negative feelings until I'm forced to explode. Sometimes it happens while driving, which isn't ideal, but what can you do?

My five minutes are up and I wipe the tears from my face. A light flicks on, and I look over to see a woman standing on the front steps of the split-level home, staring at me with what is either concern or horror. I wave, start the car, and drive away.

So my dad thinks I'm dating the guy I took to my senior prom. And, okay, so all he wants is to see me get married, which is literally never going to happen because (a) I don't want to get married, (b) I'm not dating anyone, and (c) my dad would most likely not remember a wedding, even if it happened.

I may not have the power or desire to change most of those things, but there's one bullet point I do have power over: dating someone.

In the pre-Drew days, Annie always acted like getting a date was some mystical, magical thing, but it's really not that hard. And it's not because I'm fantastically attractive or supremely confident; I think I have an average level of attractiveness. The truth is, people are usually taken aback (in a good way) when you simply ask them if they want to make out. Stop beating around the bush. Stop texting for days and weeks on end, vetting each prospective sexual partner to see if they have marriage potential, convincing yourself that this person has to be perfect. Stop talking yourself out of it, telling yourself they'll reject you, convincing yourself that they're too good for you. Pick somebody, walk up to them, look them in the eye, and say, "Hey, do you want to come back to my place?" It works. Trust me.

Annie seems to think I'm the modern-day equivalent of young Warren Beatty, sleeping my way through the town, but the truth is that I haven't had sex with that many people. And anyway, even Warren Beatty was forced to admit that he hadn't really had sex with the rumored twelve-thousand-plus women his biographer claimed he did. Truthfully, I've hooked up with a perfectly reasonable number of people, while Annie, picky as she is, could count her sexual partners on one hand, even if she had an unexpected amputation or three.

Which is fine, for her! All I'm saying is that finding a date, or a hookup, isn't difficult. And while I may not be getting married literally ever, I can at least secure someone to make out with me so that I can sort-of-honestly tell my dad that, yes, I *am* seeing someone.

Does this have the added bonus of helping me forget about Nick? Well, it's like the ancient proverb says: the best way to get over someone is to get under someone else.

I pull up to the curb in front of Mikey Danger's place, step out, kick yet another beer can out of the way, and march to the door. Fred answers.

"Hey, Chloe. You here to see Milo?"

I shake my head, my body vibrating the way it always does before I do something like this. The excitement, the possibility, the way I feel confident in the outcome.

"Is Mikey here?" I ask.

Fred gives me some side-eye but steps back to let me in. "Uh, yeah. He's in his room."

I nod my thanks, step around the empty milk jugs on the floor, and walk toward Mikey's room. I square my shoulders, take a deep breath, and knock.

"Yeah?" comes a sleepy voice from inside.

I open the door. There are tapestries on the

wall, the kind you might see in a college dorm room. Mikey's mattress is on the floor, and he's on top of it, watching something on his laptop. He is, unfortunately, still a babe, in that *Jake Gyllenhaal let himself go the tiniest bit* way.

"Mikey," I say. "Would you like to go back to my place?"

Mikey Danger was all too happy to go back to my place, where pizza boxes aren't used as decorations and there's always edible food in the refrigerator. Neither of us even brought up the idea of him spending the night, so I was in bed at a perfectly reasonable hour after reading some articles for my online class.

Nick and I are opening today, which means he's not in the back room doing Nick-stuff on the computer; instead, he's with me, getting everything set up and preparing for the morning rush. We don't open until 6:30, but at 6:15, as usual, Gary wanders up to the door, peering in as if he's not sure we'll be there, as if this isn't our routine every morning.

I flip the sign, open the door, and step to the side to let him in. "Gary," I ask, "why don't you ever bring your wife in here?"

"She likes to spend her mornings at home with the ferrets," he says. "And honestly, I feel like a fifth wheel."

I pat him on the back. "Well, you're never a

fifth wheel here, Gary. And no one can bring in ferrets because animals aren't allowed."

Gary shrugs, sitting down. "Too bad. It would really liven up the place."

"And be a health code violation," Nick says, sliding raspberry almond bars into the baked goods case. Although we're about to open, I got here a couple of hours ago to make the bars. I do all of my baking experiments at home, but when it comes to stuff we actually serve, I have to make it in Nick's kitchen; speaking of health code violations, it turns out health inspectors don't love it when you bring in random food from home kitchens. Shocking, I know.

"Did you try my raspberry almond bars?" I ask with way too much intensity.

"Yeah," Nick says, turning to face me. He looks all cool and calm and ruggedly sexy over there in his flannel shirt. I hate him and also I want to lick his face.

"They're good," he says.

I stand up straighter. "Good?"

He raises his eyebrows and walks to the speaker, where he presses some buttons. "Yeah? That's the opposite of bad, in case you forgot."

Bon Iver starts playing and I can't even be annoyed by it because I'm too busy being annoyed by this faint praise. "I'm looking for great, Nicholas."

"Stop calling me Nicholas."

"Stop changing the subject. What was wrong with my raspberry almond bars?"

He widens his eyes. "Nothing was wrong with them. I said they were good."

"But no one leaves the warmth and safety of their home to travel to a coffee shop and get something that's *good*. People are looking for great. They're looking for fantastic. They're looking for stupendous." I slam my hand on the counter.

Nick leans against the baked goods case, eyebrows raised, a look of amusement on his face.

"I'm glad the success of your business is funny to you," I mutter. "I'm trying to help you be great."

"You're trying to help me be stupendous."

I stifle a smile, which is easy to do because Bon Iver is still playing and it's hard to smile while listening to a song about a *blood bank,* for God's sake. "Yes, stupendous. Nicholas."

Nick frowns.

"I don't want Nick's to be any old coffee shop, you know?" I say. "Columbus has a lot of coffee shops. A lot of very good coffee shops. But I want us—I mean, you—to be the best, the place where people can expect the highest quality. Where our baked goods are classics with a twist, something you know you'll love that's a little bit different than what you expected. And I know you don't care about décor, but I really think that with a few small changes we can make this place more—"

"I think the bars are great," Gary calls from his table.

"Wait." I glance at the baked goods case, then at him. "How did you even get a bar?"

"Oh, I walked over and got one while you two were doing your whole . . ." He waves his hand in the air. "Thing that you do. I left a few dollars by the register."

"Huh," I say. But I can't even concentrate on the fact that apparently Gary's, like, an expert at baked good heists because the bell above the door rings.

I do a literal double take, like I'm a vintage cartoon character, when I see who steps through the door.

"Mikey?" I ask.

He squints, looking around, as if he's stepped out of a cave and into the sunlight. "Hey, Chlo," he says, his voice easy and sleepy. "This is your place, huh?"

"My workplace, yes," I say, watching him take everything in. He inspects the artwork on the walls, the nature paintings by local artists. He runs a hand over the brick wall, then ambles up to the register and picks up a napkin dispenser, eyeing it skeptically like he's never seen one before.

"What are you . . . I mean, why are you up so early?" I ask. True, I don't know Mikey's schedule, but back in high school, he routinely missed his first two morning classes because an alarm clock powerful enough to wake him didn't exist.

He shakes his head, giving me a smile. You know how most people have, like, five different smiles, minimum? Like how Nick will give me his *making fun of me* smile, his *reluctant to admit I'm funny* smile, his *Why are you so strange* smile? Well, Mikey only has the one smile—it manages to communicate the entire range of his emotions in one expression, and you know what? It's nice to be around someone so uncomplicated, so open and easy.

"Nah," he says, shaking his head like I tried to tell him that two plus two equals five. "I haven't been to sleep yet."

My mouth drops open. "But . . . but you left my place well before midnight. What have you been doing?"

He shrugs. "Little bit of this, little bit of that. You know."

I do not know, but I nod slowly. "Do you . . . want something to eat?"

His face lights up for the first time since he came in. "Yeah. Do you have, like, cereal?"

"Um." I look at Gary, and even he's giving me a *What's this guy's deal?* expression. "This isn't

93

a breakfast buffet, Mikey. We have raspberry almond bars. And some rose pistachio cookies from yesterday that are pretty bomb, if I do say so myself."

"Oh, hell yeah," he says with a fist pump. "Cookies are my favorite food."

I can't help but smile for real. "Yeah, okay. I'll give you a cookie." I grab one out of the case and hand it to him. He shoves the entire thing in his mouth and rolls his eyes heavenward. "Shit, Chlo. This is, like, the best fucking thing I've eaten in my life."

As we were leaving his place last night, Fred pulled me aside and expressed concern that Mikey's internal organs were going to disintegrate, given that he seems to subsist on a diet of Crunchwrap Supremes from Taco Bell, so I don't know if this is a huge compliment. But it feels like one, so I accept it.

"Thanks," I say with a smile, and then, as if this is a thing we do on a regular basis, Mikey leans across the register and kisses me. It's quick and casual and not designed to cause shock, but given that two short days ago I was kissing Nick in this location, it's jarring.

But not terrible. Mikey isn't a bad kisser and he tastes like a cookie right now, so things could be worse.

"Uh, thanks!" I say, and offer him a bright smile and another cookie.

"See you, babe," he says, then toasts me with his cookie. "Thanks."

I watch him shuffle out the door, a man who doesn't have anywhere to be until his evening delivery shift at Pizza Hut.

A throat clears behind me and I turn around, then jump when I see Nick. "Oh!" I say. "I didn't know you were still here."

"So . . . that guy, huh?" Nick asks, staring at the door, even though Mikey is long gone.

"Uh, I mean . . . he's a guy, and I know him and . . ." I shake my head. Why do I care what Nick thinks? I don't need to stammer my way through a defense of my actions. "He's whatever. It's Mikey. He's perfectly nice and he doesn't expect anything from me and I like that, okay?"

Nick smiles, but this is a smile I've never seen before, one I can't decode. "I can tell," he says, then tosses his dish towel on the counter and walks toward his office.

"What is that supposed to mean?" I ask, but he ignores me and keeps walking. I mutter, "Ugh. Why do you have to look so good when you're walking away?"

A noisy slurp draws my attention to Gary, who's staring at me and shaking his head as he drinks his coffee.

"What?" I cross my arms. "Would you like to critique my choice of partner, too?"

"I'm minding my own business," Gary says. "But I heard you're giving out cookies."

I sigh, then reach into the case and pull out a cookie for him. He walks up to the counter to take it. Adjusting his hat, he says, "Thanks. How about instead of money, I pay you in advice?"

I scowl. "That's not an even trade, Gary." But I listen anyway. After all, Gary seems like a happy person. He spends most of his retirement here, eating delicious (some might say great) baked goods and drinking the best coffee in town. Clearly he knows something about life, and although I fear he's going to say something offensive about who I should or shouldn't hook up with, I'm willing to give him a chance.

"You should really allow animals in here," he says. "Even a fish tank. A bird cage! It would brighten the place up."

I pat his hand as Nick walks back to the counter. "Go sit down, Gary."

The bell above the door jingles again, but this time it's a cute girl with long wavy hair and a heart-printed dress that I would kill for. I let Nick handle our first real, non-Gary customer of the day as I go back to the kitchen to get the rest of the bars for the case—if Gary's enthusiastic response is any indication, we'll sell out quickly.

When I come back out, I see that Heart-Printed Dress Girl is still talking to Nick, despite the fact that her coffee is already in hand. As is sometimes the case, I'm confused as to whether I want to *be* this cute girl or whether I want to *make out* with her.

She smiles, her eyes crinkling at the corners and her head tilted, and that's a move I recognize all too well. That's a move you do when you're flirting with someone. I watch as Nick smiles back at her, a real Nick smile, the kind he gives me when I'm lucky enough to have made him laugh.

Be her. I definitely want to *be* her.

"Do you need anything else?" I ask, butting into their conversation before I can stop myself.

She abruptly stops smiling and turns to me. "I'm sorry?"

I gesture toward the baked goods. "A stupendous raspberry almond bar? A delicious rose pistachio cookie?"

"Um." Her eyes dart between me and Nick, but come to rest on him. "No thanks. I'm good."

She smiles at him, then says, "See you," without turning to look at me again. We both watch her walk out of the shop.

When the bell jingles, I grab Nick's arm. "Um, whoa," I say.

"Whoa, what?" he asks, adjusting the finicky receipt printer.

I can't help but laugh. Of course Nick—sweet, innocent Nicholas—wouldn't know when a beautiful woman was hitting on him. I never see him go on dates and he's always at work; he probably can't even recognize that she was about ready to leap over the counter and attack him.

"That girl," I say. "She was flirting with you."

But Nick doesn't seem confused or horrified. Instead, he turns to me and waves a scrap of paper in the air. "Yeah. No kidding."

I inspect the paper, a string of numbers that slowly starts to make sense. "Is that . . . her phone number?"

"It would be weird if she gave me someone else's phone number."

The realization dawns on me. "Did you *want* her to hit on you?"

Nick crosses his arms, staring at me a little too intently for my liking. "Why do you care, Chloe?"

For once, I'm speechless.

"Because you wanted to pretend that night between us didn't happen, so I'm not sure what else you want from me. You're hooking up with a grown man who calls himself Mikey. Do you want me to be celibate?"

Of course I do is the first thought that pops into my mind. I don't want Nick to even notice other women. I want every other person on earth to be simply a pale imitation of me. The thought of Nick putting those strong hands on another woman, of his stubble rubbing against someone else's neck, of his body pressing another body

98

into the brick wall of the shop, makes me want to barf.

I'm not saying I'm proud of those thoughts, or that they're fair, but I'm saying they're mine. Part of me wants Nick to be here, in the shop, waiting for me as I stumble through life.

Reason #4: He's the scruffy-bearded hunk who's always there when you need him.

"I don't want you to be celibate." I close my eyes, because looking at his face is too much. "Go do whatever you want. Get phone numbers from whoever you want. Sleep with whoever you want. I don't care."

"Good to know," Nick says, brushing past me.

I watch him walk into his office and shut the door. There's a part of me—a large part of me—that wants to run after him, wants to throw open the door and kiss him until he forgets that other women even exist. The part of me that says, *What if Annie's right? What if the movie is right? What if what if what if you're supposed to be with Nick Velez?*

But believing that would require me to be a different type of person—one who thinks soul mates are real, for starters. Or one who believes in rom-com perfect happy endings, instead of what I actually believe in, which is the real-life right now. Those happy endings don't exist for people like me, but joy-filled moments sure do.

I put on some yacht rock, paste on my Customer

Service Chloe smile, and try my hardest to forget that Nick Velez is back there in his office, possibly texting a beautiful woman at this very second.

Chapter Eight

"Wait," Annie says on the phone, because the events of last night and today merited a phone call, not a series of texts. Annie's currently in LA, doing something-something-something related to her movie (I zone out when she gets into specifics), and I decided this couldn't wait until she was back in town. "You're telling me you slept with Mikey Danger?"

"No need to put it so crudely, Annie," I say, immersing my hands in the pie dough. I have her on speakerphone so I can work on making this vegan pâte brisée out of coconut oil and coconut milk. It's occasionally confusing and bewildering to work without butter, but I love being able to offer options at the shop.

What I'm not telling Annie because it doesn't matter is that Mikey and I didn't *actually* have sex. We made out for a while and then he left, but I feel like I should at least keep up the Chloe Sanderson mystique.

"A lady never kisses and tells," I continue, adding my chilled coconut oil to my flour.

"Could a lady confirm or deny the rumor that

Mikey has the word *Danger* tattooed on his lower abdomen?"

I make a face that only the pâte brisée can see. "Uh, that's a hard deny. I have standards, Annie."

"Sorry! I've been wondering about that since high school."

"Ew. No. All of his tattoos were normal and not warnings."

"Okay. Um." She sighs, the air rushing into the speaker. "Can I ask you a question?"

"Yes, I will be the godmother of your child."

"If we were doing the whole godmother thing, it would be you for sure. But that's not what I wanted to talk about."

I add in a small quantity of solidified coconut oil and wait.

"What did Nick think about all this?"

My hands stop moving, covered in dough. "Um, why does that matter?"

"You know why it matters."

I glance around my kitchen, at the teal backsplash I got on a deep discount from a home improvement store and had Nick install for me one weekend a couple of years ago. I shift my gaze and focus on the floral pictures with frames I painted in coral, yellow, and green, the ones I plan on hanging up at Nick's once he agrees to let me redecorate. I spin around and come face-to-face with my succulent named Geoff—the only plant I can manage to keep alive because it thrives on neglect—and remember how I tried and failed to get Nick to let me bring in some plants to brighten up the place.

No matter how hard I try, the universe won't let me forget about Nick, not even in my kitchen, the most sacred of spaces.

"Nope. I don't get why it matters if my boss cares about who I'm hooking up with."

"Because you're meant to be together, Chloe! Because—"

She keeps talking but I groan through it. There was once a time when Annie refrained from commenting on my love life. Sure, she would do this little half smile and stare off into space whenever she was around Nick and me, but I knew what she was thinking, even though she clearly thought she was being so smooth.

But that time ended when the news of her script went public, and now she thinks she has permission to tell me the grand, overarching truth about my feelings. Which is bullshit, because they're *my* feelings, and this is *my* life, and I'm the one who has to deal with everything.

It's easy for her to sit in Drew's fancy LA apartment and tell me that I should give in to my physical feelings for Nick, because she isn't the one who has to deal with the fallout. She isn't the one who has to deal with how weird things already are, and how much weirder they would be if they went any further and fell apart. I'm the one who needs this job, who needs to take care of my dad, and who apparently needs to take care of Milo on account of he's an overgrown baby. Annie doesn't get it.

But I don't say any of that, because I'm pretty sure a lot of it is mean and it violates the unwritten BFF code, which clearly states that you shouldn't give your best friend a verbal smackdown when they're trying to help you. Even if they're really, really wrong.

So instead, after I stick the dough in the fridge to chill, I take her off speaker and hold the phone to my ear as I say, "Annie. Listen, I get it. I get it that your life is a romantic comedy, because you're the one who's obsessed with romantic comedies. That's never been me."

"True. You're obsessed with stuff about murder, because there's something wrong with you."

"First off, there's nothing wrong with me, lots of women love to learn about murder and I'll forward you this article about it and—wait, no. We're not changing the subject here. All I'm saying is that I know your life is a rom-com and you love it, but that's not what my life is like. I'm not like you, all cute and tiny and tripping into movie stars—"

"That only happened one time."

"—and finding myself in hilarious situations. That's not me."

104

"It kind of is you, though. You have a great wardrobe, like any romantic comedy star—"

"I don't dress this way for anyone but me!" I shout.

"And you *are* cute, and in case you didn't notice from the hundreds of rom-coms you've watched with me, 'not believing in love' is, like, the number one indicator that you're about to fall in love."

Well, she has me there. But still. Romantic comedies are supposed to be fun, and cheesy, and above all they need to have that predictable happy ending where two people solve their problems and surmount their obstacles and kiss in a rainstorm to celebrate their perfect lives and perfect faces. None of that's going to happen here. If there were a rom-com about my real life, it would be a pretty big bummer because it wouldn't have a happy ending and it would have a *terrible* Rotten Tomatoes score.

"Annie. I love you. But my life is *my* life, and I don't have the time to fall into a makeover montage right now."

"No one ever does," Annie mutters.

"And anyway," I say with a wince. "Some other woman hit on Nick today and he was totally into it, so whatever. I don't exactly think he's pining away for me."

"He was into it?" Skepticism drips from her voice. "Really?"

"Can we not talk about this anymore?"

"Okay, okay, okay," Annie says, because this is also part of the best friend contract. Even when you're annoyingly, persistently, obliviously fixated on something, you have to drop it if the other person says so. I mean, I knew Annie and Drew were shooting heart-eyes at each other way before they got together, but when she was all "mad" at him because they had a rom-com-worthy misunderstanding, I kept quiet. It's the law.

"How's wedding stuff going?" I ask, because there's no better way to change the subject than by asking an engaged woman about her wedding.

She exhales so loudly that I have to hold the phone away from my ear. "It's fine. It's . . . fine."

"Huh. You're saying 'fine' the way a beleaguered wife in a sitcom says it, right before she starts a hilarious argument about her husband's ineptitude."

"What?"

"I'm saying there are a lot of layers in your 'fine,' and none of them sound good." I sit down on my bed.

"Oh. Well, you know I'm excited about the actual 'getting married to Drew' part."

"I've noticed it once or twice."

"But it turns out a wedding isn't about how much you love your partner. It's about flowers. And table decorations. And tasting a lot of cakes."

106

"Okay, first off, congrats on being the only person to ever complain about cake tastings. And secondly, I told you I'd make your cake!"

"Chloe! I'm not making you do all the maid of honor duties plus deal with decorating a massive cake the night before the wedding."

"I'm offended," I say, examining my cuticles.

"Plus, you know cake isn't even my favorite thing."

I remain silent.

"Frosting. Ugh. What's the point?"

I take a few deep breaths to steady myself. "I'm going to ignore the terrible things you said about cake and give you a proposition: what if you had a noncake wedding dessert?"

"You can do that?" Annie asks with wonder in her voice.

"Again, woman, get thyself on Pinterest. How are you even planning a wedding without a board dedicated to desserts?"

"So you're saying I could have . . . pie?"

I direct a silent prayer of thanks toward the ceiling. "Yes, Annie. You can have pie. And you know who makes a mean pie?"

"I would never ask you to do all that work right before the wedding—"

"Honestly, I would consider ending our friendship if you went anywhere else for the pie."

"Are you sure?"

"I'm sure. Pie dough can be made and frozen

ahead of time, and lots of whole pies can even be frozen. I'll get started this week. Tonight! As soon as we end this phone call! You tell me five to seven pie varieties you'd like and I'll get to work."

"Can you pick the pies?"

Now it really feels like this is too good to be true. Not only do I get to make the dessert for my best friend's wedding, but I get to decide what it is? "Um . . . don't you want to tell me your favorites?"

"I think I'm suffering from decision fatigue. Between picking out centerpieces and choosing my dress, I can barely expend the energy to figure out what I'm gonna eat for dinner. I swear, I snapped at Uncle Don the other day because he asked me if he should wear a *Star Wars* or *Star Trek* tie to the ceremony."

I laugh. "That sounds like Don."

"To be fair, it was the third time he'd asked me."

"Well, it's a big decision."

"You choose the pies, okay? I trust you, in all matters but especially in those of pie."

I put my hand on my chest, even though Annie can't see me. "I'm touched."

"I figure it's the least I can do, since I'm not even going to offer up a cute groomsperson for you to hook up with."

Since Annie and Drew are keeping their

wedding relatively small, they each only have one attendant. Annie has me, duh, and Drew has his fourteen-year-old brother, Louis.

"I told him you said, and I quote, 'Drew should forget about his teenage brother and choose a celebrity,' but he kept talking about how 'family is important,' and 'I've never even met Tessa Thompson so I can't ask her to be my groomswoman.'"

"Ugh," I groan. "But she looks so good in a suit."

"Sorry to crush your dreams of flinging yourself at a celebrity, but on the plus side, Louis had a major growth spurt over the past year, so at least you won't look like you're babysitting in formalwear."

I snort, grateful that I'm seeing a little bit of Annie's sense of humor. This is always how we've bonded: joking through movies, nurturing inside jokes, sending each other mental notes with our eyes when someone says something ridiculous. Between her hardly being in town and being so busy with the movie and the wedding, I haven't had much of a chance to remember why I love her so much.

"I'm blessed. How about I let you go? I'm sure you have a million things to do, and I have some pie research to get on."

"Okay. And—listen, I'm sorry if I went too far with the . . . the you-know-who stuff."

I put a hand over my face. "Nick. You can say his name. He isn't Voldemort."

"Right. Well, I didn't mean to make you feel bad, or pressured, or annoyed, or whatever, and I promise I'll cool it, okay? But since we're being honest . . . can I talk to you about something?"

"Oh no," I say. "Are you kicking me out of the wedding? Am I being replaced?"

"Chloe. Come on. Who would I possibly replace you with?"

"I don't know. Dungeon Master Rick?"

Annie attempts to respond through her laughter. "Um, first off, wow. No. He would not be a comforting presence before I walk down the aisle. He's officiating."

I pause. "I did not know that."

"Well, we needed someone right away, and we figured if he's good at running a Dungeons and Dragons campaign, he's probably good at keeping a wedding on track."

"That's just logic."

"Right. Okay." Annie exhales. She hates conflict, and I can't even imagine what she could have to say to me. "Um . . ."

"Say it! I'm starting to panic!"

"You didn't tell me you talked to Hollywood Gossip," she says in a rush. "And now there's an article with a quote from you that's all about how, like, the movie is fake and there's nothing between you and Nick?"

"Well," I say slowly. "There isn't anything between me and Nick, other than some residual sexual tension that I plan on banging out with someone else. Also, honestly, I forgot I even talked to Hollywood Gossip. I responded one night at, like, two A.M. and you know I make some bad decisions late at night."

"It's just . . ." Annie stops talking for so long that I start to think she hung up on me, and I'm checking the phone when she continues. "It doesn't really make the movie look great, you know?"

"Um . . ." I say. "No. I don't know."

"It's like, okay, everyone knows *Coffee Girl* is based on a true story, and that's part of why people find it so charming!"

"Right."

"And when you tell everyone that it's all made up and you would rather die than date Nick, then that kind of paints the movie in a bad light. It's not exactly romantic."

"First off," I say, "I would not rather die. I wasn't aware my two choices were *date Nick* or *be mercilessly executed*."

"You know what I mean," Annie says in a low voice.

"So, what," I say, my voice rising a little bit as what she's saying sinks in. "You want me to fake-date Nick so your movie gets good PR?"

"No!"

"You want me to lie to the press?"

"I don't want that either! You don't have to lie to anyone. But maybe don't seek them out to set the record straight, or whatever."

I press my lips together. So Annie wants me to cooperate to ensure her movie doesn't look bad . . . but I definitely don't remember her asking me if it was okay to write a movie based on very real aspects of my very real life. Sure, she offered to kill the script after it had gotten some attention, but at that point, what was I supposed to say? "Yes, please ruin your first chance at going after your dream career." What kind of friend would I be then?

"Okay. Well . . . okay."

"Are you mad?" Annie asks, sounding a little panicked. "I hate it when you're mad."

"You hate it when anyone's mad, Annie. That's why you only watch rom-coms instead of murder shows."

"That and all the murder, yes. But I mean it. Are we good?"

"Yes," I say. "I promise I won't tell any other news outlets that Nick and I are not in a relationship. Even though we aren't in one and we never will be."

Annie pauses. "I feel like a bitch. You know *I* don't want you to do anything *you* don't want to do, right? You know I just want you to be happy?"

"Yes, and you're not a bitch. I love you, okay?"

"Okay," she says, and I can practically see her nodding and biting her lip. "I love you, too."

"I'm gonna go draw up some pie blueprints now, so I'll talk to you later." We say our goodbyes and hang up.

I love Annie. I really do. Our friendship is the single most stable relationship in my life, and I know that I can trust her. She's been there for me through some of the roughest moments of my life, and we've been almost-roommates for years. Maybe that's why it stings so much that she's telling me I'm making her life harder. She literally wrote a fictionalized version of mine, and I didn't even know about it until it was halfway to being a real movie.

I get up off the bed and pull my pie books off my cookbook shelf. Spreading them out on my tiny kitchen table, I get to work. Because if there's one thing I know for sure, it's that a good pie can solve most problems.

Chapter Nine

The next morning at work, the Doobies are pumping, customers are happy, and I have pie on the brain. I love retreating to dessert fantasies in stressful moments. Why think about my dad's care when I could think about strawberry pie, covered in a thick layer of sweetened whipped cream instead? It's so nice to let my problems melt away like chunks of butter in a baking pie crust.

This morning I made chocolate lavender muffins, which may sound unusual, but customers are really going for them (which I knew would happen, because they're great). Lavender is one of my favorite herbs because you think it's delicate—those tiny little flowers, the barely-there color. But if your hand slips and you put too much in, you're going to be overwhelmed by lavender, because it's strong. It's assertive. It's almost *too* much.

In a way, I relate to lavender.

"Tobin?" I ask as the line snakes around the counter. "Could you grab a small hot chocolate, please?"

Tobin is in his senior year at OSU and he is

truly a good kid, but asking him to hand you something is asking for trouble. I don't know how he's worked here for years without being able to handle the concept of . . . well, handling things without dropping them. While I'm swiping a customer's credit card and Nick is putting a muffin from the baked goods case into a paper bag, Tobin gets the hot chocolate ready. And I don't see it happen, but I hear it: a loud and uncharacteristic yelp from Nick, followed by Tobin's profuse apologies.

"This is . . . scalding," Nick says, looking down at his white thermal, the one that's now soaked in hot chocolate and clinging to his body in a way that is positively *Colin Firth in any given movie* (Annie's made me watch *Bridget Jones's Diary* and the entire *Pride and Prejudice* miniseries way too many times).

Tobin and Nick both look at me and I realize I'm making an inappropriate low, guttural noise, kind of like that time we took a school field trip to the Columbus Zoo in the fifth grade and we saw the Aldabra tortoises mating.

I cough. "Sorry. Something in my throat. Um, okay, right."

I begin to apologize for the delay to the customer who's waiting, but she doesn't even notice my words because she's staring, openmouthed, at Nick and his accidental entry into a wet T-shirt contest.

And who can blame her? Certainly not me. So much of popular culture acts like men have to be super muscular to be attractive, with bulging forearm veins and abs so distinct you could vigorously scrub laundry on them. Nick's arms are thick but not scarily so, and his abs lack that washboard definition, but he's still got what it takes to entrance a line full of caffeine-seeking women (and a few men).

I grab a new hot chocolate myself, despite Tobin's offers to get one, and hand it to the customer in front of me while refraining from reaching over to gently close her mouth. By the time I'm on to the next customer, Nick is gone, presumably off somewhere changing into something less straight out of a beverage-themed rom-com.

"Uh, Chloe?" Tobin asks, an empty roll of paper towels in his hand, a smaller but still sizable puddle of hot chocolate at his feet.

He looks so helpless that I can't be annoyed. "I'll go get more paper towels, buddy."

Our "supply closet" is a shelf that lines the walls of Nick's office, so I hightail it back there. I burst through the door but stop so quickly that I almost topple over. Nick is at his desk, leaning over his wet shirt, and he is . . . not wearing another shirt.

For the record, that means he is currently shirtless, and I am in the same room with him.

"Ahh!" I shout, then grab a roll of paper towels off the shelf and throw them at him.

"What was that for?" he yells.

"Put some clothes on, you perv!" I shout, covering my eyes. "The rest of us don't parade around here naked, you know?"

"I'm in my own office," Nick grumbles. "Also, I'm not naked. I'm not wearing a shirt, which is a state many people are in when they mow their lawns. Don't act like it's so offensive."

"The sign on the door says *No shoes, no shirt, no service,*" I point out.

"We don't have a sign like that."

"Well, maybe we should!" I yell, opening my eyes. Nick is still shirtless, still dabbing ineffectually at his shirt with a wet paper towel.

He looks up. "What?" he asks. "Would it make you more comfortable if I put this wet shirt back on?"

"Yes," I say, shifting from foot to foot. "But actually . . . ugh. You're gonna work the stain deeper into the fibers."

I don't *want* to offer to clean his shirt for him, because it's not my job and he hasn't asked me. If I know Nick the way I'm sure I do, he would never even think of asking me. But after years and years of doing the laundry for our family, of getting spaghetti stains out of my dad's work shirts and the stink out of Milo's gross gym clothes, I'm unable to watch someone poorly remove a stain.

"Just . . ." I walk over to him and yank the shirt off his desk.

"Where are you going?" he asks, but he doesn't follow me as I step out of his office, because while we may not have a sign prohibiting shirtlessness, it would be super weird for the boss to waltz around the place half-naked.

The bathroom door opens as I'm nearing it, and I step in front of the one guy in line. "I'm sorry," I say, an exaggerated look of apology on my face as I hold up the shirt. "It's a hot chocolate emergency."

He opens his mouth but has nothing prepared to counter my statement.

I run cold water over the shirt for a while, flushing out as much of the stain as I can. Then I fill the sink with soapy water and leave it there to soak for half an hour.

"The sink's currently out of order," I say to the guy who's waiting when I open the door. "You can use the toilet, but don't even think about washing your hands."

"Um . . . I'll . . . I'll just wait," he says, turning around and retreating to a table.

"Thank you!" I call after him.

I return to Nick's office, but this time, I knock on the door. "Everyone decent in there?"

After a pause, I hear Nick's voice, annoyed. "Yes."

I slowly push the door open, peering around it.

"For God's sake, come in," says Nick.

"I want to be sure I'm not going to see an excess amount of flesh!" I say. "I'm an innocent girl, Nicholas."

I finally see him, sitting at his desk, wearing a gray hoodie with nothing under it. It's unzipped a little and I can see chest hair poking out. With his scruffy beard and his lanky body and the way his deep brown eyes are looking at me, he's like a photo shoot for an up-and-coming stand-up comedian who booked his first part on a sitcom.

But I don't tell him that. I say, "Your shirt's in the bathroom."

He leans forward. "You took my shirt so you could . . . leave it in the bathroom?"

I shake my head. "I mean, it's soaking in the sink. Leave it in there for half an hour, then go wring it out, and take it home and wash it on cold. Don't, under any circumstances, put any heat on it until you're certain the stain is gone, otherwise you'll set the stain."

Nick narrows his eyes. "Did you do my laundry?"

"No." I look around the room, desperate for something to look at that isn't Nick's face or Nick's body or . . . Nick. "You were doing a bad job of it, and I knew it was gonna stain, so I took care of it. It took me, like, five minutes."

Nick shakes his head, looks at his computer,

119

looks back at me. "That was really nice of you. You didn't have to do that, you know."

"Yeah, well, stop being so bad at stain removal and I won't have to."

In a low voice, Nick says, "You know I'm not another person you have to take care of, Chloe."

My heartbeat speeds up, like I've been caught doing something but I don't even know what. It's like Nick is looking into my soul and seeing something that I could be disclosing to a therapist if I had the time to go to a therapist. I feel like he's seeing me naked, and I certainly don't want him to.

I grab another roll of paper towels and chuck it at him before turning on my heels.

"What the hell? Stop throwing paper towels at me!" he shouts as I run out the door.

A woman stops me as I speed-walk toward the counter. "Um, sorry, but I wanted to let you know that there's . . . something? In the bathroom sink?"

"Oh, thank you, there was a hot chocolate incident," I say, patting her on the arm. "But you're a dear for letting me know."

She stares at me, confused, until I give her a firm smile that convinces her to turn around.

Back at the register, I'm flustered. I make a customer a hazelnut mocha when she asked for a hazelnut latte and I'm forced to remake it. The rush finally dies down and we get into the slow rhythm I love so much—a regular occasionally coming up for a refill, plenty of time to restock the baked goods case, Tobin sweeping up—and that's when I see that I have a text from Tracey.

See you tonight! Hannah made peanut butter paprika cookies so I brought some in for you!

Right. I'm visiting Dad tonight and Tracey and I made plans to get together first. Whereas we used to catch up at places like restaurants, now we're both so busy (her with married life and her wife's attempts at getting pregnant, me with . . . well, everything) that our only chance to actually talk is on my visits to my dad. About once every couple of weeks, Tracey and I find time to sit down and fill each other in on our lives. Her wife is an avid baker (clearly, she has a type) so usually she brings in something from Hannah and I bring in something I've been experimenting on and we do a trade, baker to baker. It's one of the high points of my week, especially now that Annie's rarely in town and I don't have a lot of other socialization.

Can't wait! I text back, planning to bring her some leftover muffins.

And then I text Annie. SOS. I walked into Nick's office and he was shirtless???

She texts back immediately, which isn't a surprise. No matter how busy she is, she'll always respond to a scene that sounds like it's straight out of a rom-com.

Need more details ASAP. Why is Nick shirtless at work?

It's a long story, I respond. Well, okay, it's not. Tobin spilled hot chocolate on him and then he had to go change his shirt and I walked in while he was poorly attempting to clean the stain.

Only you would insult someone's stain removal tactics at a time like this. Wow. This is like in The Proposal when Ryan Reynolds runs into naked Sandra Bullock. Did Nick have any unusual tattoos?

I was too busy throwing paper towel rolls at him to notice. And anyway, it was more like that scene from the Who's the Boss opening credits when Tony sees Angela in the shower and he's like *tortured Tony Danza scream*.

After a long pause, Annie responds, I like my references better. And for the record, you brought Nick up this time.

I scowl and quickly tap out a text. It was a moment of trauma. Forget we had this conversation. AND DO NOT WRITE A SCENE LIKE THIS INTO YOUR NEXT MOVIE.

Annie texts back the shrugging emoji. I write rom-coms. My literal job is including scenes like this.

I sigh and grab a muffin of my own from the baked goods case.

It turns out the muffins were a much bigger hit than I anticipated, because I only have three left by the time I sit down in the break room with Tracey. The "break room" is perhaps a generous name for what is really a tiny room with one table, no windows, a few chairs, and a microwave and fridge in the corner.

"Wow," she says with her mouth full. "This is good. When are you gonna start your own bakery?"

I make a loud fart noise with my mouth, and a nurse pokes her head in the room.

"That wasn't a real fart," I say. "It was my mouth."

She backs out of the room and Tracey laughs. "Uh, defensive much?"

I throw my hands in the air, exasperated. "These people deal with bodies all day! I don't want her to think I'm being disrespectful!"

Tracey shakes her head. "Whatever. Anyway. Bakery. I'm envisioning the sign . . . *Chloe's Cookies*."

I wrinkle my nose. "Definitely sounds like a weird name for my vagina. No thanks."

Tracey thinks about it. "I don't know. Might be good for business."

I ignore her and grab one of Hannah's peanut butter paprika cookies.

"Those are so good, aren't they?"

I nod, chewing. "Yeah. Wow. Think Hannah wants to share this recipe with me? I can for sure see these selling out at Nick's."

Tracey narrows her eyes.

I stop chewing. "What?"

She tilts her head to the side. "Say that again."

"I . . . can see these selling out at Nick's?"

She snaps a finger, nodding. "Yep. You guys made out."

"What?" I spit cookie crumbs everywhere in my indignation. "How did you know that?"

She shrugs. "Honestly, it was a guess, but thank you for confirming."

"Damn it," I mutter.

Tracey grabs another muffin, leaving one for Hannah. "Okay. Start at the beginning."

I tell Tracey most of the details, including the part about walking in on Nick when he was shirtless today.

"Huh," she says.

"What does that mean?" I pick tiny pieces off the cookie and put them in my mouth.

"I'm thinking," Tracey says. "So, like . . .

what's the holdup here? You like this dude, right?"

"I am physically attracted to him," I say, focusing on the cookie.

"Riiiiiight," Tracey says. "So what's stopping you from . . . you know . . ." She pounds her fists together.

"What is that gesture?"

"Gettin' it," she says.

I shake my head. "This is how I know you've been married and out of the game too long. You're making up hand gestures. That's not a thing."

"Pretty sure it's a thing."

"See, this is why I tell Annie this stuff, not you, because she's all, 'Oh, true love, feelings feelings feelings.' She doesn't give me inappropriate, inaccurate hand gestures."

"You think I don't care about true love?" Tracey asks, either mock-offended or real-offended. "In case you forgot, I'm *actually* in love. And honestly, I think you are, too."

"With Nick?" I ask.

"See?" Tracey points at me, like she's caught me doing something I'm not supposed to. "This is what I mean. It's the way you say his name."

I scoff. "How do I say his name?"

"Like this." Tracey looks off into the distance, fanning her hair away from her face. "Niiiiiiiiiiick."

"What is this? This thing you're doing with your hair?"

Tracey stops and looks at me. "It's the wind. Like, you're standing on a cliff somewhere, thinking about your man out at sea, and the breeze is blowing your hair as you wait for him to come home."

"Nick isn't an old-timey sea captain."

"Not *literally*."

"I don't even know what you're talking about."

"Well," Tracey says, suddenly looking more serious, "have I ever told you how I knew Hannah was the one?"

I shake my head. I remember when Tracey and Hannah got together, but Tracey didn't give me a lot of details. They were immediately serious, with Tracey moving into Hannah's place and the two of them talking about marriage within a month.

Tracey puffs up her cheeks and blows the air out. "Well. Okay. So I got super sick. Like, the stomach bug from hell, the kind of thing I wouldn't wish on my worst enemy. No one deserves to double-dragon in front of the woman of their dreams."

I raise my eyebrows. "I'm almost afraid to ask, but what is double-dragoning?"

"You know. Fluids spewing out of both ends. Double-dragon." Tracey does some truly unfortunate gestures to drive her point across.

I purse my lips. "Is this story going somewhere? Because I'm attempting to eat a cookie over here, and there's about seventy-five percent too much vomit talk happening."

"Right. So anyway, Hannah and I were on our first date when this started. Like, we'd gone out to dinner, we were back at her house talking and drinking wine, and all of a sudden I had to run to the bathroom. Her bathroom."

I put down my cookie. "You never told me this story!"

"Because I was embarrassed!" Tracey says, widening her eyes. "This was the worst first date ever. I was barfing all over the bathroom of this beautiful woman I had a massive crush on."

I wince, peering out from under my hand, like that will protect me from the secondhand embarrassment of this story. "Was she grossed out? Did she start sympathy barfing?"

Tracey shakes her head, a tiny smile on her face. "She made me a bed on her spotless bathroom floor, then she put a cold washcloth on my forehead. She slept right outside the bathroom door and checked on me every thirty minutes all night. And then the next day, she let me stay all bundled up on her couch, drinking Sprite and watching PBS."

"So you locked that down," I say, nodding in approval.

"I locked that down," she agrees. "And all

I'm saying is . . . when you're with the right person, you'll know. You'll feel safe and taken care of and like you can barf and shart without shame."

"The dream!"

"I think you're kidding, but I'm not."

I shake my head. "I know that Nick and I have the chemistry of star-crossed lovers on a long-running sitcom. But you know what happens when that couple finally gets together five seasons in?"

Tracey shrugs. "I don't know. We only watch baking competitions, and the contestants rarely have sexual tension."

"The show ends, because it sucks," I tell her. "And anyway, Nick's not even interested in me. Every customer who comes in is interested in him and he's probably having phone sex right now with a cute girl in a heart-printed dress."

"I seriously don't get you." Tracey checks her phone. "And my break was definitely over five minutes ago."

"Then I guess I'm off to visit Dad." I tuck the small box of cookies into my tote bag. "Get me this recipe from Hannah, please. I want to make it for the shop. Ni . . . Our customers are gonna love it."

Tracey rolls her eyes. "Oh, don't stop yourself from talking about Nick in front of me, okay?"

"There's nothing there," I mutter, rooting

around in my purse so I can avoid meeting her eyes. "We kissed once. Big deal."

"Ooookay," Tracey says. "Tell Mr. Sanderson that Tracey says hi."

"Will do." I pull her into a hug, and then we exit the break room, her going to the front desk and me going down the long hallway that leads to Dad's room. The carpet is a brown floral print, all the better to hide stains, and the walls are covered in striped tan wallpaper. This color scheme is my nightmare, but as I walk past the doors, each decorated with a resident's name, some of them accessorized by children's drawings or seasonal wreaths, I remind myself that this is the best place for Dad, even if the décor is as bleak as an Ohio winter.

But that's why I'm dressed in one of my favorite outfits. A red skirt that flares out to my knees, and a shirt with red and purple flowers, topped with a bright yellow cardigan. Some may call it "kindergarten teacher chic," but I know what it is to me: a slight pop of color in a world full of beige.

Sometimes, when I pass another visitor in the hallway here and give them a quick smile, I think about what their lives are like. They might be my age. They might be slightly older and bringing their small child along to visit a grandparent. They might look happy or sad or distracted. No matter what, I remind myself that this person could very well be having one of the worst days of their life. It's easy to slide into the monotony of visiting my dad—these hallways, his room that's always about three degrees too warm, the sitcoms he watches—and forget about why we're really here. But when it hits, the realization that my dad is gradually losing all his memories, things like who called him on the phone this morning or how to turn on the TV or who his daughter's dating . . . well, then. That's the part that really stings.

I know that everyone I pass in the hallway is having that same realization, even if it's not at this exact moment. And any person I pass on the street, or anyone I talk to on the phone, or any customer who comes into Nick's could be dealing with something as bad or worse. That's why it doesn't bother me when people are rude or snappy or downright insulting; I tell myself, silently, that they're having the worst day of their life, and I let myself be perhaps the only happy thing they'll see all day.

That's why I believe in bright colors, and cute hairdos, and elaborate baked goods, and cheerful music. Because it all counts. In a world that's often hard and cold and cruel, the tiny bits of warmth and kindness matter, too.

So I paste a smile on my face and knock on Dad's door. Sometimes it might feel like I'm drowning, but I'm still going to furiously tread water as long as I can.

Chapter Ten

Nick is always in the shop—except for Tuesday nights. On Tuesdays, we all expect him to walk out with a wave around six, and I've learned to stop asking where he's going. At first I used to joke about it. "Oh, off to spin class, are we?"

But then I started thinking about how little I know about Nick, and how he could be going to something really serious. I mean, what if he's in a twelve-step program, or what if he has a weekly therapist appointment? Or, what if he's meeting a stranger for hot sex every Tuesday night at six? It's not my problem.

This Tuesday, I'm so engrossed in my business management textbook that I don't notice the clock tick past six. When the bell above the door jingles, I stand up and paste on my Customer Service Chloe smile as I say, "Good evening and welcome to Nick's!"

A stocky dude wearing an OSU baseball cap walks up to the counter. "Is Velez here?"

I squint. I'm not used to having questions barked at me by bros. "Excuse me?"

The bro shrugs. "It's six fifteen. I've been

waiting out back for fifteen minutes. Is he skipping out on bowling this week or what?"

I shake my head. "I don't have any idea what you're talking about, my good man."

The door to Nick's office opens and Nick strides out, pulling on his jacket. "Sorry, let's go. See you tomorrow, Chloe."

The bro's eyebrows raise. "Oooooh. You're Chloe?"

I nod. "That I am."

The bro looks from me to Nick a few times. "Okay, okay, okay. I get it."

"Let's go, Mooney," Nick says, not looking at me.

The bro leans over the counter and extends a hand. "I'm Doug, but everyone in our friend group calls me D-Money."

There's a lot to unpack in that statement, so I start with the obvious. "Nick has a friend group?"

"Uh, doy?" Doug says. "We meet every Tuesday night for bowling."

"No one calls you D-Money. I'm headed out the door," Nick says.

"Nick *bowls?*"

"Hell yeah, Velez bowls!" Doug shakes his head in wonder and looks at Nick. "You haven't even told her about bowling?"

"Wow," I say, relieved that Nick doesn't have a standing once-a-week sex date with a mysterious stranger. "I wish I could see this."

Doug's smile breaks open, like he just had the best idea. "Come with us!"

"Wish I could," I say with a sigh. "But I'm working."

Doug gestures around. "It's frickin' Tuesday night. This place is a ghost town. Hey, uh, T-shirt dude?"

Doug snaps his fingers at Tobin, who up until this point has been staring into space and thinking about God knows what.

"Yeah?" Tobin asks.

"You gonna care if Chloe skips out tonight? You can . . . uh . . . lock the door, or whatever you have to do?" Doug shrugs.

Tobin looks confused. "Nick doesn't let me close. He said I can't be trusted with the keys."

"He can't," says Nick from his place in the doorway. "Chloe, stay here."

I take off my apron. "Excuse me, I have an invitation from this gentleman to attend a bowling . . . match? Game? Uh, meet? I don't know bowling terminology."

Doug claps his hands. "Hell yeah. We're out of here!"

Nick groans. "Tobin, I'll be back before close. Just . . . don't start any fires."

"That only happened once," Tobin mutters.

"Three times," Nick and I say in unison.

I place my hands on Tobin's shoulders. "I trust you. You can do this."

Tobin nods. "Have fun bowling."

Doug shakes his head as I walk out from behind the counter. "Bowling isn't about fun. It's about sport. Life. Loss. Those killer nachos they serve at the snack bar."

"Those nachos are disgusting," Nick says.

Doug puts an arm around me. "They're dope. You'll see."

"I don't think they ever clean out the cheese dispenser," Nick says, holding the door open for us and eyeing Doug's arm with an unwarranted amount of irritation. "They pour new cheese in on top of it."

"Uggggh," Doug groans, throwing his head back. "Velez, you are such a buzzkill. Let's go bowl!"

"Yeah," I say, meeting Nick's eyes and wiggling my eyebrows. "Let's bowl, Velez."

Nick sighs.

Even in my wildest theories about what Nick did with his free time, I didn't suspect bowling. But then again, he's a mysterious man. I know nothing about his past, and certainly very little about his present, because he doesn't share that information with me, or anyone. That's part of the Nick Velez mystique.

But I'm realizing there's even more to Nick than I ever suspected.

After I get my pair of actually kind of stylish

bowling shoes, Doug introduces me to the only other guy there.

"And this is the one, the only, Shivanenator," he says over the sound of bowling pins falling.

"Shivan," says the man, holding out a hand. "The nickname doesn't exactly roll off the tongue."

Doug throws his hands in the air. "What the hell else am I supposed to call you?"

"Uh, how about my name?" Shivan asks.

Doug shakes his head in disgust. "I'm trying to have some fun here, and these assholes act like I'm conducting a tax audit."

"Have we been transported back to the 1980s?" I ask, looking at the dingy, retro green carpet. "There's a surprising amount of wood paneling in here."

"Don't diss the bowling alley." Shivan points at me.

I crane my neck to look around. "And is there an arcade here?"

Doug scoffs. "Of course there's an arcade. What the hell kind of bowling alley doesn't have an arcade?"

I watch Nick grab a bowling ball out of that bowling ball dispenser thing (I don't have room in my brain to learn bowling terminology) and approach the line. He holds the ball up to his nose and then, in a movement so sudden it makes me jump, slams it down the lane. It's all very powerful and, to be honest, more than a little hot.

I unbutton the top button of my floral shirt because my neck feels warm all of a sudden. "I was *not* expecting bowling to be so erotic," I mutter.

"It is when I do it," Doug says, standing up and cracking his neck.

Shivan leans over. "It isn't."

"I heard that," Doug says. "And you're jealous."

Nick walks over and takes Doug's place. "You having a good time?" he asks me, eyebrows raised, like he expects me to say no or beg to go back to the shop.

"You know what? I am," I say, giving him a smile. "I feel as if I've traveled back in time and it smells like feet, but it's nice to have a break. Thank you for letting me leave the dungeon tonight."

Nick narrows his eyes. "I would hardly refer to my business as a dungeon."

"You're right." I nod. "A dungeon makes it sound much more pleasant."

Shivan stands up. "I feel like I'm in the middle of a romantic comedy. I don't wanna sit here anymore."

"We're not in a rom-com!" Nick and I shout at the same time.

Shivan squints from his standing position and

scratches his chin. "Yeah, what's that one? *When Harvey Met Cindy*?"

"*When Harry Met Sally*," I say flatly.

He points at me. "Yeah. And they're always, like . . ." He makes a wavy gesture with his hands. "Bantering. You know?"

"I don't know, Shivanenator," I say.

He shakes his head, then points at Nick. "Definitely a Harry." He points at me. "Totes a Sally."

I shake my head and Nick and I turn to look at each other. "Are you really okay?" he asks, his voice lower. "Because if you're not having a good time, we can leave."

"I'm having a lot of fun," I say, which surprises me because . . . it's the truth. I kind of like Nick's bro friends and their backward baseball caps and their nonsensical nicknames.

Nick offers up a small smile, one that says, *Okay, but I'm skeptical.*

"All right, Chlo-dog," Doug says. "You're up."

"You can't add *dog* to the end of everyone's name and make it a nickname," I say.

"And yet, he does," says Shivan.

"Nicknames are harder than everyone thinks," Doug grumbles.

I stand up. "Okay, I'm gonna try this, but just so you know . . . I haven't bowled since maybe fourth grade, and you guys refused to let me use the bumpers like I did back then."

Nick shakes his head.

"You got this," Shivan says.

I turn around and grab a ball, then approach the line. I try to mimic the posture I've seen on the guys. I bring the ball up to my eyes like I'm lining things up, like I have some sort of plan or strategy and I'm not flinging this ball down the lane and hoping for the best.

And then I go for it. I use all my strength to hurl the ball and then watch from behind my fingers as it slowly makes its way down the lane. It rolls, rolls, rolls, and then . . .

"STRIKE!" everyone behind me shouts. I turn around to see that they all have their hands in the air, expressions of shock and joy on their faces.

"A strike?!" I ask, incredulous. I check the screen to make sure.

"A STRIKE, Chlo-dog!" Doug says, then rushes toward me and picks me up, spinning me around. I'm laughing so hard that I can barely focus on Nick, but then I see him, staring right at me with a smile I can't decipher.

When the game is over, the four of us sit down at a flimsy table near the snack bar, the laminate peeling up at the corners, and Doug asks Nick to go get us some nachos.

Nick sighs. "Really?"

Doug gestures toward me. "This is Chloe's

first time bowling with us. She needs the full experience, and that means nachos."

Nick frowns but heads toward the snack bar.

"So . . . this is what you guys do every Tuesday? The three of you?" I ask over the sound of pins falling and a sudden cheer from someone who presumably got a strike.

"Pretty much," Shivan says. "Sometimes a couple other guys from college join us."

"T-Money and G-Man," Doug says.

"Tim and Greg," Shivan fills in. "But usually it's just us."

"Just a few dudes, getting our bowl on," Doug says, leaning back with his hands clasped behind his head. He looks at me and the smile fades from his face. "It's cool that you're here."

"Well," I say, not sure how to take this sudden change in tone. "Thanks for inviting me. Or demanding I leave my place of employment, I guess."

He shakes his head and leans forward. "No, I mean . . . Nick doesn't really open up to a lot of people, you know? We're glad he has you."

I shake my head. "Nick doesn't really open up that much to me either."

"He does, though," Shivan says, leaning forward on his arms. "He's just . . . y'know, *Nick* about it."

Somehow, this makes sense.

"He's not into getting super close with a lot of

139

people," Doug says. "You know, because of all the stuff with his dad. It kind of messed him up."

I sit up straighter. "What stuff with his dad?"

Shivan and Doug shoot each other a quick glance, then look back at me. Shivan opens his mouth.

"Nachos," Nick says, plunking them down on the table. "Enjoy your years-old cheese sauce."

"And subsequent diarrhea," Shivan adds.

"I will, dudes," Doug says, shoving a chip in his mouth.

I stare at Nick until he meets my eyes.

"What?" he asks.

"Nothing," I say, grabbing a chip.

As I enjoy this delicious-if-risky plate of nachos, I can't help wondering when the last time was that I actually went somewhere in the evening. I mean, most of my socialization takes place in Annie and Don's living room. For me, a nighttime hot spot is the break room at an assisted living facility or my kitchen table, surrounded by textbooks. Do I go out with the occasional person? Sure, but not as often as Annie thinks, and those dates are more utilitarian than they are social calls.

But I'm having *fun* tonight. It was *fun* to get that strike and hang out with Nick's dude friends. It's *fun* to be out around human adults and laugh, forgetting for a few minutes about the cloud of responsibility that usually hangs right over my head. This wood-paneled, musty-smelling, old-fashioned bowling alley is kinda growing on me, and as I listen to Doug continue to make fun of Nick for refusing to eat these nachos, I wonder if I should do this more often.

Doug drives us back to the shop, and we get there right before closing. Tobin's shoulders slump with relief as soon as he sees us. Nick sends him home after we're done cleaning, leaving the two of us to lock up.

"Thanks for letting me come with you guys tonight," I say. "It was . . ."

"Boring?"

"No," I say, grabbing my bag. "I really loved it. Doug and Shivan are great."

Nick sighs, as if he's reluctantly admitting something. "They are."

"I never thought your friends would be . . . bros," I say. "Actually, I never thought about you having friends."

"Thanks," Nick snorts.

"I mean . . . I don't know, you don't seem to enjoy talking to people."

"I enjoy talking to *some* people," Nick says, and I ignore the subtext in his comment.

"How did you guys meet?" I ask, pulling on my jacket, then leaning against the counter.

"We were roommates in college," Nick says. "Random assignment. When I walked into my room freshman year, Doug had already put up a giant motivational poster about missing one hundred percent of the shots you don't take, and I almost turned around and went back home."

"But then you were deeply inspired by that poster, right?"

"I was not. But eventually, even though Doug and Shivan were always talking about leg day and carb-loading and knew so much more about drinking than I'd ever learned in my nerdy, sheltered childhood . . . I figured out that they were good guys. They made me leave the dorm, even go to some parties."

Wistfully, I say, "I so wish I could see young Nick at a kegger. Did you stand in the corner with your arms crossed, wishing the music were more depressing?"

Nick points at me. "It's like you were there."

"Well, they seem nice."

Nick shrugs. "They are nice."

After years of knowing Nick but not even knowing about the best friends he's had since college, now I'm curious to learn more. "What was your major?"

"Philosophy."

"Ohhhhh," I say, nodding my head. "So you've always been like this."

He looks at me, eyes narrowed. "What's that supposed to mean?"

I smile.

"Anyway, uh." Nick grabs his jacket. "Thanks."

"For what?"

"For coming tonight. It was . . . fun. To have you there." He clears his throat and doesn't meet my eyes.

I'm glad he's not looking at me, because this innocuous statement makes me start to blush.

"Yeah," I say softly as we walk out the door and Nick locks up. "It was a good time."

It was the best time I've had in a long time and a rare opportunity to get out of my own head for a minute . . . but it also made me wonder how much I don't know about Nick Velez.

Chapter Eleven

"What are you doing this weekend?"

I look up from my business management textbook and blink a few times. It's Wednesday evening and hardly anyone's in, which means prime homework time as long as Annie's not around to distract me (and she rarely is anymore). And I know I've been in a business management haze, but I could swear I heard Nick ask what I was doing this weekend.

"Um . . ." I say, standing up from my hunched position. I rub my sore back; I'm getting old. When have I ever worried about a *sore back?* "Why? Are you inviting me to go bowling again?"

"Bowling's on Tuesdays." Nick taps his fingers on the baked goods case. "There's this coffee convention in Indianapolis . . ."

I furrow my brow. "There's an entire convention dedicated to coffee?"

Nick puffs out an exasperated breath. "Chloe. I go to this every year."

I smile and poke him in the arm. "I know. I was kidding."

Nick runs his hand through his hair and, with

his head tilted down, gives me this annoyed look that is, like, too much for me. When he looks at me that way, it's like his hands are all over my body even though we're several feet apart.

"So!" I say more loudly. "Coffee convention. Do you need me to work another shift to cover for you?"

"No. I want you to come with me."

My mouth drops open, and I quickly close it. "What?"

Nick sighs. "You know how you're always on my case to freshen things up here? Be more adventurous with what we offer?"

I nod. "Yes, stop being such a boring old man. I do say that often."

"I'm only two years older than you."

"Biologically. Spiritually, you're an elder."

"Maybe I should rescind this invitation."

I wave him on. "Keep talking."

"Since you have some, well . . . good ideas about how we could change things up, I thought maybe you could come, too. See if there are any new roasters we should try in the shop."

I close my eyes.

"What . . . are you doing?" Nick asks.

"I'm soaking in this moment. The moment when you finally admitted that my ideas are good."

"I said *some* of your ideas are good."

"I believe your exact words were, 'Chloe, you're a goddess and a genius and everything you say is golden. I should always listen to every single idea you have.' "

"You're ridiculous," he says, but I can hear him smiling as he says it. I open my eyes and feel a jolt when I see him staring at me, his brown eyes looking right into mine with unnerving intensity.

"Indianapolis," I say, eager to smash the moment into smithereens. "That's, like, two and a half hours away, right?"

"If you're a speed demon, sure. More like two hours and forty-five minutes. But it's gonna be a long day, so I'm planning on spending the night."

It hits me both quickly and slowly what this means. First the words *spending the night* go into my ears, then they swirl around in my brain for a moment, then they find their way to my heart and the jolt hits me again and I realize what this means. This means I would be spending the night with Nick in another city.

"Um," I say, rendered momentarily speechless, able to make only noises.

Nick holds out his hands. "Separate hotel rooms. I'm not . . . whoa. This isn't—"

"I knew that," I say, squaring my shoulders. "Obviously. Duh."

"Duh."

"Okay. So . . . leaving on Saturday morning?"

"Yep. Staying there Saturday night."

I nod a few times, chewing on my lip, like I'm thinking this over. Because, frankly, I should say no. I need to keep a wide physical distance between Nick and me, not spend hours with him in a truck while traveling to another state. Everyone knows that all bets are off when you cross state lines.

"You don't have to," Nick says. "But it would be helpful for me, to get your opinion—"

"Can I think about it overnight?" I ask, my voice strangely high-pitched.

"Yeah, sure," Nick says quickly.

"Okay." I smile. "Um . . ."

I don't know how to end this conversation, and Nick is just staring at me, so I hold out a hand for a high five.

Nick looks at it skeptically. "What are you doing?"

"I'm high-fiving you. Totally normal way to conclude a conversation."

"I'm not really a high-five kind of person," Nick mutters.

I grab his wrist, ignoring the zing that zaps through me as I do, and smack his palm against mine. "Looks like you are now, dude."

He doesn't move his hand, and we stand there, our hands raised in the air, palms touching like we're in a still shot from an awkward couples yoga video.

My phone buzzes from under the counter and I yank my hand back as if his hand is the top of a hot stove.

It's Mikey Danger. **Hey.**

Somehow, I'm not surprised that Mikey Danger texts like this. Everything new I find out about him supports my initial hypothesis, which is that he is about as uncomplicated as it gets.

I put my phone down to ask Nick more about the coffee convention, but when I look up, he's gone.

After his eloquent opening text, Mikey and I make plans to get together on Thursday night, since I'm not working. He invites me to his place, and as soon as I step in the door, I regret not suggesting my place. For starters, because his kitchen is so full of empty pizza boxes that I can barely step inside. But also because Milo.

"Hello, sister," he says, narrowing his eyes when he sees me.

"A pleasure to see you, brother."

He lowers his voice and leans in. "What are you doing?"

My hands stop moving. "I'm breaking down pizza boxes so I can put them in the recycling container outside."

"No, I mean . . . Well, yes, sure, keep doing that, we're living in filth over here. I mean what are you doing hanging out with Mikey Danger?"

I open my mouth, mock-offended. "Oh, so it's okay for you to live with him, but I can't hook up with him? Double standard much?"

"Nice try, but I'm not putting my tongue in his mouth. It's a little different."

"You guys are sharing a toilet seat. Same level of intimacy, if you think about it."

Milo stares at me. "Why are you like this?"

I shrug and grab another pizza box.

Milo gets even closer to me and whispers, "Do you actually *like* him?"

I concentrate on the pizza box. "It's nice to be around someone who isn't complicated, you know? The rest of my life is a pretty big mess, and all Mikey wants to do is watch randomly selected movies on Netflix and eat pizza."

Milo gestures at the pizza box pile. "Clearly."

"Have you seen Dad lately?" I ask, tossing another pizza box on the pile and finally looking Milo in the eye.

"Uh, yeah," Milo says, suddenly evasive.

"When?"

"The other day! Geez, Chloe, what are you, my mom?"

"Obviously not, as proven by the fact that I'm standing here and talking to you."

Milo rolls his eyes, but in a measured voice, he asks, "Speaking of which . . . do you ever think about, you know . . . getting in contact with Mom?"

I raise my eyebrows and look at him as if he suggested I get in touch with Prince Harry to see if he wants to get coffee sometime. "Uh, no?"

"Why not?"

"Oh, I don't know. Maybe because she walked out on us when we were children, leaving our family in shambles and making me the de facto head of the house?"

"People change, Chloe," Milo says, tilting his head the way he always does when he's trying to convince me of something.

"Leopards don't change their spots," I say.

"Lepers?" Milo asks, squinting. "Do they get spots? I thought that was when your limbs fell off in olden times."

"*Leopards,* Milo. Listen, I've enjoyed the catch-up sesh where you casually berated my life choices, but where's Mikey?"

Milo gestures over his shoulder. "Watching an infomercial about knives on the futon."

I nod. "Cool. That's . . . pretty much what I expected. Wait, I keep meaning to ask. Do you have a job yet?"

Milo nods. "I'm working at a denim purveyor."

I stare at him for a moment. "So . . . a jeans store?"

He sighs. "There's no poetry in your language, Chloe."

I look at Milo again, into those eyes that look just like mine. "Hey," I say, reaching out to touch his cheek. "I'm glad you're back."

"Yeah." He ducks slightly to get out from under my hand, but he's smiling. "Me too. Go make out with your boyfriend."

"On a futon? Never," I say in a low voice, then walk into the living room.

Mikey Danger is, indeed, watching an infomercial about knives, and he's so into it that he barely notices when I walk in.

"Uh, hey," I say, because I've never been in a situation where I've had to compete with an infomercial before. Am I supposed to announce myself?

He looks up. "Oh! Hey, babe!" He stands up and pulls me into a quick and sloppy and not-altogether-unpleasant kiss. As previously discussed, Mikey Danger is good looking, but he's also a more than competent kisser. I'm in no danger (ha) of falling for him, but he certainly has things to recommend him.

He sits back down so I do, too, my legs folded up underneath me, the metal bars of the futon poking my shins through the thin cushion. "So what's happening here?" I ask, gesturing toward the TV.

Without taking his eyes off the knife that's currently chopping a potato, Mikey says, "This is, like, the sharpest knife in the world. It's hypnotizing."

And you know what? He's right. I get sucked into this infomercial, too, so much so that I jump when Mikey Danger softly strokes my milkmaid braids. "I like these," he says in a low voice, and I'll admit, something kinda flips in my stomach, that half-nausea-half-pleasure feeling of attraction.

"You look cute tonight," he says, running his fingers over the hem of my sleeve. I'm wearing a white billowy blouse embroidered with orange and red flowers and a pair of ripped jeans. It's not my dress-to-impress look, but I'll take the compliment.

"Thanks," I say, leaning into him and kissing the side of his face. "You wanna go back to my place?"

He points to the TV. "Yeah. I kinda wanna see how this ends first, though. Okay?"

I nod, deciding against telling him that it's an infomercial and there isn't really an end. But I get sucked back into this knife demonstration, and after a few minutes, as the audience applauds for the last time and an infomercial for copper cookware comes on, I look at Mikey Danger.

His head lolls back on the futon, his mouth open and his breathing slow and steady.

He's asleep.

I grab my tote bag before walking toward the kitchen. I'm about to reach for the door handle when it opens and Fred steps in.

"Oh! Hey, Chloe," he says, taking out his AirPods. "What's up?"

I jerk my head toward the living room. "Mikey Danger fell asleep on the futon and my lust remains unfulfilled."

"Still weird that you're into his whole . . . thing, but whatever," Fred says.

"Where were you?" I ask. "Working?"

"The gym," Fred says. "It's kinda my second job."

"Right. Because of . . . you know." I gesture vaguely toward his body.

He nods. "Yep."

"So . . ." I don't know Fred that well, and I feel like I probably should know my brother's boyfriend, especially since Milo seems convinced that they're soul mates. Maybe now, while Mikey Danger slumbers, is a good time for a heart-to-heart. "What are you guys doing this weekend?"

Fred narrows his eyes at me. "Why? Do you want us to be out of the house so you and Mikey can turn it into your own personal love den?"

I snort-laugh. "I can only imagine that a Mikey Danger love den would be constructed entirely out of pizza boxes," I say, gesturing toward the stack of broken-down boxes.

Fred does a double take as he looks at them. "Whoa. Who organized those? I was leaving them all over the kitchen on principle, like, I didn't put these here in the first place, it shouldn't be my responsibility to clean them up."

"It was me. But anyway, no, this isn't love den related. I was just wondering if Milo was available to be on Dad duty if I'm gone."

"Let me guess," Fred says. "Mikey Danger rented a room in a lovely B&B and you're getting out of town for the weekend."

Both of us laugh, and maybe it should be sad that the idea of Mikey Danger making a reservation or even setting foot in a B&B is a joke, but whatever. I'll take what I can get right now.

"Uh, no. I was thinking about going to a coffee convention with Nick."

Fred stares at me.

"Oh. He's my boss."

Fred nods and points at me. "Right. Movie Guy."

"I . . . What?"

"Milo told me all about it. The movie, the flirty banter, I know the drill."

"The flirty . . . wait, what? Milo's never even been into Nick's."

Fred shrugs. "Well, you know. The Internet."

"Ugh. The stupid Internet causes so many problems for me. Listen, can I ask you a question?"

"As long as it isn't about Mikey Danger. I already have to share a bathroom with him. I deeply don't want to know anything about his love life."

"No, it's about Nick and the trip. Should I go? I mean, Milo's right. We do have flirty banter. And, okay, we did kiss once."

Fred raises his eyebrows.

"But it was during a thunderstorm!" I point at him accusingly. "Don't say you've never made poor romantic decisions under the influence of lightning!"

Fred shakes his head. "I'm honestly afraid to disagree with you right now."

"Anyway, is it a bad idea to go to the convention with him?"

Fred presses his lips together, then pulls out a chair, removes junk mail from it, and sits down. I do the same.

"No offense, but . . . why are you telling me this?" he asks, steepling his hands.

"Because I'm desperate, Fred!"

He tilts his head. "But couldn't you talk to Milo about this?"

"God, no."

"And don't you have friends?"

"Of course I have friends!" I snap, because duh, I have exactly two friends and one of them is usually out of town and the other one I only see at her place of work. I'm doing *just fine,* friendwise. "But you're a neutral party. I can trust your opinion."

Fred nods. "Okay. So the problem is you wanna hit that, but you don't *want* to wanna hit that."

I think about it for a second. "In a nutshell, yes."

"Well, this is a tricky situation. Because

he's your boss, and it sounds like he's doing everything possible to make this less creepy. I mean, you're getting separate rooms. This isn't, like, an HR violation."

I roll my eyes. "Trust me, I'm the HR violation here. Not him."

"And you do want to go, right?" Fred asks, leaning forward.

I shrug. "Well, yeah. I've been trying forever to get Nick to update things at the shop because I think we could be doing so much better. And I'd like to be there to help Nick make decisions."

"Sounds like a pretty easy choice to me," Fred says, leaning back and holding his hands out in an exaggerated shrug. "Go. It's not like you're gonna jump him while you're on the convention floor. And then you can retreat to your solo room and watch bad TV while lounging in the bed your boss paid for."

"When you put it that way, it does sound nice," I say. "You convinced me!"

I smack the table for emphasis, and it starts to tilt left. "Oh no," I mutter. "Don't tell anyone that was me."

Fred shakes his head. "This is why we have to get out of here. There isn't a reliable puzzling surface in the entire house. I have a puzzle mat on the floor of our room but it's *not* ideal and it's making my back hurt. The hot air balloon puzzles deserve better than this."

"Okay, well . . . tell Milo I left. I assume he's back in your room."

Fred nods. "We don't spend a ton of time in the common areas."

I look around us, at the scuffed cabinet doors caked with food residue. "That's such a generous description."

"It was good to see you, Chloe," Fred says, standing up as I dodge the pizza box pile and make my way to the door. "And, hey."

I pause in the doorway, my hand on the frame.

"I know Milo isn't big on talking about feelings, but you should know that he appreciates everything you're doing for your dad."

"Did he tell you that?"

Fred shrugs. "He didn't have to. I can tell."

My heart aches for a moment, to imagine what it must be like for Milo and Fred, to have another person you can communicate with without even saying a word, a person you can do a puzzle with, side by side, working toward a common goal.

I mean, sure, in a lot of ways that's what I have with Annie—we've always had entire conversations with our facial expressions and a shared history of inside jokes that could fill an encyclopedia. But imagine having that *and* make-outs, too. It's almost enough to make a girl consider having an adult relationship.

But then I push that feeling away and smile.

"Good luck with the hot air balloons. And thanks for doing this for Milo."

Fred looks at me with confusion in his eyes. "Doing what?"

"You know." I point around us, the gesture meant to encompass both the house and the entire city. "Giving up your glamorous city lifestyle to come to the Midwest."

Fred coughs out a laugh. "Oh wow, is that what you think happened? That I selflessly followed Milo here?"

I nod. "I've done a lot of selfless things for Milo."

"That's sweet, but no. Milo wanted to be here for you and your dad, and other reasons . . ."

I frown, wondering what Milo's other reasons could be, but Fred keeps going.

"But I was ready to get out of the city. Like, so ready. I mean, I'm thirty-one, which is basically eighty-five in model years."

I shake my head. "You have the body of a twenty-five-year-old."

Fred places one of his hands on mine. "Bless you. But I was ready for a change, and my family lives in Detroit, so it's nice to be a little closer. This move was for both of us. A relationship shouldn't just be about one person giving everything and the other person taking."

I swallow. But what if I stop giving everyone everything, and then they don't give me anything back to fill the void?

I keep that question to myself.

"I'm glad you guys are happy," I say sincerely. "And thanks for talking to me. I'll see you soon."

Fred holds up his hand in a wave and I shut the door behind me. The air is slightly chilly, but there's a promise in the air. It might be rainy and cold and, okay, it wouldn't be unheard of if it started snowing in April, but warm weather is coming. Things are growing, and I can feel it.

Chapter Twelve

We're busy on Friday, like usual (people like to roll into their weekends highly caffeinated, I guess), so it takes me a while to notice the two unexpected guests sitting at Gary's table. Random tablemates in general aren't unusual for Gary; he'll hold a conversation with anybody, at any time, about any topic. But the guests themselves aren't our typical patrons.

I leave Tobin in charge of the counter and head toward the table. "What are you guys doing?" I ask Doug and Shivan.

"I was telling D-Money and the Shivanenator about the girls," Gary says, taking out his wallet and opening it to reveal several photos of his ferrets in their (admittedly impressive) habitat.

I lean in to look at the pictures, then shake my head. "That's great, Gary, but I mean . . . *why* are you guys here?"

"We were just talking about how weird it is that we never come in here," Shivan tells me. "And then Doug was in here the other day . . ."

"And I was like, damn, this place rules," Doug continues. "Great coffee, great conversation."

He gestures toward Gary, who nods. "And great service." He smiles in my direction.

"I can't give you anything for free," I say. "Nick has a strict policy about that. I mean, maybe you can have a day-old muffin, but that's it."

"That's not why we're here. Wait, are you serious about the free old muffins?" Doug asks.

Shivan points at him. "Focus."

Doug shakes his head. "Right. We want to talk to you."

I smile. "Do you want me to start bowling with you every week because I'm so great?"

"No way. That lucky strike aside, you really suck. No offense," Shivan says.

My smile fades. "Muffin offer rescinded."

"Did I ever tell you guys about the time I almost lost a finger bowling?" Gary asks.

Doug and Shivan look interested, but I wave a hand. "Not now, Gary."

He shrugs. "It's a good story. It has everything: intrigue, lust, a late-night trip to the emergency room to reattach an appendage . . ."

I rub my temple. "Guys. What do you want to talk to me about?"

"We're signing Nick up for a dating app," Shivan says, cutting straight to the point.

"What?" I stand up straight. I suddenly feel like I swallowed one of Gary's ferrets, like something is twisting and tumbling in my stomach.

"Velez isn't getting any younger, and he's

always working," Doug says. "It's not like he's gonna meet a new chick at the gym every day like I do."

Doug misinterprets my stare of confusion as one of interest and points to his legs. "I mean, look at these calves. They scream virility. Ladies *cannot* resist them."

"I had the same experience as a young man," Gary says, sipping his coffee.

"Why are you telling me this?" I ask.

"Because." There's no trace of a smile on Shivan's face. "We don't want you to miss your chance."

"My chance to what?" I ask, starting to sweat.

Now Shivan looks at me like I've just asked him to wear a shirt that covers his arms. "To date Nick."

"I don't want to date him!" I spit out.

"Right," Doug says slowly. "I saw the way you were looking at him when he was bowling. And I've heard him talking about you. You guys have a thing."

"A real *will-they-won't-they* energy," Gary agrees. I scowl at him.

"And all I'm saying," Doug continues, "is a guy like that is gonna get snatched up fast on the apps."

"He has those soulful eyes," Shivan says.

"And that hair!" Gary shakes his head in amazement. "Gimme a break!"

"Nick will never let you put him on an app," I say. And he won't. I know him, and a dating app is his idea of hell.

Doug points to himself. "I can be very persuasive."

"And also we're going to do this without his permission, then present him with a veritable buffet of available women." Shivan pauses. "Maybe I need a less creepy word than *buffet*."

"This is just like the Olsen twins movie *Billboard Dad*," I whisper, with a little bit of awe even though this sounds like a horrible idea.

"Exactly!" Doug practically leaps out of his seat as he points at Shivan. "He's never seen it!"

"You're missing out," Gary says. "It's some of their best work."

Shivan rolls his eyes, then looks at me. "We just want Nick to be happy."

"Yeah, well, me too," I say, then glance over my shoulder to see a long line and Tobin moving far too quickly. He's going to drop something any second now. "I've gotta get back. But . . . Nick can date whoever he wants. I'm not in charge of him."

Doug and Shivan exchange a look, one that I can't read. "Whatever you say," Doug says, and I roll my eyes at him before I make my way back to the counter.

"Thank God you're back," Tobin says, his voice as panicky as it gets.

163

I pull off my apron. "I have to go talk to Nick. Be right back."

He lets out a whine like a golden retriever who needs to pee, but I can't focus on Tobin right now. I march to Nick's office and swing the door open without knocking.

Nick looks up from his computer. "What's wrong?"

"I'll come," I say, then wince. "I mean . . . I'm going with you. To the convention tomorrow."

Nick raises his eyebrows. "Yeah?"

I nod. "Yeah. It promises to be an educational and informative weekend."

He presses his lips together. "Everything okay?"

"Yep!" I spin on my heels and march back toward the counter.

What the hell did I just sign up for?

"You know we're only gonna be gone for one night, right?"

Nick stares at my bags, which are in the (roomy, as Milo noted) back seat of his truck.

"Yes," I said. "That's why I only have two bags."

Nick points to his bag, a small, nondescript black duffel. "How could you need more than that?"

I give him an incredulous look. "Um, I had to bring several dresses, because I don't know what the weather's going to be like in Indianapolis."

Nick looks at the truck ceiling. "Chloe. Indianapolis isn't going to have a vastly different climate from Columbus."

"But I can't predict the weather, Nicholas," I say, and he shoots me a weary look. "And then I have various cardigans depending on which dress I wear, and they're all different colors so different shoes are required, and then it's like, no color of lipstick is going to go with *all* those outfits. I needed to bring options. Plus two books, because I don't know what I'm going to want to read to help me fall asleep."

Nick stares at me.

"Fine. Five books."

"Is it exhausting being you?"

I sigh dramatically. "It is."

"All right." Nick starts the truck. "We're off."

"Oh wait! I forgot something!"

"You brought all your earthly possessions. Are you kidding me?"

I smile. "Yes. I'm kidding. Let's motor, baby."

Am I nervous about being hours away from my dad for most of a weekend? Of course. But Tracey reassured me, passionately and at length, that he would be fine for a couple of days. She reminded me that sometimes I go more than one day without visiting him and he manages, so what's the difference?

I mean, the difference is that if something *does* go wrong, I won't be able to be there within a

165

few minutes, and I'll blame myself for it for the rest of my natural life. But, you know, no bigs.

If I'm to believe Tracey, it will be good for me to take some time for myself. She might've even used the term *self-care,* which I always thought referred to drinking rosé while taking a bubble bath and wearing one of those paper face masks that make everyone look like a serial killer, but I guess in this instance it refers to going to a coffee convention with my boss.

Whatever. All I know is that I am pumped for this, and as I reach over to plug my phone in, I can feel the stress leaving my body, like it can't sink its grubby little claws into me once we leave the Columbus city limits.

"What are you doing?" Nick asks, not taking his eyes off the road. He's a responsible driver, I think as I stare at his hands, firmly placed at ten and two on the steering wheel. It's a turn-on, in an *authoritative, responsible adult* kind of way.

I wave off his question. "Shush. How are we supposed to have a road trip with Father John Misty playing? Do you think I want to spend this drive thinking about the collapse of capitalism?"

Nick sighs.

"Let me . . . okay. Here we go," I mutter, scrolling through my phone until I find my playlist. The opening notes of Hall and Oates's "You Make My Dreams" fill the car.

With his eyes on the road, Nick calmly states,

"I am going to grab your phone and throw it out the window if I have to listen to Hall and Oates all the way to Indianapolis."

I let out a cackle as we keep on driving.

We get stuck in some nasty traffic and end up getting there later than we planned, and Nick doesn't want to miss anything (he was being a real dad about this, talking a lot about "making good time" on the road), so we decide to check in at the hotel later tonight and go straight to the convention center now. As we get our name tags from an alarmingly perky young man (I assume he's been sampling the coffee all morning), I'm struck by how huge this place is. I mean, it's an entire convention center, filled with coffee shop owners, employees, distributors, and roasters.

"Oh shit," I say as we step onto the convention floor and I flip through the schedule we received. "Are we gonna take this workshop on Espresso Machine Preventive Maintenance? It sounds positively scintillating. I could run that workshop, and it would be, like, 'Do NOT let Tobin use it when he's distracted.' Problem solved."

Nick ignores me, looking through his own schedule.

"Hmmm, a workshop called '10 Ways to Lose Employees'? I wonder if 'badger them incessantly about their amazing musical taste' is anywhere on that list?"

Nick glances up at me, a half smile on his lips, then points to his schedule. "We're going to this one. 'An Introduction to Roasting Your Own Coffee Beans.'"

I lean toward him to look at his schedule. "Seriously? Are you suddenly into roasting your own?"

He shrugs. "It's not really sudden. I want to do some new things with the shop."

I stare at him and narrow my eyes. "Who are you? What have you done with Nick Velez? Who is this man talking about change?"

"Leave me alone," he mutters, looking at his schedule again.

Nick and I visit the booths of lots of coffee roasters and try about one million samples, some better than others. We sample biscotti, muffins, and cookies, and Nick maintains that everything I bake is ten times better (I agree, but it's nice to have the confirmation). We even attend a couple of workshops, including the one on coffee roasting, which I fall asleep during (although Nick seems to find it fascinating).

It's a long day, and by early evening I'm full of nothing but sugar, caffeine, and anxious energy. I need real food and a long soak in a hotel bath.

"Hey, do you want to go to this networking party thing?" I ask Nick, pointing to my schedule. "There's supposed to be food, and I feel like there's a ninety-five percent chance they'll have pigs in a blanket."

Nick snorts. "I'm not going to that. I came here to learn things and try coffee, not *network*."

I stifle a laugh. "You don't have to say the word like it's a communicable disease. You know, there are benefits to meeting new people. In fact, some of us enjoy it!"

Nick meets my eyes. "I already know all the people I want to know."

I'm about to keep arguing with him when a cute, redheaded woman approaches us. She has on a lanyard that identifies her as the representative of some coffee company, and she's looking at us expectantly.

"Um, can we . . . help you?" I ask her.

"I'm really sorry to bother you," she says with a nervous smile. "But are you, um . . . are you the people from the movie?"

Oh, no. I should've worn a disguise, sunglasses or a fake mustache or a large, face-obscuring hat, anything that would've disguised me. I'm looking as Chloe as I've ever looked (hair in an elaborate bun decorated with a tiny butterfly pin, a blue-and-white striped dress and my yellow cardigan, bright red lipstick), and obviously a room full of coffee enthusiasts is going to have at least a passing interest in a movie called *Coffee Girl* that's set in a coffee shop. What was I thinking?

"Nope," Nick says as I wince and say, "Yeah, that's us."

She squeals. Like, the response you might give

if you were a teenage girl in the late '90s and the Backstreet Boys walked into the room. And listen, I'm no Brian Littrell. My eyes dart around nervously and I cross my arms, trying to make myself as small as possible and hoping no one else is paying attention.

"I can't wait to see the movie. I'm *so* excited and it makes it so much better that you guys are dating in real life."

"Ohhhh, no, sweetheart," I say, gesturing between me and Nick. "We're not together."

Her face falls. "You're . . . not?"

"Nope. No way. Uh-uh." I shake my head, wishing I could teleport myself to my hotel room bathtub. I know the last thing Nick wants is extra attention, and I certainly don't want strangers commenting on my lack-of-love life. "It's just a movie. In real life . . . I mean, yeah, there's some sexual tension, okay? People have picked up on it. But we're not acting on it. Or maybe we did, but that was a onetime thing. It was a mistake."

She stares at me, eyes wide and mouth slightly open.

"Bottom line, we're not dating," I finish.

"Okay, um." She points behind her, then almost runs away.

"Well, that was awkward," I say, turning to Nick and expecting him to be relieved that she's gone.

Instead, he looks back at me with anger and irritation.

"Whoa. You're kinda Hulk-ing out over here," I say.

"Because it would be so awful, right?" He raises his eyebrows.

"What?"

"If someone assumed we were dating. Glad you set the record straight."

"I'm sorry, I didn't know you wanted me to lie to random rom-com fans!"

"You didn't have to lie," Nick says, shaking his head. "But you didn't have to act like it's such an unthinkable prospect."

"I didn't—"

He mutters, "This is like the article."

I stiffen. "What article?"

He laughs, but there's no humor in it. "Oh, are you not familiar? The one where you told a reporter we would never, ever be in a relationship? The one where you essentially told the entire world you couldn't even fathom it?"

"That is not what I said, and I thought you only used the Internet to listen to playlists on music blogs for old men."

"I have a Google Alert," Nick mumbles. "On our names."

"Uh, okay." I throw my hands up in the air. "It's not my fault you're a fame-hungry monster. I don't have a Google Alert for us. Who are you, Kim Kardashian?"

"I don't know who that is."

"Well, maybe you should get a Google Alert for her!" I almost shout.

We glare at each other. The crowd at the convention center has thinned out since it's the end of the day, but the people disassembling their vegan muffin booth stare at us.

I break first. "Listen, we're both tired and we've only had sugar and massive amounts of caffeine all day. Let's go to the networking event and eat all the appetizers."

"I am not networking," Nick says, sounding so irritable that I drop the subject.

"Whatever. You're being a cranky baby. Let's go back to our rooms."

"I'm not a baby," Nick mutters, but he follows me anyway.

Chapter Thirteen

By the time we get to the check-in desk, after retrieving our bags from the truck in the parking garage, I'm fuming. And tired. And hungry. And ready for a hot bath and a fluffy bed and one of the five book options I brought.

I don't feel the need to accompany Nick to the desk, so I sit down in a faux-leather chair in the lobby and check my phone. It's a text from Annie, and I brace myself for a barrage of questions about my time with Nick.

> Hey, how are things going with your dad? Is there anything I can do to help? Remember that we can always jettison the pom wall if you don't have time!!!

I sigh and shove my phone back in my purse. I know Annie's concerned about me, but she has enough to deal with right now, what with planning a wedding to a celebrity and growing said celebrity's spawn in her womb. I'm not going to make her handle my problems, too.

I close my eyes and although the chair isn't exactly comfortable, I'm tired enough that I almost fall asleep to the ambient noise of the hotel lobby. Nick's voice jolts me into consciousness, interrupting my daydreams about pizza slices and burgers and hot, salty French fries.

"So, uh . . . there's a problem."

I sit up from my slumped position and study his face. His eyebrows are knitted together in concern, not furrowed in anger like they were on the convention floor. I stand up and we're face-to-face. "What is it?"

He shakes his head, not meeting my eyes. "I guess the room I thought I reserved yesterday didn't go through and now . . . we don't have two rooms."

I stare at him, waiting for him to continue.

"We have one room." He sounds out the words slowly, like it's my fault for not understanding this preposterous and unbelievable situation. "And all the other ones are occupied."

I shake my head. "It's fine. It's whatever. Two beds, right?"

Nick's lips are pressed together in a straight line. "One bed."

I begin shifting away from anger and into crisis management mode. "Okay, have them send up a cot and—"

"They're out," Nick says slowly, "of cots."

"Wait," I say. "This sort of thing happens in real life?"

This is one of Annie's absolute favorite

174

romantic comedy tropes: when two people are forced to share the same bed (or sleeping bag, or whatever). Usually it's people who hate each other but have sexual tension simmering beneath the surface of their anger. Like in *Leap Year*, when Amy Adams is stomping around Ireland and Matthew Goode is always angry at her but, of course, they end up at a B&B where they have to pretend to be married and share a bed. Or in *What If*, when Zoe Kazan's and Daniel Radcliffe's friends leave them stranded and naked on a beach and they have to share a sleeping bag. It's one of those situations I always roll my eyes at because there's no way this ever happens; I mean, how many times has a real live person been forced to share a bed with someone?

Well, at least one time, because it's happening right now. I get the feeling that wherever Annie is, she's laughing.

Nick shakes his head. He looks embarrassed, which isn't an expression I see on him often, not even when I'm making jokes that are NSFW. "You stay here tonight. I'll just . . . I'll go find another hotel for myself."

"Nick, no," I say, my vehemence surprising even me. "Get real. We're two adults here; I don't think we need to put an entire building between us."

"I'll sleep in the chair," he says. "Presumably there's a chair in this room."

I wave him off, standing up and grabbing my bag, all traces of my earlier anger evaporated. "Whatever. I'll sleep in the bathtub. I have a near-legendary ability to sleep anywhere."

And a near-legendary, at least among Annie and our other high school friends, tendency to talk in my sleep. Which might be a problem if I'm sharing a room with Nick, but I'm not about to banish him to another hotel.

"*I'll* sleep in the bathtub," he says loudly as we walk to the elevator, getting a few looks from people.

"You're an old man," I say as the elevator door closes. "I'm not making you do that. It would be bad for your back."

"*Two years older,* Chloe."

I shrug and stare at the buttons lighting up.

After a silent walk to our room, Nick swipes the key card and the two of us attempt to walk through the door at the same time, bumping shoulders.

Nick closes his eyes and inhales deeply. "Go ahead."

I walk in ahead of him and sit down on the bed, then realize where I'm sitting and stand up again. "I'm gonna go get a pizza."

"From where?" Nick asks.

"Um." I point out the window. "There's a Little Caesars across the street."

Nick stares at me.

"Listen, if you don't instinctively take stock of all food sources when you enter a new environment, then I don't know what to tell you, but I made a mental note of that Little Caesars when we pulled in today and I'm going to get a Hot-N-Ready pizza before my stomach eats itself."

I attempt to walk past him but he blocks me. "You're not getting a Hot-N-Ready pizza."

"Why not?"

He looks at me as if he's explaining why I shouldn't eat a hot dog that someone dropped on the sidewalk. "Because that's disgusting."

"Oh, so you're too good for yacht rock *and* fast-food pizza?"

"You can't call that pizza. I'm not eating that."

"That's fine, because you're so high up on your horse that I couldn't throw a slice to you even if I wanted to."

"Good one."

"I know." I smile smugly. "Now if you'll excuse me, I have six dollars burning a hole in my pocket, and a pizza that's both hot *and* ready is calling my name."

Nick sighs and stares at me for a moment. I let myself study the line of his jaw.

"Sit down," he says. "I'll go get your gross pizza."

Mere minutes later, Nick returns, carrying a pizza box as begrudgingly as possible. I'm sprawled out on my stomach across the bed, scrolling through Instagram.

"My hero!" I shout, tossing my phone aside. "I was about two seconds away from eating this probably disgusting comforter!"

"I'm not sure you're better off with this pizza," Nick says, handing it to me gingerly as if he's passing me a bag of dog poop he picked up off the street.

"Whatever." I sit cross-legged and open the pizza box, then pat the bed beside me. "Sit down. Have a slice."

"I will do no such thing."

"Nick." I level him with a stare. "There's no other food here. I know you're hungry."

He looks skeptical, but he pulls off his shoes and sits down beside me. It's a big bed, and there's room for an entire other person in between us, which is perhaps the only thing that would make this situation more awkward.

I grab the remote and turn on the TV. "Oh, okay. *Steel Magnolias* is on."

"What is that, a reality show?"

I almost drop the remote. "Nicholas. It is a film. It is *the* film. It's about the South and female friendship and big hair and Dolly Parton looking amazing at all times."

He grabs a piece of pizza and inspects it. "I thought you only watched stuff about murder. Is this one of Annie's rom-coms?"

"It's sweet that you refer to all romantic comedies as belonging to Annie, but no. I mean, there's some romance in it, but the entire film is about the bonds between women, and how all their husbands, boyfriends, and sons are completely useless until they're not. And it's cheesy, but in, like, a pleasant way. You're going to make fun of it, but also you're going to be emotionally affected and Sally Field's sobs will haunt you for the rest of your life."

Nick nods slowly. "Sounds like a blast."

I reach over and pat him on the knee, then instantly regret it. "You'll love it."

We start almost halfway through, but I'm able to catch Nick up pretty quickly on account of I have this movie memorized. He leans over a few times to whisper-ask me who someone is or what they're doing, which is hilarious, because we're in a hotel room alone and not in a movie theater. And by the end, as usual, I have tears rolling down my face.

"Are you crying?" Nick asks as the credits roll and minimize to make room for a commercial where bears use toilet paper.

I look at the pizza box, empty except for a greasy pizza outline on the cardboard. "We ate that entire pizza. You liked it."

"It was . . . passable."

I lean toward him. "Admit it. That Hot-N-Ready pizza *ruled*."

It hits me that Nick and I are on a bed and I'm leaning toward him while making what can only be described as bedroom eyes (well, hotel room eyes). The sensation of being so close to him on a bed isn't unpleasant; in fact, I'm afraid to say, the pizza isn't the only thing that's feeling hot and ready.

I lean back. *Get a hold of yourself, Chloe.*

"Don't change the subject," Nick says. "You're crying."

I wipe my eyes with the back of my hands, probably smudging my winged eyeliner. "Shut up. No. Yes. Okay, so I'm crying."

I look over at him and bark out a short laugh. "You're crying, too."

"I'm not."

"Then what is this?" I ask, gesturing toward his eyes.

"It was an emotional movie, okay? My eyes are wet."

"Wet with . . . tears?" I say through a smile. I sniffle a little bit. "I'm not making fun of you. Really. I never should have let us watch this. This is what I put on when I need a Five-Minute Cry."

Nick blinks a few times. "I'm afraid to even ask."

"It's so I don't have to spend all day feeling upset about the terrible things in life. My dad being sick, Milo being selfish, Mikey Danger falling asleep before we can even make out,

180

wars, climate change, people starving in other countries, people starving in *our* country, gun violence. So I, you know. Confine it all to occasional, five-minute bursts of emotion and get it out of my system." I shrug.

Nick looks at me and runs his tongue over his lower lip. It is sexier than any lip-based gesture has a right to be. "Mikey Danger fell asleep before you made out?"

My shoulders slump. "That's what you got out of that?"

"I don't know if your method sounds healthy."

"Excuse me. The Five-Minute Cry, trademark pending, has been tested and approved."

"By a therapist?"

"By me."

"Alternatively, you could ask someone to help you. I mean, you talk to Annie, right?"

I feel a pang of guilt as I think about the text she sent that I never responded to. "She has her own problems. She doesn't need to be burdened with mine."

"Nothing you say is ever a burden, Chloe," Nick says, and his eyes hold mine with such a powerful force that I feel like someone in an old movie who gets beamed up by a UFO. Like I'm standing there in the light, unable to move, knowing that whatever comes next is gonna be bad.

"I don't know how you're doin' on the inside,

honey," I say in a Southern accent. "But your hair's holdin' up beautifully."

The intenseness in Nick's eyes is replaced with confusion. "Was that a bad Dolly Parton impression?"

"Um, it was a great Dolly Parton impression, thank you very much," I say. "Now if you'll excuse me, I'm going to abscond to the powder room to get ready for bed."

"And was that supposed to be a British accent?" Nick asks.

There is no way to explain to Nick that I'm nervous and I guess when I'm nervous I start deploying terrible accents to distract from my feelings. "Lovely artwork," I say, gesturing to a bland picture of a flower as I scoot off the bed and take my bags into the bathroom.

I do a few deep-breathing exercises in an attempt to convince myself to be more normal. "Chill out," I whisper to my reflection. I consider leaving my makeup on, but wouldn't going to bed with my makeup intact be an admission that I care about how Nick thinks I look, when I very much do not want to? And anyway, my eyeliner is gonna stain the pillowcase. So I take off my makeup and change into my full-coverage pajamas—thick sweatpants and my Pizza Slut T-shirt, the one that matches Annie's because we used to order pizza back when we actually had girls' nights.

I frown at myself in the mirror as I brush my teeth, thinking about how much I miss Annie and the way we used to see each other before she got a real job and a fiancé and a pregnancy. I make a mental note to plan an actual girls' night with Annie soon, one where our biggest concern is which movie we want to fall asleep in front of.

I rinse out my mouth and throw my yellow cardigan over my Pizza Slut shirt because I'm not about to wear a bra to bed but also I don't think Nick and I are at a point where I want him to see my nipples through my shirt. I mean, not in a work situation, anyway. Not in any situation. I shoot myself a stern look in the mirror. *Behave, Chloe.*

Nick uses the bathroom after me, and I take a moment to settle myself into bed, my entire body covered by the fluffy white comforter. *This is fine,* I remind myself. *It's just Nick. It's just sleep. It's just . . . one bed.*

Nick comes out of the bathroom and doesn't meet my eyes as he grabs a pillow from the other side of the bed, then sits down in the desk chair.

"What are you doing?" I ask.

"I told you," he says, his entire long body stretched out, closing his eyes as if he's going to drift off to sleep right this second. "I'm sleeping in the chair."

I groan and sit up. "Nick. You're making this

even worse than it already is, I swear. This bed is, like, one mile wide, okay? Just sleep here."

He opens his eyes and looks at me.

"Please," I say, and the thought crosses my mind that I'm begging Nick to sleep with me. Or sleep next to me. You know, in a purely platonic way.

"Does your shirt say *Pizza Slut?*" he asks, standing up and stretching, his shirt riding up to show more lower abdomen than I'm comfortable with. He has a lot of body hair, but I guess if loving a thick carpet of man fuzz is wrong, then I don't want to be right.

"Yes," I say, sliding back under the comforter. "It's a joke with Annie. Don't worry about it."

I reach one arm out from underneath the comforter and pat the bed beside me. "Come on, dude."

Nick groans, lifts up the blankets, and starts to get in before I shout, "Whoa whoa whoa! Are you wearing street clothes in here?"

He stops, halfway into the bed. "I'm sorry. Did you say 'street clothes'?"

I gesture to myself. "I'm wearing my comfies. My pajamas. Clothes that haven't been out in the world, picking up germs and aromas and stress."

"Clothes can be stressed?" Nick asks, a small smile playing across his face.

"Put on your pajamas."

He pauses long enough for me to put two

184

and two together and realize that I'm getting an incredibly uncomfortable four. "Wait. Do you . . ."

"I'm gonna stay in my jeans."

"Do you sleep *in the nude?*"

Nick throws his hands in the air, exasperated. "I sleep in my boxers, okay? I didn't think you were gonna be in my room. Boxers are a perfectly normal thing to sleep in, but don't worry. I'm staying fully clothed."

I shake my head. "Big bed, Nick. Just . . . get under the blankets and sleep whatever way you normally sleep. The idea of jeans in bed is so much more upsetting to me than the idea of your half-naked form."

"Wow," Nick mutters, sliding under the blankets. "Thanks for the compliment."

I realize too late that he's misinterpreting the way I mean "upsetting." He thinks I mean unattractive, but what I actually mean is . . . well, *too* attractive, and disruptive to my sleep.

It's just as well that he thinks it's the former, though. I lean over to switch off the light on my nightstand and he does the same, meaning that I'm forced to listen to the rustle of him removing his clothing as I lie in the darkness. My entire body feels like a malfunctioning toaster, like I'm too hot and shooting off sparks and someone's gonna get burned.

I close my eyes and try to go to sleep—after

all, I'm bone tired after a long trip in Nick's truck plus the entire day of us arguing on the convention floor—but it's sort of like when a small child pretends to be asleep. I'm about two seconds away from pretending to snore.

I've resigned myself to spending the entire night awake when Nick says, "I'm sorry, Chloe."

I jump, the nearness of his voice in the dark a shock. "For what?" I ask, staring at the ceiling.

"For being an asshole today. About the interview, and Mikey Menace—"

"It's Danger and you know it."

"Fine. Mikey Danger. But . . . it's your life. You can do whatever you want."

"Yeah, well," I say lightly. "You're my boss."

"At work, not anywhere else. And I think we both know I'm your boss in name only."

I turn to face him, not that I can see him in the darkness. "What does that mean?"

The pillow crinkles and the mattress groans as he turns to face me. "You do everything at the shop. You're always working, you know our customers better than I do, your ideas are way better than mine . . ."

I snort. "You don't have to flatter me to get me into bed, you know. I'm already here."

"I'm not joking, Chloe. That shop is as much yours as it is mine."

"Maybe we should name it Nick and Chloe's," I say.

"It does have a nice ring to it."

"Yeah," I say softly. "It does."

My eyes are adjusted enough to the darkness now that I can see the outline of his face in the slight glow of the streetlamps shining in through the curtains. I can't see his expression, but I can tell he's looking at me. It feels like he's looking at *all* of me, like he's seeing something I don't even have words for. Part of me wonders what would happen if I said, "Hey, Nick, remember that thing we pinky swore about? The thing we promised not to talk about?" Part of me wonders what would happen if I cut out all the preamble and leaned over and kissed him. Would he want me to? Should I ask him? Should I . . .

"What do you want, Chloe?" Nick asks.

My breath catches in my throat. "What?" I ask in a gurgle.

"What do you want to do with the rest of your life?" My heart rate starts to return to a normal speed. "After you get your degree."

I bite my lower lip. "Promise you won't laugh. Or at least laugh silently so I won't see it in the dark."

"I'm not going to laugh at you."

"Okay. Well." I inhale and exhale. "What I really want is . . . my own bakery."

I let the words hang there for a moment. It's the first time I've ever said this out loud, and I thought it would feel weird to admit it, but it doesn't. Maybe it's the darkness or maybe it's Nick, but it feels good to say the words.

"I want my own bakery," I repeat with conviction. "A place where the desserts are classic but unconventional. Someplace where people can sit down with coffee and a scone and talk to their friends, or have a piece of pie while working on their laptop. Somewhere with tons of plants, and bright artwork, and flowers and butterflies everywhere. It's warm and it's comfortable and none of the chairs or cups match because I found them all at antique stores. And the music is fun and upbeat, not that sad, quiet coffee shop music you like."

Nick doesn't say anything, so I keep going. "I know it's ridiculous. I know, like, ninety percent of businesses fail and it's not like Columbus needs another bakery and I don't even have a bachelor's degree yet, let alone the kind of education I need to become a business owner, but—"

"It's not ridiculous," Nick says. "Chloe. It's not."

I'm so relieved to hear him say that, I almost can't swallow or breathe. "Yeah?" I ask.

"This is everything you're good at. Like I said, I couldn't run the shop without you. You're good at everything I hate. Decorating. Coming up with new ideas. Being friendly to the customers. Picking out music that doesn't make people want to cry."

"Thank you for admitting that last one," I whisper.

"And all the business stuff—finances, bookkeeping, making sure we actually make money. That stuff's such a pain in the ass for me, but you're good at it."

I exhale slowly. "I am pretty great, aren't I?"

"What's the name of the bakery?"

I snort. "I haven't named my hypothetical bakery."

"Come on," Nick says in a low voice. "I didn't just meet you. You named your succulents. You definitely named your not-yet-existent bakery."

"Fine, but—"

"For the last time, I'm not going to laugh."

I bite the inside of my cheek. "Okay. It's . . . the Butterfly."

Nick doesn't say anything.

"Do you think it's bad?" I ask quietly. "Is it too cheesy? Or girly?"

"No." I can hear the crinkle of Nick's smile. "It's perfectly you."

I frown. "What does that mean? Because 'perfectly you' can mean 'perfectly terrible.' "

"It means it's perfect."

"Oh." And all of a sudden, it feels like my heart is beating somewhere in the vicinity of my throat, threatening to leap out and say a bunch of stuff I don't really mean. So I decide to keep talking.

"What about you?" I ask. "What do you want to

do when you grow up? I mean, you're practically at retirement age already, right?"

"Can it," Nick growls.

Neither of us says anything for a moment, and then I say, "So?"

"I guess . . . I don't really know. I opened a coffee shop with one of my friends because I needed something to do, and I liked coffee, and I liked food, and he had the money to do it, and it seemed like a good idea at the time. And then he moved away and I decided to keep it going myself and . . . here we are, years later, and I still haven't thought about what I really want to do."

"Wait."

"What?"

"If you opened the shop with a friend . . . then why is it named after only you?"

Another pause. "His name . . . was also Nick."

I sit up in bed. "Are you telling me, this entire time, the shop has been called Nick's when really, it should've been called Nicks'? As in, 'belonging to multiple Nicks'?"

"We called it Nick's because it was a lot less confusing. People have enough trouble with apostrophes as it is."

I settle back down on the bed. "Wow. I feel *more* confused, because I've been lied to for years."

"You haven't been lied to. Don't be so dramatic."

"You're too *mysterious,* Nick. You're like a crossword puzzle, but one that's specifically about, like, Victorian literature or golf or something else I know nothing about. And unlike crossword puzzles, I can't look up Nick Velez answers by flipping to the back of the book."

I hear the mini fridge click on as neither of us says anything. "Hey," I say, rolling on my side again.

In the dark, I can see the outline of his face on its side. His ear, his hair slightly puffed out, the roughness of his cheek visible even in the darkness.

"Yeah?" he asks.

"I'm sorry I talked to that gossip website. That was maybe not my best decision."

He exhales. "It's okay. I just don't like anything about my personal life being available online . . ."

"You would be terrible at Instagram."

"Social media is for children. But with the movie coming out . . . well, it's out there anyway. I can ignore it, and eventually, another movie will be out and people will forget all about this."

"Except for the shippers," I say. "They're gonna keep writing some extremely steamy fic."

"I have no idea what you're talking about."

"It's—"

"Nope. Don't explain it."

I snort. "You're the one with the Google Alert, dude. Even *I* don't have a Google Alert."

He sighs. "I want to make sure no one's saying anything bad about you."

"There's nothing bad to say," I try to joke, but my voice cracks. It's kind of touching to know that Nick is looking out for me online, even if he doesn't fully understand social media.

"I know this is weird for you, too," he continues. "And you're allowed to tell the truth about how you feel. I shouldn't have gotten mad about it."

I lick my lips. "But . . . but what if I wasn't telling the truth?"

Nick doesn't say anything.

I scoot closer to him, moving my body across the soft sheets of the king-size bed. He may be one big mystery, but the Nick Velez clues are falling into place and I feel like I'm getting closer than ever to solving this crossword puzzle. We're so close now, our noses an inch apart, and I know if I reached out a hand I'd feel his bare chest, his heart thump-thump-thumping underneath his skin and bones.

"What if I changed my mind?" I whisper, and there it is. A telltale hitch in Nick's breath that tells me I have him right where I want him. I thought this wouldn't be a good idea—and I was probably right—but we're here now, and this is Nick. He believes in me. He's the first person

I've ever told about The Butterfly, and he's the first person who's ever encouraged me to do anything about it. My lips part. Would this really be so bad?

"Chloe," he says, his voice a low growl.

I close my eyes. This is the moment. And this time, we're not in the shop, and I'm not worrying that this is a bad idea when I should get out of my head for once and do what I know would feel good. Maybe the world won't fall apart if I let myself have this one thing I want, this thing my entire body has been crying out for, for weeks and months.

"You have a boyfriend," Nick says, and I press my lips together.

"I don't think Mikey Danger would call himself my boyfriend," I clarify. "He's just . . . a guy I see occasionally."

"Still. I didn't ask you to come to Indianapolis with me so I could do this. We were supposed to have separate rooms. I didn't plan all this as some elaborate way to get you to sleep with me."

"I know that—" I start to say, my voice tinged with frustration.

"And I'm not saying I don't want this. Believe me. I want this," he says, and hearing him say the word *want* is almost too much for me. It takes everything in me not to launch myself on him, but I do have *some* pride.

"But you were right. God, it sucks to admit

that you were right about us, but you were. We shouldn't do this. I want you to keep working with me, and I want you to have more responsibility at the shop, and I don't think we can do those things if . . . well . . ."

"If we have a night of crazy passion in a hotel room in Indianapolis," I say, morose.

Nick exhales, short and frustrated. "I wouldn't be done with you in one night, Chloe. That's the entire problem."

I swallow hard and make a noise that sounds like someone smashed a bunch of keys on a keyboard.

"Get some sleep," Nick says. There's a rustle of sheets, then the sensation of his fingers on my cheek. It's so sudden and unexpected that I jump, but then I arch toward his hand, so desperate for anything he'll give me right now. His hands, the ones that make coffee and install tile in my kitchen and grabbed me with such powerful desire on that rainy night I can't stop thinking about, those hands belong on me and I know it, which makes it almost unbearable when he pulls his hand back.

But the other thing I know: he's right when he says this would be a bad idea. I know Annie thinks this is the beginning of a rom-com, just a woman who claims to have "no time for a relationship!" when she's really waiting to be swept off her feet. But I don't even think I have the ability to be swept off my feet, and if I did, who would catch me when I fell? Who would take care of Dad if I was devoting my time and energy to taking care of someone else? What if I abandoned everything, my school and my dreams and my family? And what if—when—it all goes bust? The romantic comedies don't show that, but I know what happens in real-life relationships. Love fades, and lust fades even faster. Nick might find me charming at the moment, but if he was around for even one of my Five-Minute Cries, that would change.

So Nick's right. I guess we're destined to have these secret moments in the dark, getting to know each other with our faces in shadow, always stopping before things get too far. That's never gonna be in a movie, but it's the depressing reality of my real life.

"Good night, Chloe," Nick says.

I exhale shakily. "Good night," I whisper, so softly I'm not even sure he hears me. I don't move, staring at the ceiling and feeling horny and sad at the same time (the worst combination of feelings). It's only when I hear Nick's breath slow down, minutes or hours later, that I finally let myself drift off to sleep.

Chapter Fourteen

I wake up feeling warm and cocooned. I keep my eyes closed for a few minutes, letting my brain run through everything I have to do today while my body relaxes. I have reading to do for class, and there's at least one pie I want to get to, and do I have to work? I should probably get out of bed, throw on my silky bathrobe that's covered in bright flowers, shove my feet into my kitschy bunny slippers, and stumble into my kitchen . . .

Wait.

Where am I?

I blink a few times as an unfamiliar room comes into focus. Despite what Annie might think about my crazy lifestyle, it's pretty rare that I wake up anywhere more unusual than my kitchen table, my head surrounded by open textbooks.

The white comforter pulled around my shoulders. The ceiling that is decidedly not sloped. The hairy arm draped around me—

Holy shit. I'm spooning with Nick.

I stifle a groan that is either an expression of panic or lust; I'm genuinely not sure. Nick's bare chest is pressed up against my back and it feels so good that I want to drift off to sleep for the rest of the day—but eventually he's going to wake up and realize that he's cradling me, his slow breath in my ear and his right hand grazing my boob and his . . .

Holy shit, part the second. Nick has a boner.

I'm familiar with the physiological phenomenon of morning boners, but I absolutely do not want to be near Nick's. Or, okay, I do. I very much do. But after last night's conversation, I want to *not* want to and that means that I need to get away from him, which is gonna be hard because we're still two high-powered magnets, pulled to each other even when we're asleep.

I arch my back and make my body as horizontal as possible, letting my feet dangle off the bed, then do an impressive almost-backbend as I let my body slide to the ground. I rest there on the floor for a moment, breathing heavily.

It's fine. This is fine. I'm huddled on the rough carpet of a probably disgusting hotel room floor, trying to forget about the sexually charged discussion Nick and I had last night while dealing with the fact that he has a boner.

I crawl toward my bag, then slide carefully into the bathroom, where I shut the door with a click.

"Whew." I exhale and stare at myself in the mirror. I look flushed and panicked, like I ran a mile at gunpoint. I shake my head quickly, then strip down to get into the shower. I double-check that the bathroom door is locked, because the absolute last thing I need right now is another rom-com-worthy accidental nudity scene.

I crank the water up as hot as it will go, until it's practically peeling my skin off. The hotel-issued washcloth and bar soap aren't what I would call luxurious, but I scrub my body as if I'm removing all memories of last night. If only I could exfoliate my feelings away.

Nick was right, of course, and now that we're no longer under the cover of darkness, I'm so glad he stopped me from doing something I'd regret. I *do* want more responsibility at the shop, and I like knowing that Nick's compliments are about my work, not about his desire to sleep with me.

Although. I can't get what he said last night out of my head.

I wouldn't be done with you in one night, Chloe.

"Arrrrrrgggghh," I grumble out loud, and then I crank the water to cold.

After I'm dressed in jeans, a black shirt with white polka dots and a red collar, and red flats, I put on my bright red lipstick and smooth down my milkmaid braids. I look good, and my button-up shirt is buttoned right to the collar. Not even any visible neck. I'm trying to send a message of "absolutely nothing sexual will ever happen between us and I am okay with that."

Honestly, though, I should apologize to Nick

for what happened last night, and the way I basically asked him to kiss me while he was half-naked in the bed we were sharing. And I should tell him it's okay that he turned me down, that it's *more* than okay—that it's for the best!

But when I open the door, I see Nick, fully dressed, standing in front of the hotel room desk, arranging food.

"What's going on?" I ask.

"You take a long shower." He turns around. "So I went downstairs and took advantage of that continental breakfast. Their pastries aren't exactly up to Chloe Sanderson standards, but I think I got a pretty good spread."

He points at each item as he describes it. "I got a blueberry muffin and a chocolate chip. Skipped the lemon poppy seed because I know poppy seeds are your sworn enemies."

"They get stuck in your teeth and they're pointless," I say softly.

"Several varieties of yogurt for the protein, and every kind of sugar-filled cereal they had. I left the bran flakes down there because I know you think bran is boring. Oh, and I got you a coffee."

I take a step toward the desk, then notice that the bed is made. "You made the bed?"

Nick shoots me a confused look. "Were you planning on going back to sleep?"

"No, it's just . . . we're in a hotel, Nick. One of

the very few opportunities you have to pawn the bed-making off on someone else. And besides, the cleaning staff will unmake it so they can wash the sheets."

Nick shrugs. "I'm used to making the bed every morning."

You're just such an adult. I don't even realize I said that out loud until Nick says, "You're constantly reminding me that I'm an elderly man, remember?"

Ugh. Why is it such a turn-on that Nick has his shit together? That he can make a bed and obtain food? Maybe it's pathetic that I'm so touched by various packaged food items pilfered from a continental breakfast, but other than the meals Don sometimes cooks for us at Annie's, I can't even remember the last time someone took care of a meal for me. The kind of people I go on dates with don't tend to focus on meal preparation, and even when Dad was living at home and able to use the stove, he didn't make meals for us. Milo and I fended for ourselves, which led to me learning to make basics like spaghetti for us every night in high school.

Also, I would bet my meager life savings that Mikey Danger doesn't even know how to make a bed.

"Okay. Um. Thank you, then," I say, grabbing a coffee and a blueberry muffin. "This was really nice of you."

Nick meets my gaze. "I went downstairs. Not a big deal."

I take a sip of the coffee and grimace. "Wow. This certainly isn't Nick Velez coffee."

Nick smiles, the half smirk that means we're both in on a joke, one of my favorites. "They can't all be winners."

"I'll take what I can get right now," I say. I reach for my phone and realize that, in all the drama of last night, I left it in my bag. I cross the room, shoving the muffin in my mouth, and dig it out. When I touch the screen, I have multiple missed calls from Tracey.

"Oh, no," I say, spraying muffin crumbs onto the screen.

Chapter Fifteen

I know Nick is taking it easy on me because he lets me listen to yacht rock the whole way home. It might have something to do with how I started crying right after I called Tracey back. She reassured me that nothing was seriously wrong, but Dad got into a shouting match with Ralph across the hall because he swore, again, that Ralph was sneaking into his room and attempting to reprogram his TV. This happens a lot and, like Tracey said, it's not urgent, but I want her to call me every time Dad has an episode. If I don't go check on him and calm him down, then who will?

"I don't know why, but he keeps pressing the input button on his TV remote, and then the TV doesn't work because he can't figure out how to switch it back, and then he blames poor Ralph across the hall for the problem," I explain to Nick.

"What does Ralph do about it?" Nick asks, keeping his eyes on the road.

I shrug. "I don't know. Ralph seems to spend most of his days watching his own TV. I don't think he's ever been in my dad's room."

Ralph also, I note only to myself, has

multiple children who visit him often, not one beleaguered daughter who has to shoulder all the responsibility. All that and a TV that reliably works! What *doesn't* Ralph have?

I lean my head against the truck window. "I'm sorry I panicked back there."

"Chloe. You don't have to apologize. Anyone would freak out if they were worried about their parents."

I turn to look at Nick. "And your parents?"

"What about them?"

"Are they, like, around? Did one of them abandon your family to run off to Ann Arbor with a man she met on the Internet in the '90s?"

"Is that what your mom did?"

"Yes, but we're talking about your parents now."

"My mom's great. My dad's out of the picture."

He says it with a finality that shuts me up. For once, I don't want to badger Nick with questions, because I think about what Shivan and Doug said about him at the bowling alley—that he doesn't open up to everyone, that something happened with his dad. Maybe, for once, I'll have to trust Nick to tell me when he's ready.

We pull into the parking lot of Dad's facility and Nick turns off the truck.

"Thanks for bringing me here. And thanks for . . . um . . . last night?" I wince. "I mean, you were right."

Nick looks out the window, then unbuckles his seat belt.

"Anyway," I say, narrowing my eyes. "I'll find a ride back. You don't have to wait."

Nick opens his door and steps out of the car.

"Um," I say, opening my door. "What are you doing?"

Nick shrugs. "I'm going in."

I shake my head. "You really, really don't have to do that."

And yet, Nick Velez, unpredictable and confusing as always, walks with me to the front door and waits with me as I buzz in.

"This might be weird," I say, turning to him.

He looks at me, his brown eyes laser focused on mine. "I'm gonna stay with you," he says, and then he grabs my hand.

At this point we've kissed and shared a bed, but nothing—nothing—has been close to the total-system shock of Nick holding my hand. It's like I can feel his heart beating against my palm.

The door clicks open and we walk in together. Tracey looks up from the front desk and smiles her typical, reassuring smile, but her eyes widen as she takes in Nick, and Nick's hand in mine.

I can almost see her tell herself to be professional, and she plasters on a generic smile. "I'm so sorry I bothered you while you were gone."

"We were headed back anyway," Nick says. "I'm Nick, by the way."

He lets go of my hand to shake Tracey's, and I'd be dreading the conversation she's gonna have with me later if I weren't so worried about my dad.

"Tracey," she says with a smile in his direction, and then she turns to me. "So your dad's fine, as always, but I know you want me to keep you updated—"

"I do." I nod.

"Okay. So, there was a lot of yelling. He threatened to hit Ralph because he thinks Ralph broke his television."

I groan. "Okay. Um. I'm going to go talk to him. And I'm sorry he's so confused, and so angry, and—"

Tracey shakes her head, her real smile back on her face. "Hey. That's literally why he's here, okay? You don't need to apologize for it."

I give her a grateful smile and start walking toward Dad's room, Nick trailing behind me.

"This is a nice place," Nick says, looking around as we walk down the all-beige, all-the-time hallway.

I look over my shoulder at him. "Did you think I put my dad in a shithole?"

"No," he says, his long legs taking a couple of steps to catch up to me. "It's just, when you picture a place like this in your head, you think of it as being clinical. Hospital beds and tile. I bet your dad's really happy here."

We stop in front of Dad's door and I give Nick a tiny smile. "Yeah. Well. This is where pretty much all the money I make goes, so it had better be nice. But what am I supposed to do? Put my dad in a dump and spend my leftover money on a cruise?"

"You're a good daughter."

I exhale, feeling like I'm about to cry. "Are you sure you want to go in here with me? He won't know who you are and it might get uncomfortable."

"I'm not leaving you alone right now," Nick says, and the idea of him protecting me makes me feel half happy and half scared.

I knock on the name tag three times, then push the door open. "Dad?"

Dad sits on the couch, eyes on the TV. "Chloe!" he says with a wide smile. His eyes catch on Nick and he falters.

"This is Nick," I say, and Dad nods, even though I can tell he's confused. I glance at the TV, which shows a bull-riding competition. "Since when have you been into bull riding?"

"Since never. But the damn thing's broken." His voice rises as he continues. "That asshole Ralph across the hallway keeps coming in here while I'm sleeping and messing with it. I've got half a mind to punch him next time I see his ugly face."

I purse my lips together, risking a glance at Nick to see if he's totally freaking out, but he's listening to my dad as if everything he's saying makes sense and isn't threatening and profane. Dad used to be strictly antiprofanity, but that's another way he's changed. It's like he doesn't know, or care, what's socially appropriate. This is why it hurts when people say that Alzheimer's uncovers someone's "real" personality, without the filter—because this person, the one ranting about his TV, isn't any realer than the one who scolded me for cursing twenty years ago.

"Dad," I say as gently as possible. "Do you remember how I told you not to press any of these buttons?"

"I didn't!"

"And how I left you a note telling you not to press the buttons? Where's that note?"

I get down on my hands and knees and find it—a little yellow Post-it note under the TV cabinet, my handwriting in all capitals: *DO NOT TOUCH THESE BUTTONS*.

"Okay, listen. I'm gonna make a new note and I'm gonna tape it on here to remind you or Ralph or whoever not to press any of these buttons, all right?" First I press a few things to fix the TV and make it show something other than bull riding, and then I make another note. As I work, I remember that Nick is still here, and I turn to see him and my dad talking quietly, each of them shooting the occasional glance at me.

"Uh," I say, standing up. "What's going on over here with you two?"

"I'm telling Dave here that a girl like my daughter isn't gonna wait around for his sorry ass forever," Dad says, pointing at Nick.

I wince. "Dad, this isn't—"

"And I'm telling him, neither of you's getting any younger. Maybe it's time to shit or get off the pot, if you know what I'm saying."

I look back and forth between Nick and my dad, suddenly understanding exactly what people mean when they say that their heart is breaking. Because that's what this feels like, like something deep inside my chest is splitting apart and crumbling into a million tiny pieces as my dad thinks he's having a typical parent heart-to-heart with my boyfriend, when really he's talking nonsense to my boss.

"Dad," I say again, sitting down beside Nick on the love seat.

"All I want," Dad says, looking at both of us, "is to know someone's taking care of you when I'm not around."

I press my lips together and hope that if I just shut my eyes tight enough, this moment will be over. I won't be stuck here beside Nick, both of us listening to my dad mistake him for a long-ago boyfriend and—

"Mr. Sanderson," Nick says, interrupting my depressing train of thought. "Forgive me if this sounds rude, but Chloe has no problem taking care of herself. I've known her way less time than you have, and even I know that."

My dad smiles a little. "Well, that's true, but still. I just want some sort of promise that you're not jerking her around, you know?"

Nick grabs my hand, making me jump, and he leans forward toward my dad. "I promise you," he says, looking my dad straight in the eyes. "I'm going to take care of Chloe for as long as she'll let me."

I'm glad Nick isn't looking at me, because my jaw has permanently dropped to the floor. I know Nick and I just agreed to never do anything physical again, but right now I'm filled with the urge to rip every single last item of his clothing off his body. I've been part of several sexual conversations that were hot enough to almost make my phone spontaneously combust, but I've never heard anything as sexy as what Nick just said. I can think of about five hundred ways I'd like him to take care of me right now, and none of them involve buying me breakfast or making the hotel bed.

But instead of saying that, I just force myself to close my mouth as my dad says, "Well, it's not a proposal, but I'll take what I can get. Chloe, you've got a good one here."

I shake my head, remembering where we are and what's happening. Right. We're sitting across from my dad in an assisted living facility, and he thinks Nick is my high school boyfriend, and also he's engaging in paternalistic thinking that I would definitely complain about if not for his health.

Nick's hand is still on mine, and he rubs my thumb with his in a gesture that feels both casual and electrifying. *This is real for now,* I tell myself. *This is real in this room, in front of Dad. Just pretend. Just let yourself.*

We talk to my dad a little longer before we leave. I make him promise not to touch the buttons on his remote even as I know that his promise means nothing. Nick puts his arm around my shoulder as we walk down the hallway, and I don't say anything. I can't say anything. Tracey sees us coming and stares, her mouth attempting to form words, and I widen my eyes in an attempt to communicate that I'll explain all this to her later.

She buzzes us out and we walk to Nick's truck without saying a word. When we stop in front of the passenger door, I finally pull myself out from under his arm and turn to face him.

We're not in the building anymore. The spell is broken.

"What *was* that?"

Nick twists his arm to rub the back of his

neck. He winces. "I'm sorry. I don't know. I kept thinking about what you told me, about how all you wanted was for your dad to know you were taken care of, and I know I'm not Dave, but—"

I launch myself at him, pulling him into a hug, my arms around his neck and my face pressed into his shoulder. He hugs me back, his arms wrapped around my waist, and he feels so good. Even after a night in a hotel and hours in a truck he smells like Nick, and being held by him is a thirty-second break from my real life. A tiny respite from my responsibilities.

"Thank you," I say, my voice muffled by his shirt. "He won't remember that tomorrow, and I know it was weird for you, but he was so happy for a minute there. It was . . . it was nice to pretend. Thank you."

Nick rubs my back, his strong hands sliding against the fabric of my shirt. "You're welcome, and it wasn't weird. I liked being Dave."

I laugh into his neck. "In addition to the bowling, do you also secretly do improv? You were really 'yes, and'-ing back there."

Nick ignores my question. "Is Dave at least hot?"

I pull back and look Nick in the eyes, my hands still around his neck. "Dave had bleached blond spiky hair, like a teenage Guy Fieri, but without the flaming button-down shirts or the love of diner food."

"So . . . the answer is yes?"

I laugh for real now, my shoulders shaking.

"Can we go home?" I ask, wiping my eyes. "I mean, can you take me to my home?"

"Yeah," Nick says, giving my shoulders a squeeze. This is all normal friend behavior; I would act this way with Annie or Tracey. And I know that both Annie and Tracey check in on me and offer to help me when I need it. But with Nick, I can't ignore how different it all feels. Electric. Exciting. I think about what my dad said. *You deserve someone to take care of you the way you take care of everyone else.*

I'm going to have to bake, like, five pies to work through all this.

Chapter Sixteen

Annie's finally back in town, praise the Lord, so we do something we haven't done in quite a while: we hang out at her house while Uncle Don makes dinner.

"Geez," I say, settling in on the floral couch where Annie and I have watched approximately one million rom-coms. "It's been ages since my butt has graced these hallowed cushions."

"You mean you don't come over while I'm gone and watch movies with Uncle Don?" she asks, taking a sip from a can of sparkling water.

I point at her. "I did come over here when he was doing his annual *Lord of the Rings* rewatch, but he and Tyler did *not* like it when I fell asleep and started snoring."

After not being in a relationship for, oh, his whole life, Don surprised all of us by bringing Tyler home after a convention. She's since moved to Columbus, and although she hasn't moved into the house yet, she's here pretty much all the time.

"So," Annie says, setting her can down on the coffee table and wincing. "I hate to have to do this, but are you ready to talk . . . wedding stuff?"

I clap my hands together. "I've never been so

excited for anything in my entire life." Part of me is being hyperbolic, but also, I feel guilty for not telling Annie about Nick's and my unplanned confessional hotel sleepover. It feels too private, and I don't want to hear her thoughts on how it's like a rom-com or how Meg Ryan was once in a similar situation or whatever. I'm happy to talk about something else.

"Okay." Annie pulls a binder out from under the couch and smacks it onto the coffee table. "There's one month left until the wedding, which means that a lot of stuff is done but there's so much to do."

She flips toward a tab marked *pies*. "So, what types of pie are you thinking?"

"Hold up." I grab the binder from her and flip through it. There are tabs marked *twinkle lights* and *vows* and even one that says *pom wall*. "Did you make your own IRL version of Pinterest?"

Annie smiles a little guiltily. "Actually, um . . . Drew's mom made this binder for me. She's very crafty and organized."

Not getting along with your mother-in-law is such a joke in popular culture that it even made its way into a rom-com, *Monster-in-Law* starring Jennifer Lopez and Jane Fonda. But Annie loves Drew's mom, probably because she misses her own parents so much. She looks positively giddy to have this nerdy binder.

I nod. "Okay, well, bitch better not step on my pom wall. That's all I'm saying."

"Please don't say stuff like that when she's here," Annie says, taking the binder away from me and flipping back to the *pie* tab. "Carol is one hundred percent not going to get our sense of humor."

"So. Pie." I start counting off on my fingers. "I'm thinking . . . an apple whiskey. I know that sounds like fall but people love it and I already baked three and stuck them in the freezer, so please don't hate the idea. Lemon chess, chocolate silk, blueberry lavender, and bourbon pecan."

Annie nods, writing all this down. "Very boozy. I love it."

"Are you sure? Because I can think of five to ten alternative pies."

"Chloe." Annie stops writing and puts a hand on my arm. "I love these pies."

"You do?"

"Yes." She resumes writing. "If it were legally possible, I would marry these pies."

"You're marrying Drew."

"These pies would be my sister wives," she says, then flips to another tab. "On to . . . bridal party. You have your dress, so we're all good there . . ."

I give her a thumbs-up. Annie went through a moment of wanting me to wear the gold dress

Kate Hudson wore in *How to Lose a Guy in 10 Days* and I had to remind her that there aren't enough Spanx in the world to make me feel comfortable in a clingy number like that. Also no one would even pay attention to Annie in her dress because my boobs would be *fully* out.

She finally decided I should pick out my own dress, since I'm the only bridesmaid, which was both fun and stressful. I found a long, sparkling blush pink dress with fluttery elbow-length sleeves that (a) is perfect for a spring wedding and (b) makes me feel like a romantic mermaid. Annie approved it, and I can't wait to wear it.

"Okay, so on to . . ." She flips to the next tab, but I interrupt her.

"Wait. Wait, wait, wait. What about your bachelorette party?"

She wrinkles her nose.

"What are we going to do? Do you want to *Magic Mike* it up? Admittedly, I know less than nothing about the world of the male revue, but I'll ask around. Or a bar crawl where I make you wear a tiara covered in penises?"

"Covered in penises?" Annie asks, horrified.

"Not real ones," I clarify. "Or do you want to go full-on *The Hangover* and fly to Vegas and totally ruin your life? Because I don't think we have the funds for that, but maybe we could do a Columbus version. The zoo definitely has at least one tiger."

"I don't think the zoo's going to let us borrow a tiger."

"You know what I always say. Don't ask, don't get."

"Hey." Annie closes her binder. "I really, really appreciate you being so enthusiastic about this, but I'm not sure I have time for a bachelorette party."

I throw my hands in the air. "What do you mean? You only get married once, probably! You've gotta do it up."

"I mean . . . the premiere's this Saturday. And even when I'm not focusing on that, I have so much to do for the wedding. Oh, yeah, and I'm growing a human life inside me." She sighs heavily. "This is probably the busiest time of my entire life."

"All the more reason to let your yayas out in the form of a regrettable wedding tradition."

Annie laughs a little. "Also, um, who else am I going to invite to this bachelorette party? It's just going to be you and me. That's not exactly a party."

I sit back. "Um, ouch."

"Hey!" Annie widens her eyes. "That's not what I meant. You know that's not what I meant."

I nod.

"Every day with you is a party," she says, smiling. "You, yourself, are a walking party."

"Keep complimenting me," I mutter.

Annie shakes her head. "Hey. How about this? Let's plan a movie night, just you and me, okay? Like the old days. We'll eat pizza and you can tell me how terrible my favorite movies are and it'll be so fun."

I didn't even realize movie nights had turned into the old days. I thought they were still our current days. But I guess that's what happens when people move on and you're stuck in time. Every day, things slip away and become part of the past without you even knowing it.

But there's not really any point to saying any of this . . . I mean, what do I want Annie to do? Quit her dream job, start living with her uncle again, and *not* marry the love of her life? Go back to being lonely because I'm unhappy? None of that would be possible anyway, since she's going to have a baby with Drew soon. Her life is hurtling forward, whether I like it or not.

"Yeah, okay. That sounds great," I say.

"Anyway, I don't want you to spend a ton of time planning a ridiculous party when you're already doing so much for me, and I know you have your own stuff going on. How's your dad? How's Milo? Are things going okay?"

I hold back a wince and wave her off. I know she means well, but the last thing I want to do is let one of our rare evenings together devolve into a Here's What's Wrong with Chloe's Life session.

"It's fine. It's all fine. But I don't want to talk about that right now . . . tell me how Drew Jr. is doing." I reach forward and place a hand on her completely flat belly.

Annie hesitates, then smiles. "As if we would ever name our baby that," she says, but then she starts talking about baby names and registries and the merits of different cribs and even though none of this means anything to me, I'm glad she's telling me. It almost helps me forget that apparently I'm just part of her past now.

Chapter Seventeen

"I don't understand how I got sick," I say, blowing my nose for the fortieth time in the last hour.

"Probably because you never sleep, don't take care of yourself, and have worn your body down into a desiccated husk?" Milo says with an innocent shrug.

"Watch out." I wave my used tissue in his direction. "I'll infect you."

A woman walking past us in the cookie aisle holds her box of Nilla wafers closer to her chest.

"I'm not really spreading disease," I call after her. "This is my brother and he's being an asshole."

Milo and I are attempting to do a typical "siblings hanging out" day, which entailed him coming with me to Target to pick out some stuff for Dad. I almost didn't want him to accompany me into this sacred space; Target is where I go when I feel lost and untethered (so, most days). There's something about the overhead lighting, so bright that it sterilizes all my worries away. Pushing the cart fills me with a sense of purpose. And there's always the belief that this endcap or this clearance rack will hold the answer to something, that the next aisle over will have the solution to a problem I didn't even know I had.

But Milo offered to come and I don't want to discourage him from helping me. You know what they say: don't look a gift horse in the mouth, even if that horse is your twin brother who basically abandoned you.

"Wave that thing somewhere else," Milo says with a grimace. "If I wanted what you have, I'd go straight to the source and suck face with Mikey Danger myself."

"Real mature," I say, tossing some snack-size packages of Oreos into our cart.

"So . . . snacks, coloring books, colored pencils," Milo says, looking through our cart. "Are we shopping for our dad or your secret toddler?"

The parallels between taking care of a relative with a degenerative disease and caring for a child have occurred to me before. There's a lot of yelling, confusion, poor communication, defiance, and yes, snacks. But the thought sends me into a bad place where I start thinking about Dad's mortality and my mortality and then it's really hard to get my Target on, so I change the subject.

"Where's Fred today?"

Milo always fights back a smile when he talks

about Fred, like he's afraid to share his unbridled joy with me. Frankly, it's annoying.

"He's doing a shoot for some discount chain store. I think he's going to be wearing a lot of out-of-season track suits and, like, pulling the hoods off his head while staring at the camera like this."

Milo stares toward the graham crackers with his lips pursed.

"I can see why Fred is the model in your relationship," I say. "You're terrible at smizing."

"Great reference to a television show from like ten years ago," Milo says, throwing a box of Chips Ahoy into the cart.

"Dad hates Chips Ahoy."

"They're for me. Duh," Milo says. "Oh, can we stop by the frozen food aisle? I am in desperate need of pizza rolls."

I turn to look at him. "Are you a teenage stoner?"

"Have you *had* pizza rolls lately? Teenage stoners are onto something. Anyway, Mikey ate an entire family-size bag the other night and I was like, 'Um, answer me this: are you a family or are you one dude on a couch watching infomercials?' and while he did *not* give me an answer, the point is I now have no pizza rolls."

"He's still into that infomercial, huh?"

"It's entrancing. That knife can chop through anything. I'm thinking of getting one."

I raise my eyebrows at him as I push the cart toward the frozen food aisle. "For all the cooking you do?"

Milo shakes his head. "Someday I'm gonna want to slice a tomato into paper-thin slices and I'm not going to have the knife to do it."

He reaches into the case and pulls out the largest bag of pizza rolls I've ever seen. "Okay, what else?"

"Dad needs sweat pants."

"And sweat pants he will get!" Milo says, thrusting a fist in the air as if he's leading the charge. A wide-eyed baby in a shopping cart laughs at him, and Milo stops to examine him. "Well, aren't you cute. How old?"

As he talks to the baby's mother, cooing at the appropriate times (as if he knows anything about babies!), I'm reminded that this is Milo's thing. He's charming and friendly and strangers love him. Everyone is his friend and I'm sure in a month he'll have scammed his way into a guest room in a nicer place, and then a few months later he'll end up sharing one of the fanciest apartments in town. I'm not even sure if he knows he's doing it, but Milo can give you one look and make you do whatever he asks. All these years later, it's still incredibly annoying.

I inspect the individual frozen meals while he talks to the mom, and when he finally starts walking away he calls over his shoulder, "I'm serious about that sleep training book. It's the best one out there!"

"What the hell do you know about sleep training?" I whisper as we walk toward the clothing department. "You don't have a child. Do you even know anyone with a child?"

Mock-offended, Milo puts a hand on his chest. "Chloe. I know things."

"Right," I mutter. "Hey, when's the last time you went to visit Dad?"

"Yesterday," Milo says smugly. "Did you know his TV doesn't work?"

I groan and fill Milo in on the situation.

"Uh, wow," he says, inspecting a pair of sweat pants before making a face and putting them back on the shelf. "And here I thought Ralph across the hall was some sort of TV-busting freak."

"He very well could be, but I doubt it," I say, picking up the pair of sweat pants Milo put back. "What's wrong with these?"

Milo wrinkles his nose. "They're so . . . sweat pants."

I give him an incredulous look. "What, you're some sort of fashion expert now that you have a model boyfriend and you sell jeans? They're supposed to be sweat pants. Dad has too much trouble getting any other pants on and off these days."

I toss them in the cart and look at Milo when he doesn't say anything. "Hey," he says, meeting my eyes. "Until I visited him, I didn't . . . I didn't know how bad things were. With Dad."

I nod casually, like we're talking about our weekend plans and not the deterioration of our father. "Yeah, well. I tried to tell you."

Milo exhales, absentmindedly running his fingers over the sweat pants on the shelf. "I guess I didn't listen because I wanted to pretend it wasn't happening, you know?"

"Not really an option for me."

"I know, I know." And then Milo surprises me by leaning in for a hug. "I'm sorry I wasn't here."

Tears spring into my eyes, but I bat my eyelashes quickly until they go away. *Save it for a Five-Minute Cry,* I tell myself. If I start crying here, under the fluorescent lighting of the Target men's department while a Rascal Flatts song plays, I may never stop. Those ugly sweat pants will float away on a river of my tears.

"I'm sorry you weren't thcrc, too," I say, reluctant to let Milo off the hook, even though every cell in my body is crying out to forgive and forget, to file this away with all the other ways Milo has let me down, all the things I've never complained about.

"I'm here now," he says into my ear.

"I know," I say, and I decide to let myself believe it. To give in to this moment right here, to let the magic of Target fix all my problems, to let Milo be Milo.

• • •

By the evening, I'm so sick that I can't get out of bed. You know how everyone says that sharks have to keep moving constantly or they'll die? That's how I feel as I huddle in bed, my knees pulled up to my chest under my blankets, watching whatever sitcoms are on Antenna TV (right now, *Welcome Back, Kotter*). I stopped baking pies and working and studying and running around and now I'm forced to be in bed, alone, thinking about my own life, and I feel like I'm going to die.

I text Nick that I can't come in on account of snot is pouring out of my head and customers tend to find that gross. He texts to ask me if I need anything, but I ignore him. First off, no one ever means that when they say it (it's too vague; what is *anything?* Could I ask you to pay my dad's rent for a month? Be more specific!), and second, the kids on *Welcome Back, Kotter* are really in a scrape this time.

Typically I like to watch shows about murder investigations, but on the rare occasion I'm sick, my go-to comfort viewing is sitcoms. It's probably because they remind me of my dad— he always had an episode of *Happy Days* or *The Partridge Family* or *One Day at a Time* playing. Sometimes he even mixed it up and watched sitcoms that were at least relatively new, like *Family Matters* or *Full House* or

Step by Step. He would get home from his job selling insurance, exhausted and usually kind of cranky, and I would serve him whatever I made for dinner. And then he'd turn on the TV and we'd watch something old or something new, laughing at the predictable jokes and well-worn plotlines.

But as much as I loved watching those shows with my dad—it was, after all, pretty much the only time we got to spend together—they always broke my heart a little. Because no matter how charmingly dysfunctional those families were, they were all TV perfect. They all loved each other and helped each other and there certainly was never a teenage girl taking care of two sad, emotionally checked-out men.

Welcome Back, Kotter ends and *Rhoda* starts playing. "Oh, I love *Rhoda*," I croak, even though no one else is here and I should probably be saving my voice. "Such elegant scarves."

I hear a knock on my door and sit up straight in bed. Annie's not in town right now. Uncle Don always sends a polite text or call rather than coming up to my apartment. Mikey Danger is working, and even though I texted him, Can't hang out later; too sick, he hasn't responded. I mean, he's probably driving his car and making deliveries. It's fine.

Since I live in the carriage house, solicitors don't ever knock on my door. Which leaves one person: Milo. Maybe Milo needs me for something; maybe he was visiting Dad and there was a problem!

I swing my feet over the bed and get up too quickly, feeling dizzy. "Ugh," I say, holding my head in my hands. I cross the apartment in a few steps, then swing open the door, only to come face-to-face with someone who is decidedly not my twin brother.

It's Nick, and I'm staring directly at his mouth, because I assumed I'd be meeting Milo's eyes.

"Um . . . hi?" I say, my eyes moving up to meet his.

"Hi," Nick says, a smile forming for a second before he wipes it away. I look down and remember that I'm wearing pajamas, my hair is in a truly unfortunate and lopsided topknot, and I'm not wearing any makeup. Not my signature bold lip; not my typical winged eyeliner; not the blush that gives my deathly pale skin the slight touch of pink it needs for me to not look like a sexy ghost.

My non-penciled-in brows contract. "Why are you here?"

Nick lowers his head to meet my eyes. "I'm checking on you. You said you were sick."

I narrow my eyes. "Did you check on Tobin last week when he was sick?"

"No, but I knew he wasn't really sick."

"Touché."

Nick gestures toward the sky with one hand. "It's starting to rain."

"Are you asking to come in?"

He sighs. "If I may be so bold, Chloe."

I smile with faux-sweetness and step aside, gesturing as if I'm a butler. "Come in, sir. Welcome to my humble abode. Wait, what's in the bag?"

I close the door as Nick walks to the table. He sets a paper bag on it and pulls out a Tupperware container. "Soup."

"You brought me soup? Like, you went to the store and purchased soup for me?"

Nick looks at me quizzically. "You've set such a low bar for the people in your life. No, I didn't buy you soup from a store. I made soup."

I sink down into one of the chairs at the table, feeling dizzy. I could certainly blame it on whatever strain of the flu I have, but also Nick's behavior is making me feel kind of light-headed. It's not that no one's ever made me soup before— Uncle Don makes a mean zuppa toscana. But for reasons I'd rather not examine, soup doesn't evoke quite the same feelings when Don makes it for me.

"What kind of soup? Chicken noodle?"

"Even better. Chicken tortilla. Extra spicy to clear out those sinuses." He gestures toward the kitchen. "I'm gonna get a bowl for this."

"Let me—" I attempt to stand up and fall back into the chair. "Whoa."

"Nope." Nick places an arm around me and easily hoists me out of the chair, directing me toward my bed. "Get back in bed and let me take care of this."

I want to make a joke about how the two of us have once again found ourselves in a situation involving a bed, but I'm struck by what he said. *Let me take care of this.* Nick is taking care of me. There's a person in my kitchen reheating soup in a bowl for the express purpose of making me feel better.

"I can do it." I attempt to get up again, but this time my traitorous body doesn't move. I let my arms flop back down at my sides. "This sucks."

A few cabinet drawers bang shut, and even though I can only sort of see him over the half wall, I can tell Nick's looking for something in my tiny kitchen.

"Spoons?" he calls.

"Right drawer, by the sink," I croak.

"You're extremely disorganized," he says as the microwave beeps and starts its comforting hum. "This kitchen is a nightmare."

I groan. "Sorry to offend your delicate sensibilities, Bobby Flay."

"Watch it," he calls. "I'm gonna take this soup over to Uncle Don."

"You wouldn't," I attempt to say, but my words are drowned out as I blow my nose.

The microwave door opens and shuts, then

Nick is walking toward me. "I brought extra for Don, and I already dropped it off. Here."

Nick fluffs the pillows behind me so I can sit up comfortably. "You have . . . so many pillows."

"I have a reasonable amount of pillows," I say, sniffling.

Nick shakes his head. "I've never seen this many pillows in my life. Why do you even need this many?"

"Um, aesthetics," I say. "And also for situations such as this one, when someone brings me soup and I must be propped up like an elegant lady."

Another Nick smile, the one that means he thinks I'm funny. "Oh yeah? Do you have a lot of people bringing you soup?"

I lift one shoulder. "Now and then."

"Eat," Nick says. Thankfully he doesn't attempt to spoon-feed me.

As I take a bite, he turns to look at the television. "Uh, why are you watching '70s television?"

"Good Lord," I say. "This soup is amazing."

"Yeah?" Nick turns to me and smiles, the smile that means he knows he's great. "You like it?"

"Nick." I nudge his hip with my foot under the blanket. "This is so good. This should be on the menu."

"I don't think soup really fits in with our menu of coffee and pastries."

"Okay, wow, wait, your comment about '70s

TV just registered. Have you never seen *Rhoda*?"

"Who?"

I'm holding the bowl with both hands, so I nod toward the TV. "Rhoda. As in, Mary Tyler Moore's best friend who got her own spin-off sitcom."

Nick shakes his head.

"She's wacky and she wears so many scarves."

"Do you ever consume any pop culture from *this* decade?"

"Not unless it's about murder. Why, what do you watch? Oh, wait, you think TV is beneath you, right?"

Nick's silence says it all.

"Let me tell you," I say. "You'd be a lot happier if you watched sitcoms from the '70s and '80s."

"What even is this channel?" Nick asks as Rhoda goes to commercial. "Antenna TV?"

"It's exactly what it sounds like and it primarily shows old sitcoms and also it rules," I say. "I think its viewership consists of retirees and me."

Nick nods. "I'm plenty happy."

"What?"

"You said I'd be happier if I watched old sitcoms. But what makes you think I'm not happy?"

"Uh, your whole . . . thing?" I scrunch up my face in my best approximation of a Nick glare. "The whole grouchy, cranky, grumpy—"

"I get it," Nick says. "I'm bad-tempered."

"It's not even that, it's just . . ." I take another bite of soup and let out an involuntary moan. "Ugh. This is good."

"Hey." Nick pats me on the foot. "Stop talking. You're supposed to be resting."

"This is how I relax. By bothering you."

Nick looks around my place, taking everything in. He's been here before, of course, but only to work on projects or to do things like help me move the refrigerator when I was sure there was a mouse hiding behind it (there wasn't, which led me to believe there's still a mouse loose in my apartment). But he's never been here on a purely social call.

"You're good at this," he says, looking at the walls.

"At . . . being sick? Eating soup? Watching *Rhoda*?"

He shakes his head and gestures around us. "No, at . . . this. Making a place look nice. Cozy. Giving it a personality."

My place is objectively cute—the soft blue walls, the colorful picture frames, the twinkle lights I hung in the kitchen because they made all of my baking experiments look cheerful, even when I didn't feel that way on the inside. And the slanted roof may make it small, but it also makes everything seem warm and pleasant—even this conversation with Nick.

"Thank you, and may I remind you, Nicholas,

that I have offered to do the same thing for the coffee shop."

"Yeah." He meets my eyes and smiles at me, the smile that says I'm right and he's wrong. "Okay."

"Okay what?"

He shrugs like this is no big deal, like it's not something we've been arguing about for literal years, him telling me the shop was fine the way it was and me insisting that it could be better. "You can redo some things. Paint stuff. Bring in that artwork you're always going on about."

I almost spill my soup. "Are you serious?"

He points at me. "Let's start small, though. The bathroom. Make whatever cosmetic changes you want to the bathroom, and then we'll move on from there."

"This is perfect. I know a great wallpaper guy, and I have this mirror I've been saving in my closet for this very day." I reach for my phone to look for a picture of my ideal wallpaper to show Nick, but he grabs my hand first.

"Hey," he says. "We can get to work later. Right now, you're resting."

He keeps his hold on my hand, and I stop breathing. This goes on for so long that I start to think the lack of oxygen is going to cause problems, and I can't hear anything but the laugh track on TV as I stare at Nick.

"Nick," I start.

He drops my hand. "I should probably go."

"Can you stay?" I ask, my mouth spitting out the words before I can even think about them. "For another episode?"

The credits start rolling for *Family Ties*. "Oh, Nick. Have you ever seen *Family Ties*? Michael J. Fox is this little '80s Republican in a family full of bleeding hearts. It's amazing."

Nick leans back against the wall. "One episode."

"One episode." I smile and push my feet, under the blanket, onto his lap. When I finish my soup, he takes the bowl from me and I scoot down under the blankets and get comfortable. One minute I'm laughing at something Meredith Baxter Birney said, and the next thing I know, I'm blinking as the end credits roll.

"Uggggggh," I groan, then look for Nick at the end of the bed . . . but he isn't there. Did he leave?

And then I hear a sound from the kitchen. Running water and dishes clinking. "Uh, hello?" I ask.

"You're up." Nick steps around the half wall, drying a bowl with a dish towel.

I squint. "What are you doing here?"

He shrugs. "It seemed wrong to leave while you were asleep, so I washed some dishes."

"You washed my dishes?"

"It was either that or keep watching *Family Ties*, which I had no interest in."

"I'm offended, but thank you."

Nick gestures with his head. "Tea on your bedside table."

"Oh." I reach over and take a sip of something surprisingly boozy. "Uh, whoa."

"Hot toddy," Nick clarifies. "So there's some whiskey involved. Mama Velez always swears it will cure your ills."

I take another sip. "I like the way Mama Velez thinks."

Nick retreats into the kitchen, where I can see him at the sink, washing, drying, and putting away.

"Where is Mama Velez, anyway?" I ask.

"New Mexico," Nick says. "Where I grew up."

"Your dad, too?"

"He's dead," Nick says without pausing his work.

"Oh," I say. "I'm sorry."

"Don't be. He was an asshole."

I don't say anything, because I'm not sure what I'm supposed to say. I spent years working with Nick without knowing a single thing about him, and now it's like I'm learning every single fact about his past in the span of a week. He likes to bowl? He can cook? His father is a dead jerk?

"I have an asshole parent, too," I finally say. "But my mom is alive, just currently in parts unknown."

"Sucks, right?" Nick walks toward me, drying his hands on his flannel shirt.

"Yeah," I say. "Whenever people complain about how their parents are overbearing or whatever, I'm like, 'Ha-ha, okay, my mom abandoned our family and never looked back.'"

Nick sits down on my bed.

"What about your dad? What was his particular brand of suckitude?" I ask.

"He cheated on my mom. Not just once. Over and over."

"And did your mom just deal with it?"

"She's one of those old-fashioned types who think people should stay married forever, no matter what happens."

"That was . . . definitely not my mom," I say. "So did they stay married until he died?"

Nick shakes his head. "She finally got fed up with the constant cheating and confronted him about it. There was yelling and screaming and then he tried to hit her."

My eyes widen. "Tried? What happened?"

Nick shrugs. "He got me instead."

I swallow hard. That sounds like Nick; jumping in front of someone else to take a hit. Always taking care of someone, even if it means he gets hurt.

"How old were you?"

"Twelve. My sister was only eight. And my mom was willing to put up with just about anything from him, I guess, but once she saw him hit me, it was like a switch flipped. And after that, she took us to my grandma's and we didn't hear from my dad again, until we got word that he died."

"Wow," I say. "That's *really* bad. I'm sorry I led with the story about my mom; at least she never laid a hand on us."

Nick smiles, this one a tiny, sarcastic thing. "I don't really think anyone's keeping score."

"You mean there's not an official ranking of parents somewhere?" I ask. "At the top is, I don't know, Barack and Michelle? And at the bottom is . . . what celebrities are really bad parents?"

"You're asking the wrong guy."

I take another sip of my hot toddy. "You know, I'm feeling better already. I think it's the hot toddy. Tell Mama Velez thank you."

"Or," Nick says, nudging my left foot, "it may be the fact that you actually slept for once."

I make a fart noise with my mouth. "Sleep is overrated."

"Says the girl who's stuck in bed because she made herself sick with her unhealthy lifestyle."

"Um, okay. Have you been talking to Milo?"

"Why, did he say the same thing?"

"In so many words."

"Well then. Milo's smart."

"Nicholas, Milo is many things, but smart is not one of them."

238

"Stop calling me Nicholas."

"Never." I slouch back into my pillow nest. "Do you want to watch more sitcoms of the '70s, '80s, and sometimes '90s with me?"

"Believe it or not," Nick says, "I have to get back to the shop. You know, the one I own?"

I squint, shaking my head. "Never heard of it."

"But I left you some soup in the fridge. And there's some extra hot toddy mixture in there, too; heat it up in the microwave when you're ready for it."

I don't say anything; I stare at Nick.

He looks at me uneasily. "Are you . . . okay?"

I nod slowly.

"Your eyes are really big and glassy and . . . oh, God. You aren't going to throw up, are you?" Nick jumps off the bed.

I bark out a laugh. "I'm not going to puke on you! Are you kidding?"

"I just . . . I just don't like vomit," Nick says, running a hand through his hair.

I gesture toward my hot toddy cup. "You've basically been nursing me back to health over here, but a little bit of puke is crossing the line for you?"

"Vomit is different," Nick says. "It's very different."

I wave my fingers in his face. "Vooooooooomit."

"Okay, well, you're feeling better, so I'm out of here," Nick says.

"No, don't leave!" I cajole him. "I was kidding! I won't puke on you! I promise!"

"The fact that you even have to say that proves that this conversation has gone too far," Nick says, shrugging on his jacket. It's olive green with a lot of pockets and it looks like something the hip dad of a toddler would wear and he looks damn good in it.

I don't know if it's the Dayquil or the alcoholic power of the hot toddy, but the words spill out of my mouth. "That jacket looks good on you."

Nick stops moving, his hands paused on a snap. He looks up at me, one eyebrow raised. "Yeah?"

I nod, slowly, my head feeling like it's moving through the molasses I use for my shoofly pie. Maybe I need to go back to sleep. "You look like a hot dad," my mouth says, before my brain can stop it.

"Is that . . . a compliment?" Nick asks, now not even focusing on his jacket at all.

"Ugh." I flop back on my bed and put a pillow over my face. "Just go. Get your hot-dad jacket and leave my apartment."

I'm not sure he heard me since the pillow muffled my words, but when he doesn't respond I peer out from underneath the pillow, expecting to see him standing there, smiling at me, doing one of our classic Chloe-and-Nick bits.

But instead, he stares at me with his jaw set and his eyes narrowed.

"Don't say stuff like that, okay, Chloe?" He crosses his arms.

I throw the pillow toward the end of the bed. "What? Why? We were kidding around. I was being my typical, hilarious self."

He looks at me, then looks away. "You know why."

And then he turns and leaves.

Chapter Eighteen

Without Nick around to warm my feet and make me hot toddies, I can't fall asleep. I toss and turn, feeling feverish and sweaty, pulling the blankets up to my chin and then kicking them off. The TV is a blur of sitcoms, miscommunications, mistakes, laugh tracks.

I need to talk about this with someone, but I can't call Annie. She'd be like, *Omg, this is your romantic comedy, you found your Tom Hanks or Hugh Grant or Colin Firth or whoever and now you're gonna ride off into the sunset!* and I am so not in the mood for that.

Hey, I text Tracey. Can we hang out? I need to talk.

Tracey texts back immediately.

Is everything okay with your dad? He seems fine today. He complained about the meat loaf, but honestly the meat loaf here sucks so he was in the right.

Not Dad. Nick stuff.

Tracey responds with various suggestive emojis.

How do you even know there are so many dick-shaped emojis? I text back.

Lesbians have access to the same emoji keyboard as everyone else, bitch, she responds.

Okay. Well. I'm not sure I should visit Dad today because I'm sick.

Please don't, she responds. Remember that time that Edith Clancy brought the norovirus in and everyone got infected and we had to quarantine the place for three weeks? I don't want a repeat. How about I come over tonight after work.

Yes please, I text, and in a few hours, Tracey shows up with three bottles of Gatorade.

"Gatorade?" I ask. "What, am I LeBron James?"

"You're welcome," she says, putting them in the fridge. "Gatorade is good for you when you're sick. You know, electrolytes. Also, what is this delicious-looking soup?"

"Nick made it," I groan. "Therein lies the problem."

Tracey heats up the rest of my hot toddy for me and makes herself a cup of tea, then sits down at the table ("I'm not joining you in your den of infection," she says).

"Okay, spill," she says. "Not the hot toddy, I mean. All the dirty, dirty deets."

"Lower your expectations," I say, and then I unload the whole story to her. How Nick and I shared a physical-contactless night in a hotel in Indianapolis (well, aside from how I woke up snuggled against him). How Nick brought me soup and hot toddies and watched wonderful horrible television with me. How I told him he looked like a hot dad and he left.

"Ohhhh," Tracey says, taking a slow sip of her tea. "I see what's going on here."

"What?" I ask, sitting up straight in bed. "What do you think is happening?"

She shakes her head. "You've purchased yourself a one-way ticket to bonetown, girl, and your scheduled departure is any day now."

I flop back down on my bed. "What the hell are you talking about?"

"Do you remember," she says, pointing at me, "when I told you about how Hannah took care of me during my Barfapalooza performance on her bathroom floor?"

"I'm unable to forget."

Tracey raises an eyebrow like this proves something.

"Um, what?"

"Nick came over here to take care of you," she says. "He made you food."

"That's what friends do!" I say, my voice rising in frustration, which makes me cough. "You came over here to take care of me."

Tracey waves me off. "I brought you Gatorade, like a normal person. I didn't slave over a stove to cook you a meal and then share a treasured family recipe for a therapeutic cocktail."

"It's a popular drink," I mutter. "It wasn't, like, personal."

"And then," Tracey says, clearly ramping up to something, "you admitted to me that you not only thought he looked good, but told him so. My case is closed. Bonetown: population you and Nick."

I sit in silence for a moment before saying, "This is why we never worked out, you know. Because we're way, way too similar and we would've driven each other crazy."

She smiles. "Hannah thinks it's cute when I get like this."

"I think it's annoying," I say, but I can't help smiling.

"So where's your boyfriend?" Tracey asks, looking around as if there's someone stuffed behind my bed.

"Who?" I ask, confused, then realize who she's referring to. "Oh, you mean Mikey Danger."

Tracey snorts, sloshing tea on the table. "Okay, wow. You've gotta cut this Mikey Danger character loose."

"What are you talking about?"

"Did you even tell him you were sick?"

"I had to cancel our plans to Netflix and chill last night, so yeah, I texted him and said I wasn't feeling well."

"And?" Tracey gestures around the room. "Where is he?"

"I don't know!"

"I'll tell you where he's not." She leans forward. "Making chicken tortilla soup."

"That's because Mikey Danger can't cook," I say. "Fred told me he had to throw out a pan last week because Mikey burned Kraft Macaroni and Cheese onto it."

"I think you need to ask yourself: is that what you deserve? A grown man who can't make a meal meant for children?"

"Not being able to cook isn't a character flaw," I say.

"And what did Michael Dangerous say when you told him you were sick?"

I check my phone and see that he's responded. *"Bummer babe."*

Tracey sighs, then leans back in the chair. "You're right. Not being able to cook isn't a character flaw. But not checking on your girlfriend/friend with benefits? That kinda is."

I don't want to give Tracey the satisfaction of acknowledging that she's right, so instead I bite my lip. "Interesting theory."

She smiles. "Did you catch how I called him Michael Dangerous back there?"

"Yes. That's . . ." A giggle escapes from my lips. "Okay, that's actually hilarious."

She cackles. "I know."

My laughs turn into coughs and eventually Tracey leaves with the promise to check on me again soon, but I can't stop thinking about what she said.

And then there's the other thing. The rom-com thing. I'm trying my hardest to resist the candy-coated, artificially sweet, totally fake rom-com narrative that Annie would love to impose on my life. Well, that she *has* imposed on my life. But I've seen enough romantic comedies to know how this works.

Take, for example, *You've Got Mail*. It's one of Annie's favorites because she's obsessed with Tom Hanks, but not, like, when he's stuck on an island and befriending a volleyball. She loves the Tom Hanks of romantic comedies, the one who shows his emotional side and has touching monologues and makes her cry, even though she's seen this movie *one thousand times,* as I always remind her.

Because no matter how many times I'm like, "Uh, Annie? Joe Fox put Kathleen Kelly's store out of business and this movie is about how capitalism destroys lives, not how love conquers all," she adores it, which means I've also seen it one thousand times. And I remember, so well that I could probably quote it, the scene where Tom

Hanks comes over when Meg Ryan is sick. He takes care of her and he brings her flowers and he asks if she will be his friend, because he's almost certainly already in love with her and wants her to fall in love with him, too.

And what else does he do? Well, he makes her tea, because, as Tracey said, that's what you do when you care about someone. You take care of them.

All of this gives me an uneasy feeling in the pit of my stomach (and not, as Nick feared, because I'm about to puke). After all of my complaining that I don't like romantic comedies, that they aren't realistic, that happy endings don't exist and true love is for suckers, I can feel myself slipping. I'm thinking about Nick, and I'm liking what I'm thinking about, and it feels a hell of a lot like a romantic comedy.

This is all Annie's fault. My finger hesitates over the call button as I wonder whether it might help me to talk this out with her. I know she'd drop everything to go over the Chicken Tortilla Soup Incident in exhausting detail. But I just can't do it—I need to handle this situation by myself. I fall asleep with my phone in my hand.

Chapter Nineteen

I knock on the door, holding my pie like a peace offering. In retrospect, I regret making a pie for this situation. My reasoning made sense; a pie is comfort, a salve for wounds. But pie represents joy, and it seems offensive to place something so joyous into a breakup situation. The pie didn't ask to be dragged into this drama.

Mikey opens the door and takes in the sight of me in my red raincoat. "Chloe!" he says with his genuine childlike surprise. "Perfect timing! I just got my knives!"

"What?" I step in, brushing my hood off my head. Normally I would apologize for spraying water droplets everywhere, but something tells me Mikey Danger doesn't mind. "Oh."

Mikey now stands at the counter, a plastic grocery bag full of round, red tomatoes in front of him, his knife poised over one on the cutting board. "Watch this."

He slices through it with no effort. The knife, just like it did on TV, glides right through, leaving a perfect, paper-thin slice of tomato in its wake.

"Wow," I say with genuine surprise. "That infomercial wasn't lying."

Mikey shakes his head in wonder. "This is killer. Oh, you should stick around! Milo went out to the store to get more produce to practice on."

I raise my eyebrows, surprised but glad that Mikey and Milo are bonding, even if it's over knives.

"Actually, I came over here to talk to you. Can you, uh . . . sit down?" I gesture toward the table, which is covered in junk mail.

"Yeah!" Mikey says, pushing a stack of papers off one chair.

I sit down across from him. "So, Mikey . . . I don't think this is working."

Mikey shakes his head. "Are you kidding? It's working great. You saw that tomato."

"Not the knives, Mikey," I say, trying and failing to keep the annoyance out of my voice. "Us."

"Us?" Mikey asks, confusion in his beautiful, ridiculous eyes. "But you're so chill, Chloe."

"Yeah, that's the thing," I say. "I'm not. Like, at all. No one in the history of ever has called me chill. I came out of the womb and the doctor was like, 'Whoa, get this newborn into a baby yoga class, she's stressed.' "

Mikey's eyes wander, and I realize he's thinking about those tomatoes, so I keep it brief.

"You're nice, Mikey," I say, meaning it. "But

250

I don't think we should waste any more time together."

Mikey nods. "I respect that. But damn, Chlo. I'm gonna miss you."

I shrug. "Yeah, well. My brother lives here, so you'll probably see me around."

We smile at each other for a moment, and then I remember. "Oh! I brought you a pie!" I pull the dish towel off the blueberry basil pie with an oat crumb topping. It looks objectively beautiful, like something that should be in a bakery case. I know we could sell the hell out of this pie at Nick's.

Mikey waves me off. "I'll save it for Fred and Milo. I don't like pie."

"You don't . . ." I trail off, willing my mouth to form words. "You don't like pie?"

Mikey shakes his head.

"But there are so many different kinds of pie," I say. "Saying you don't like pie doesn't even make sense. I could understand, theoretically if not personally, how someone could dislike fruit pies. Or custard pies. But all pies? A pecan pie is a fundamentally different beast than an apple pie, and a key lime pie is in its own category. How can you *not like pie?*"

Mikey shrugs and shakes his head, unconcerned.

I lean forward, studying those beautiful eyes, trying to find a real human in there. "What is it you don't like? Do you not like crust?"

"I just . . ." Mikey appears to think for a moment, although there's no telling what's going on inside that head. "The filling is all, you know, gooey. And the crust is always hard."

"My crusts," I say in a measured tone, "are never hard."

"Not your pies specifically," Mikey clarifies. "But, like, all pie."

I inhale and exhale a few times, attempting to calm myself. "My crusts are flaky and crisp. And . . . you know what? I think I should go."

"You sure?" Mikey asks. "Milo's gonna be back any minute with a butternut squash."

I pause, tempted for a moment. "Those are so hard to cut."

"I know, right?" Mikey says.

But I know I should leave. Mikey and I don't have anything more to say to each other.

"Chloe." Mikey tilts his gorgeous head and holds open his arms. "You're the best."

"Yeah, okay." I step into the hug, which feels nothing like one of Nick's. "Good luck chopping random vegetables."

"Thank you," Mikey says.

I'm about to leave when I turn around and pick up the pie. It doesn't deserve to be treated this way. "I'm gonna take this."

"See ya." Mikey waves with his knife, then goes back to the tomato.

Chapter Twenty

Annie's bachelorette party is the night before the premiere. Or maybe I should refer to it as her "bachelorette party," because she's refused to let me do any of the fun things I want to do. Example: she threatened to end our friendship if I hired a stripper who was pretending to be a pizza delivery man. I did convince Uncle Don to help me decorate the living room: we strung up a garland of multicolored penises over the dark wood fireplace mantel, I put penis cutouts all over the floral-wallpaper-covered walls, and there are streamers everywhere. I'm not saying Don loved it, but he was remarkably helpful, and he even had some great ideas, like ordering a life-size cardboard cutout of Drew from when he was shirtless in an action movie. Every time I see him standing in the corner by the decorative fake palm frond, I jump, thinking he's a shirtless, ripped robber who showed up to steal all of our phallic decorations.

Arms crossed, I survey our handiwork. "You know, Don, I'd say this looks pretty great."

Don nods. "The penis confetti is gonna be a pain to clean up, but that's what the vacuum is for, I guess."

"Thanks for helping me, and for agreeing to turn your living room into a den of iniquity." I pat him on the back. "Do you want a fruit skewer for your troubles?"

Earlier today, I threaded long banana slices on each skewer, topped them with a strawberry, then covered some in white chocolate and some in dark chocolate. I've made a lot of things in my life, but these fruit and chocolate penises might be some of my best work.

Don shakes his head. "I saw them on the platter in there. All of them together, with the spikes sticking out? It's . . . disturbing."

"They're not spikes, they're skewers," I clarify, but Don shakes his head again.

"It's too much," he mutters.

I hear a noise outside and run to the window, where I push the curtain aside. "She's here, she's here, she's here!"

Penis spikes forgotten, Don looks energized. "What do we do? Do we hide?"

"Um . . . I don't think so. She knows this is her bachelorette party. But we should do something!"

Don and I look helplessly at each other as the door creaks open and Annie steps in.

"Uh . . ." she says, taking in the streamers in every shade of pink hanging from the ceiling.

"Surprise!" Don and I yell, which makes her jump.

"Wow, um, okay!" She laughs, then hugs each

of us. "I thought we were having a movie night! You guys didn't have to do this! And . . ."

She steps back, noticing the cardboard cutout of Drew in the corner. "What is this?"

"Do you like it?" Don asks.

She walks over to it and rubs her hands over its smooth abs. "Aw. This is when he was all buff."

When Drew and Annie first met, he was coming off an action movie that required him to be in intense physical shape that was basically unsustainable unless he kept working out three times a day and eating nothing but chicken breasts. So now he has a slightly rounder face and significantly less defined abs (not that I've seen his abs; I'm relying on hearsay). Annie, who's always liked her rom-com heroes on the dorkier side, much prefers him this way.

"I love it," she says. "I'm gonna put this in our apartment in LA."

"I bet Drew will be so excited," I say.

"He'll hate it," she says with a smile.

"Well," Don says, "as much as I'd love to stay and have a girls' night, Tyler and I have plans."

"You should stay!" I say, handing Annie a headband that's topped with penis-antennae.

"I never imagined my uncle would be at my bachelorette party, but honestly, it feels right," Annie says, sliding the headband on.

"It does." Don nods. "But I promised my lady pizza, and pizza she shall get."

Don leaves, and I show Annie into the kitchen, where I've arranged a spread of food on the kitchen island.

"Not all of them are penis-themed," I say, gesturing toward the fruit skewers. "But I did try to fit the theme."

"Last-night-of-freedom frics." Annie reads the card in front of a platter of hand-cut baked fries with a trio of dipping sauces.

"I know this isn't the night before your wedding and the concept that your 'freedom' ends with matrimony is outdated and patriarchal, but, like, it's a fun name."

"It is," Annie agrees. "Nonalcoholic Jell-O shots? So . . ."

"So it's Jell-O in little cups, yes."

She looks at the next plate. "Matri-baloney sandwiches?"

"I was running out of ideas," I admit. "And I know you can't eat deli meats, that's why there's only half a sandwich there. Don ate the other half."

"Chloe." Annie looks at me with an unreadable expression on her face, and at first I think she's mad.

"I mean . . . I can make another sandwich if you want. You can eat deli meat if it's heated, right? Fried matri-baloney sandwiches? Is that a thing?"

But then she crushes me in a hug, and I realize that she's crying. "You are the best friend in the world, you know that?"

I hug her back. "I've suspected it for a while, but it's nice to have confirmation."

She reaches behind my back and grabs one of the fries off the tray. "You made me a multitude of sauces? You know how much I love dips."

"Your love of dips is one of your most defining personality traits," I say. "Also, let's order pizza, because I don't want to eat that baloney sandwich."

"Deal."

We pick at the plate of fries and eat an unhealthy amount of Jell-O, avoiding the fruit skewers (turns out Uncle Don is right . . . they are kind of unappetizing), until the doorbell rings.

"I sincerely hope that's a real pizza delivery man and not a pizza-delivery-themed stripper," Annie says, heading toward the front door. I toss back another Jell-O shot, then hear her scream from the living room.

"What's wrong?" I run in after her, only to find her doubled over in laughter, pointing toward shirtless Drew in the corner.

"He scared me," she wheezes. "I thought we had a dirty, buff intruder hiding behind the palm frond."

I snort a laugh, then answer the door and pay for the pizza.

"Whoa," Annie says as I place three large pizzas on the coffee table. "That is more pizza than we can eat."

"It's your bachelorette party!" I say with force. "You can't drink and you wouldn't let me take you to a campy, tongue-in-cheek all-male revue, but damn it, we're gonna get buckwild one way or another. I got extra cheese on these babies."

Annie leans forward as I open one of the pizza boxes. "You really did go all out."

We eat as much pizza as we humanly can while watching Annie's choice of films (a Hugh Grant retrospective: *Four Weddings and a Funeral*, followed by *Music and Lyrics*, skipping *Notting Hill* because for *some* reason Annie doesn't want to watch a movie where a regular person hooks up with a celebrity).

After we put the rest of the pizza in the fridge for Don to eat later, I lean back on the couch, full and content. "You know who I like?"

Annie looks at me, hands on her stomach. "Who?"

"That Hugh Grant. What a charmer."

"A bold opinion. Oh geez. I ate way too much."

"Look at you, getting into the spirit of hedonism. Do you want a Sprite?"

Annie shrugs. "Why not? It's my bachelorette party."

She gets up to get herself a drink but I wave her back down. "Stay on your pregnant butt. I'll get your drink."

"Again, I'm glad you're not a doctor. The baby's not in my butt."

"Not yet." I point at her and head to the kitchen.

"Not ever," I hear her say with confusion as I pour her Sprite into a penis goblet I ordered online. As I stick the bottle back in the fridge, my phone vibrates, and I look down to see a text from Nick. Oh.

Feeling better?

That's it. Just a question. No banter, nothing romantic, no suggestive emojis. This is normal.

Much better. In fact, I felt well enough to make sexually suggestive fruit skewers, I respond, then text him a picture.

This is for Annie's bachelorette, I add in a separate text.

Don't act like this isn't what you'd be doing on a typical Friday night, Nick texts back.

"What's this about?"

I look up to see Annie standing on the other side of the island, looking at me expectantly.

"What's what about?" I ask, dropping my phone in a way that isn't suspicious at all.

". . . is that a penis goblet?" she asks slowly.

I hand it to her and she takes an uncertain sip. Apparently satisfied with the experience of drinking out of a penis, she continues.

"That smile. Does Mikey Danger make you smile like that? If so, I regret all the uncharitable things I said and thought about him."

When I don't say anything, a grin makes its way slowly across Annie's face. "Ohhhhhhh."

"Oh what?" I ask, barely suppressing an eye roll.

She leans over the island. "It was . . . Nick."

"So what if it was Nick?" I grumble.

"Well, I promised I wouldn't say anything." Annie takes another sip. "And I'm nothing if not a superb promise-keeper, so I'll take this and go into the other room and—"

"We slept in the same bed, okay?" I blurt out, then clamp my hand over my mouth.

Annie gasps and jumps in the air, sending her penis antennae bobbing and sloshing Sprite out of the penis goblet. "*Yes!* I'll clean that up later. But *yes!* I knew something was up! I mean, more up than usual. You guys finally did it."

I laugh, my insides feeling as bubbly as the Sprite that's currently forming a sticky puddle on the floor.

"We didn't *do it,* and what are you, twelve? I love you so much."

Annie claps her hands together, then stops. "Wait, what do you mean you didn't do it? You said you slept together."

I sigh and start at the beginning, explaining the whole thing at the hotel as Annie stares at me with rapt eyes, occasionally sucking in a breath or whispering, "Yes!" And then I get to Nick making me soup and hot toddies, and

Annie's gleeful reaction reminds me why we're best friends. This is why I tell her things—because her enthusiasm makes me feel more excited about my own life. Everything seems more real when it's reflected back to me in her eyes.

And also because, for once, it feels good to be the one sharing the fun story. For so long our talks have been about Drew, the movie, and now the baby, while I've been talking about taking care of my dad, Milo coming back into town, and school. Sure, sometimes I get to share a fun story about a bad date, but those stories last for, at most, a few minutes of laughter. This feels bigger. This feels like more.

"Wow," Annie says on an exhale. "Am I allowed to say I told you so?"

"You are not."

"In that case . . . I will remain silent." She tents her hands on the table, then says in a rush, "I told you so. Ugh, I couldn't resist."

I roll my eyes, even though I can't help laughing. But then I see Annie grab her phone and start tapping the screen.

"Don't tell Drew!" I say, reaching across the island to still her hand. "Are you gonna be one of those married ladies who's like, 'my husband is my best friend' and tell him all my secrets?"

"I'm not telling Drew," she says, shooting me a look. "I would never. I'm taking notes."

An uneasy feeling starts in my stomach and blooms throughout the rest of my body. "Notes?"

"Yeah," she says, looking at her phone. "That cute stuff Nick said when you guys were in bed. That's good. And the way he made you a family recipe."

"No," I say, my voice so loud that Annie jumps.

"No, what?" she asks, looking at me in confusion.

"No notes," I say, my voice rising even more. "Stop taking notes!"

Annie gives me a slightly condescending smile, like there's something here I don't understand. "Writing love stories is my job."

"And this is my life."

"Everything is copy, like Nora Ephron said." Annie starts typing on her phone again. "And besides, I would never put anything directly from your life into a movie. You know that. I'd mix it up and disguise you."

"You mean like how you named my character Zoe?" I say flatly. "And gave her a job at a coffee shop and a sick dad?"

Annie stops. "Wait, are you being serious right now?"

I shrug. "I guess I am."

She squints at me and tilts her head, like I'm a dog and she's trying to figure out why I won't stop chewing on the sofa. "You didn't tell me you were upset about this."

"When would I get the chance?" I mutter. "You're always off in LA, making movies about my life."

"Excuse me?" Annie's voice rises, which is unusual for her. She's the queen of avoiding conflict, and I'm not a fan of it either, which means that the one and only serious argument we've ever been in happened in fourth grade when she insisted that Howie was the cutest Backstreet Boy (a statement that was categorically false).

"What did you want, Chloe?" she asks. "For me to not take a shot at my dream job? For me to not marry the love of my life? For me to stay here being miserable forever?"

"Oh! So the entire time I thought we were having a swell time, watching movies here on the couch and hanging out at Nick's, you were miserable? Good to know!"

"That wasn't what I meant and you know it."

"Actually, I don't. I don't know much of anything about you these days, since you're always off hanging out with Drew and having babies."

"I haven't even had my *one* baby yet," Annie says in a low voice. "Why are you being like this?"

"You mean, why am I stating my perfectly valid feelings?"

She shakes her head. "I know you don't mean any of this. This isn't like you. The Chloe I know wouldn't want other people to be unhappy just because she is."

I pause, pressing my lips together as I let that statement hang in the air like it's a physical object. And then finally, my voice as calm as I can make it, I ask, "You think I'm unhappy?"

"What I think—" Annie starts, but I'm not done. I cut her off.

"Oh no, I have more questions. See, I thought we were best friends, but do you think I'm some jealous bitch? Do you think I want what you have?"

"That's not what I—"

"I get it. You're off living your glamorous life now, all movie premieres and rubbing elbows with directors and, oh yeah, marrying movie stars, and I'm back here in the sticks, living my sad, pathetic life."

"Okay, no, let me talk," Annie says, her face flushed red. She bites her lip, then keeps talking. "I don't think you're jealous. I don't think you want my life. And I sure don't think you're sad and pathetic—I love you. But I do think you're stressed out and you're overworked and for some reason, you won't let any of us help you, because you've got this pathological need to do everything yourself. I've been asking you and texting you over and over, trying to get you to talk to me, but you won't. I mean, I had to get updates on your dad from Milo."

I freeze. "You talked to Milo?"

"Because you won't tell me anything!" she says, exasperated, flinging her arms in the air. "I'm trying to be here for you, Chloe. You can talk to me, you can let me help you! You don't have to make twelve pies for my wedding by yourself, or take care of your dad by yourself, or do *everything* all by yourself. Let someone in. Let someone take even the smallest burden off your shoulders."

I swallow. "Uh, okay, thanks for the advice. Glad to know you and Milo have been discussing my life behind my back."

"Chloe," Annie says, eyes wide. "Please don't be like this, okay? We're best friends. I don't want to fight."

"I'm not a Real Housewife, Annie. I don't love to fight either. But guess what? We're fighting. I'm mad. Your movie ruined my life."

She gasps and takes a step away from me. The two of us stare at each other, not saying anything, until tears appear at the corners of her eyes. The penis antennae bob sadly and I'm too mad to even appreciate what a hilarious detail that is.

"Okay." She turns and walks into the living room. "I'm just . . ." She grabs her bag, then looks around. "Oh. Yeah. I'm staying here tonight."

I hold up a hand, like I'm volunteering to bring cups to a party. "I'll leave."

Annie's shoulders slump. "Wait. Don't leave."

I shake my head. "Great party, huh? I'm sorry. Great 'party.'" I do air quotes.

"You're coming tomorrow, right?" she asks in a small voice.

I turn to face her, and the two of us have an entire conversation with our eyes before I say, "Yeah."

I'm filled with a lot of anger, about the movie and about Annie thinking she's some sort of lifestyle guru who can tell me how I need to "let people in" when she has no idea what it's like to be me.

But Annie's also my best friend, and I'm not going to throw away our friendship over one (huge, blowout) fight. Even if it means I have to sit through a movie about a fictionalized, glossy, happy-ending version of my own life.

"Okay." She nods, swallows, and turns around. And that's when I go out the back door.

Chapter Twenty-One

Back at my place, I check my phone and see that my last text was from Nick, a joke about my sort-of-anatomically-correct fruit skewers. For some reason, that makes me feel even worse about the way tonight went. Twenty minutes ago I was joking around about fruit penises; why did I have to ruin a perfectly good night?

I put on my favorite yacht rock playlist and flop onto my bed as the opening notes of "Arthur's Theme" fill my apartment. "Sing it, Christopher Cross," I mutter.

Perhaps no artist embodies the spirit of yacht rock like Christopher Cross—the man has a song called "Sailing," for Pete's sake. But this song is all about getting lost between the moon and New York City, and even though it logistically makes no sense (so . . . get lost in the sky? Is Christopher Cross talking to a confused airplane pilot?), it still bums me out because it reminds me of Annie and how we flew to New York City back when she wanted to confess her love to Drew on live morning television. That woman loves a grand rom-com gesture.

And, of course, Nick was there, too. But this

was before the movie, before things got weird, before the whole world knew a fake version of our lives. Back when things were simple.

So what are they now?

I hesitate, my finger on Nick's name in my phone. And then I do it. I press call.

I rarely call anyone. Annie, when she's out of town, although thinking about that gives my heart a pang. Milo, in a true emergency. Tracey, but only if it's something with my dad. Dad, never, because it confuses him too much.

The ringing of the phone echoes the ringing in my ears as I wonder if I'm doing the wrong thing. Should I even be calling Nick? What am I doing? I've been clear—to him, and everyone, and myself—that I'm in no way interested in anything but a casual coworker relationship, but the soup and the hot toddy and the bed sharing—

"Chloe?"

The raggedness of his voice startles me so much that I gasp.

"Is . . . is everything okay?"

He sounds like he just woke up, and all of a sudden I'm picturing him waking up, imagining me next to him in his bed, sharing a quilt and smelling his morning breath. I wish it weren't such a turn-on.

And then I realize why he sounds like he just woke up: because he probably did, because it's 2 A.M.

"I'm sorry," I say. "I didn't realize it was so late."

"S'okay," he says, then coughs and sounds more alert. "Is everything . . ."

"Everything's fine. It's good. I . . ." I exhale, then whisper, "I just wanted to talk to you."

He doesn't say anything for a second, and then I hear the creak of a bedspring. I imagine him rolling over in bed. "Yeah? Okay."

I smile, then press my lips back into a neutral expression, as if anyone's here to see me. "Yeah? I don't have to work tomorrow, but don't you have to be up, in like . . ."

"A few hours. Uh-huh. But go ahead. Talk. Tell me about your big wild night full of dicks."

"Please don't say it like that. That makes it sound creepy."

"You're the one who put a chocolate-covered fruit penis on a spike and then sent me a picture, like a threat."

"For the last time, it's not a spike! It's a skewer!"

"I know you have a lot of creative ideas for the shop, but I do *not* think penis spikes are gonna be big sellers for us."

"I swear, Nick."

Neither of us speaks for a moment, and he asks, "Do you have yacht rock playing?"

"Arthur's Theme" is still going (it's a long song). "Perhaps."

"Is this what you do at two in the morning, Chloe? Listen to yacht rock and call your coworkers?"

"Sure, but I usually call Tobin."

"Really?"

I snort. "No."

"So," Nick says. "Why are you calling me instead of playing penis-themed party games?"

"Well . . ." Suddenly it seems silly to explain the entire ludicrous story to him, but why did I call him in the middle of the night? Because he makes me feel better. Because he's my friend. Because I want to talk to him.

"Annie and I got in a fight," I finally say. "About the movie."

Nick pauses for a moment. The two of us don't talk about the movie. In fact, we haven't even discussed the premiere tomorrow; I don't know if he's planning on going. On the one hand, it would be unusual if he didn't go, seeing as how the movie is kinda based on him, and Annie was his most loyal customer for years. But on the other hand, it would be a real Nick move to not care and stay home.

"What about the movie?" he asks.

"Uh," I say. "The fact that it's based on me and you?"

"Oh. That."

"Yeah. Anyway, she started taking notes on what I was saying tonight, like my personal life is mere fodder for her creative genius, and it . . .

I don't know, it was too much for me. Like, I'm a person, not your story inspiration, and my life isn't going to get a happily-ever-after in an hour and a half. It will keep on going after the credits roll, and it will keep on being hard."

I don't know what I expect Nick to ask, but it isn't "Why don't you get a happily-ever-after?"

I laugh, but there's no humor in it. "Because of my life? It's a shitshow."

"You keep saying that, but what makes it a shitshow, Chloe?"

"You've met my dad, Nick. Most days, he can't even remember what he had for lunch, or *if* he had lunch, and eventually he's going to forget me, too. He's not going to get better. And no one's coming along to save me, to make it easier to take care of him or pay for his place, and I have to get my degree on the Internet during whatever free time I have, which means I'll have a bachelor's degree maybe by the time I'm seventy-five, if I'm lucky. And all I want to do is have my own little bakery, my own happy place, but I don't even know if that's possible. I think it might be the stupidest thing I've ever believed in, because the world doesn't need another bakery. Columbus sure doesn't need another bakery, which means I'd have to go to some other city, but I couldn't go to another city until . . . well, until after. With my dad. Which I don't like to think about."

I take a breath, on the verge of tears, but I don't

271

have a Five-Minute Cry scheduled right now and I'm not about to have an impromptu one with Nick on the line.

"I don't want to see this movie," I say. "But also I *have* to see this movie, in a theater full of people, with my best friend who probably hates me. This blows."

Nick breaks his silence. "Is Mikey Danger coming with you to the premiere tomorrow? Or, I guess, tonight?"

"Why would Mikey Danger be coming?" I ask, confused.

"Um . . . because you're dating him?"

"Oh. Oh, yeah, I forgot. I broke up with him."

Silence.

"Nick?"

"You broke up with him?"

"Yep," I say. "Dumped his ass. I mean, okay, sorry, that sounds cruel. He's fine. Mikey Danger is perfectly fine for some other person who wants to spend every evening eating takeout in front of infomercials and then falling asleep. But, as it turns out, that person is not me."

I can't see Nick, but I can hear him smile through the phone. "Let's go to the premiere together, okay?"

I swallow. "Yeah?"

"Yeah."

I nod, even though he can't see me. "Okay."

Being with Nick will make it better, like being

with Nick makes everything better. He'll be there for me to lean into and on, there to talk to me if it's too much, there to leave with me if I can't or don't want to handle it.

I should go to sleep. I should *definitely* let Nick go to sleep. In fact, he isn't saying anything, so he might already be asleep.

"Hey, Nick?"

"Hmm?" he says, his voice low and sleepy.

"You ask me all the time what I want. But what about you? What do you really want to do with your life?"

Nick exhales. "Big question. Not all of us have as much drive and talent as Chloe Sanderson."

"I don't—"

"You do, but that's not the point. The point is . . . I'm not even sure what I want to do, but I know what I don't want to do. I don't want to keep running this coffee shop."

My heart drops into my stomach. "Wait, are you closing the shop?"

"No," Nick says quickly. "That's not what I mean. There are things I like about it, sure, but running a business isn't my idea of a good time. I would so much rather be somewhere behind the scenes, making food. Somewhere I could make a good salad and not have to worry about doing the taxes."

I smile. "You do make a mean chicken tortilla soup."

"Thank you. I'm not closing the shop. Don't worry. I would never do that to you."

"Gary would flip if he had to find a new coffee shop," I say. "There's no way he would fit in at Starbucks."

"There aren't a lot of places Gary fits in in this world."

I sigh, then blurt out, "I wish you were here."

Nick doesn't say anything, and I realize I've overstepped. I was being honest, but maybe that was too confusing, so I quickly say, "I mean, in a completely platonic way."

"I wish I were there, too," Nick says at the same time.

I exhale. "I don't even know what Antenna TV is playing at this time of night, but it's probably something good."

"Why don't you check?"

I roll over and grab the remote from where it fell underneath my bed, then turn on the TV. It's playing . . .

"It's that knife infomercial," I say in shock. "I guess they don't play sitcoms at two A.M."

"Maybe this is a sign," Nick says. "Maybe this means you have a special connection with Mikey Danger."

I snort. "The only thing Mikey Danger has a special connection with is his new knife. Oh, and I didn't even tell you. He doesn't like pie."

"Pie in general?"

"That's what I said!" I shout, vindicated.

"Chloe," Nick says. "We should go to sleep."

"Mmm-hmmm." I know that Nick means we should go to sleep separately, in our own beds, in our own homes, but I pretend for a moment that he means we should sleep right next to each other, like we did that night in the hotel. We don't even have to hook up; I want the nearness of him, his body heat, his smell. I want him to help me fall asleep, so I don't have to sit here at 2 A.M. and think about the fact that I'm now in a fight with one of my very few friends.

But adults don't really have chaste, snuggly sleepovers. Probably because boners get in the way.

"Good night, Chloe. See you tomorrow."

"Good night," I say, and hang up, then feel a tiny shock of electricity as I think about Nick being my date tomorrow night. Sure, I don't want to see this movie. Sure, I'm going to spend the entire time squirming in my chair and wishing I were anywhere else. But Nick will be beside me, holding my hand, being my friend. It will be okay.

Chapter Twenty-Two

Nick looks so fucking ridiculously hot that I almost want to punch him in the face.

When he picks me up, he doesn't honk his horn or text me to let me know he's here. He gets out of his truck and knocks on my door, so when I open it I'm greeted with Nick in a suit. And he has a *beard*.

"Why do you look like this?" I ask, horrified. How in God's name am I supposed to stop myself from tackling him to the ground when he shows up somehow looking hotter than he did yesterday?

He looks down at his suit. "Am I overdressed?"

"Yes, but that's not what I mean." I shake my head. My entire body is on fire; Nick looks like he's a lumberjack who moonlights as a J.Crew catalog model. "Did you get that tailored?"

Nick fidgets with one of his buttons. "Yes. I'm tall and skinny. I have to get everything tailored or else I look like an awkward teenager in borrowed clothing."

"And what is this?" Before I can stop myself, I reach out and stroke my hand over his short beard. *Bad idea, bad idea, bad idea* blares the alarm in my head. Flames consume my hands and burn off my fingerprints. "How did you grow a full-on *beard* since the last time I saw you?"

He shrugs, looking uncomfortable. "I didn't shave. This is what happens."

This is a personal affront. Only Nick could grow a beard from scratch in a day for the express purpose of sexually tormenting me.

I exhale, then grab my purse from the hook beside the door. "All right. Let's get this over with."

"Hey." Nick stops me and puts a hand on my arm before we descend the stairs. "You look amazing."

I can feel myself start to blush, which is silly, because I don't blush, not even when people are making much more suggestive comments than this. I do, however, know that I look good. I chose a sexy/funky dress, one that shows off my body while still mixing patterns, with stripes on top and a green-and-purple floral pattern on the bottom. It says, *Yes, I'm quirky, but also, boobs.* It's kind of like if ModCloth and some skanky store at the mall had a baby.

"Thank you," I say, holding my head high. "And thank you for escorting me to the premiere."

Nick stares at my lips a little too long, and for a moment I think he's going to kiss me. But he doesn't, and after a short and slightly awkward ride in the truck, here we are, about to walk the red carpet at—I can't believe this is real—the premiere of a movie about us.

I knew this premiere wouldn't be like the movie premieres I saw on TV or in magazines. I mean, it's in a small, one-screen theater in Columbus, not Hollywood, and most of the people attending are our friends and family, not celebrities. Yes, Drew's here, but the actors from the movie didn't even come; the Columbus premiere is more a favor the film studio's doing for Annie, on account of how she wrote the movie and all.

And yet there is a red carpet, albeit the most pathetic one the world has ever seen, shoved onto the sidewalk outside the theater. There is exactly one photographer, but I don't know if she's from local media or some website or if the theater hired her.

I stop to check my phone, but there are no messages from Milo. He promised to be on duty if Dad's facility calls, and it feels strange to abdicate responsibility for even a moment, like I'm forgetting my purse when I walk out the door. I try to remember what everyone has been telling me—it's okay to take the tiniest bit of time for myself.

Even if the last time I tried that it ended in us rushing back from Indianapolis.

I tuck my phone into my purse, pushing it out of my mind.

"We can turn around and go home," I say as

278

the one photographer takes a series of photos of Dungeon Master Rick (this is the moment that I realize the photographer is definitely hired by the theater or movie studio to make us feel important; there's no way any media outlet would care this much about Dungeon Master Rick and the various poses he's doing with his fedora).

"We're not going home," Nick says, grabbing my hand. "How about this? You want to leave, you squeeze my hand twice, and that's it. We'll get up and leave."

I look at him and swallow, then nod. "Yeah. Okay."

We walk past the lone photographer and I give him a quick wave as Nick refuses to stop. "Nope," he says, pulling me along. "I'm not doing that."

The lobby is crammed with everyone I know; for Annie, this must be like a pre-wedding, a celebration not of her and Drew but of the piece of entertainment that she made. Even though things are tense between us now (or however you would describe it after we yelled insults at each other while surrounded by fake penises), I'm exploding with pride for her. I may not fully support the content of her movie, but she did this. She made the thing she's been talking about forever—not everyone can say they achieved their biggest dream.

"Chloe."

Annie stands in front of me, her eyes wide and uncertain. She glances down at Nick's hand holding mine, then looks away, like she wants to ask but is going to restrain herself.

"Hi," I say, then add, "Congratulations. This is amazing."

She gives me a tentative smile, and then I lean forward and wrap up her tiny body in a hug. Sure, I'm mad, or upset, or disappointed, or whatever (I do *not* have time to examine my feelings right now), but she's my best friend, now and forever. That's not going to change because of a fight.

Over her shoulder, I see Uncle Don and Tyler, plus all their D&D friends. Gary is here, although I'm pretty sure he primarily watches *Wheel of Fortune*, not rom-coms. Even Tobin is here, which means his roommate Marcus is filling in (Marcus takes over only in the case of emergencies, but Nick trusts him because he's less accident prone than Tobin, although that really isn't saying much). This room is packed full of people who know and love Annie, and, by extension, people who know and love me. And now those people are going to watch a fictionalized version of my life play out onscreen.

"Thank you for coming," Annie says, smiling at me. "I was afraid . . ."

I shake my head. "I would never miss this."

Drew appears behind Annie, looking less like a hulking action movie star and more like a rom-com lead in his suit. He puts his hand on her back. "Sorry to interrupt, but I think they're ready for you to introduce the movie. Oh, hey, Chloe."

I wave, and Nick lets go of my hand for a moment to give one of those brisk dude handshakes. But then his hand finds mine again, and it's a relief to have him to hold on to.

Annie nods, biting her lip. "Okay, well, I guess I'm gonna head in. Oh, be sure to grab some popcorn. It's free!"

I place my free hand over my heart. "Free popcorn? Why, you've pulled out all the stops."

Annie leans over to give Nick a hug, too, which is a funny sight since she's so small and he's so tall. "Thank you for bringing her."

"Yeah. Well." Nick stiffens, uncomfortable with physical contact (although, as I remind myself, he seems plenty comfortable with physical contact from me).

Everyone files into the theater, and even though Nick starts to walk toward the front, where Annie and Drew are headed, I pull him toward the back. I'm pretty sure the last time I sat in the back of a movie theater, it was for clandestine make-out purposes, but right now I don't think I can handle being up near the front. And also I want to be able to make an easy exit if necessary.

People keep filing in; so many people. People I don't know, people that must've just wanted to see this movie. My heart starts to beat faster to the rhythm of *oh no oh no oh no*. I knew there were people in the world who cared about this movie and wanted to see it; why would my picture be in blog posts if they didn't? But actually seeing them here, sitting in the plush red theater seats, makes it all so real.

A hush settles over the crowd as Annie steps up to the front. "Hi, everyone," she says with a smile and a self-conscious wave. She may be Big City Annie now, but she still looks like the Annie I know and love up there, just with a more expensive haircut and a nicer dress.

"I'm so glad you were all able to make it for the Columbus premiere of *Coffee Girl*," she says, and the crowd erupts. Like all Ohioans, we're trained to clap and cheer whenever anything from Ohio is mentioned (LeBron James, spaghetti with chili on it, Jeni's ice cream, and now, Annie Cassidy).

"This movie is an homage to the love stories I grew up with, and I hope it makes you feel as good as romantic comedies always made me feel when I was going through hard times. I know sometimes it can seem like quiet love stories don't matter, but I think they do. I think they're kind of all that matters."

I look toward Drew in the front row just in time to see him give her a thumbs-up. She smiles, just for him, then looks back at the crowd. "I hope you guys enjoy the film."

Everyone claps and the lights dim. I'm anxious

and jittery and I wish I had some of that popcorn; at least it would give me something to do with my hands.

"You can relax," Nick says, leaning over, his breath warm in my ear.

"I have never once in my life relaxed," I say, staring at the screen as the credits start.

The movie starts in the comforting way of a classic rom-com, with an upbeat pop song and a slow pan over a city skyline. Watching a prettier, more stylish, better-coiffed version of me onscreen is strange (and also, it feels a little Liberace-esque to be attracted to myself), but the feeling passes quickly. The onscreen Nick, however, doesn't hold a candle to the real one sitting beside me.

I'm relaxed enough to forget, for a moment, that this is a movie about us. Soon, I'm just watching a movie with Annie, even if this time it's in a theater full of people instead of sitting on the soft couch in the living room.

But about an hour into the movie, there's a scene where Zoe's dad tells her he's in remission. His cancer, the treatment of which has been making him sick and weak as she cared for him the whole movie, is gone. He's better.

Zoe smiles at him hopefully, and he smiles back, the two of them living in this wonderful, happy world that my dad and I will never inhabit. It's a world where people get better, one where their sickness doesn't get worse and worse and worse. One where their burden eases, instead of getting so, so heavy that it breaks their backs.

My eyes fill with tears, but this is no place for a Five-Minute Cry.

I stand up, pushing my way past a few people as I mumble my apologies. I don't even know what I'm doing, but I know that I have to get out of this theater now or else I'm going to explode. I clomp down the carpeted aisle, then stomp through the lobby, my heels click-clacking across the tile. I push the doors open and the chilly air hits my face in a refreshing burst, which precisely coincides with the moment tears start to leak out of my eyes.

Well, *leak* might be too delicate a word. Something grosser would be more accurate: *gush*. *Spew.* There are tears gushing and spewing out of my eyes as I lower myself onto the curb and rest my head on my knees. It started raining while we were in the movie, and now a cold drizzle coats me, probably ruining my hair and my dress.

"Hey."

I feel his hand on my back before I turn to see him. It's Nick, of course.

"Sorry I didn't use our secret hand-squeeze language," I say through my tears.

He moves his hand in small circles. "It's okay. You want to talk about it?"

I motion toward the movie theater.

"Maybe in words, instead of vague gestures."

I shake my head, staring at my knees. "I've never walked out of a movie before. Annie and I stayed for the entirety of *The Break-Up*, even when it became clear that they weren't going to get back together and would, in fact, break up. Annie was so upset she cried."

"Chloe." Nick's head dips as he tries to meet my eyes. I look back at him.

"This isn't about *The Break-Up*," he says.

I exhale a long, shuddery sigh, looking at my knees again. "Her dad gets better. In Annie's movie. He has cancer, and his treatment works, and he gets better."

Nick nods slowly.

I chew on my lip for a moment, then turn toward him. "That's never going to happen for me. Never, ever, not unless I wake up tomorrow and there's some magical, Alzheimer's-reversing drug in the news, which seems pretty unlikely at this point. My dad's not ever going to get better. He's only going to get worse, because my life isn't a movie. My problems can't be solved in an hour and a half. I can't have a romantic epiphany that coincides with my dad's improving health and then, like, walk around the city purposefully while a cover of a '90s pop song plays. That's not how life works."

Nick puts his arm around me and I lean into him.

"I should check my phone," I say, because even though Milo's on Dad duty, old habits die hard. I dig through my purse, then find it and gasp. There are multiple missed calls, from my dad's facility and the *hospital*.

"Fuck." I stand up. "Milo was supposed to be fucking handling this. What the fuck?!"

"Chloe." Nick stands up and grabs my arm, holding me steady. "What's happening? What's wrong?"

I call Brookwood back, my heart pounding as the phone rings. "I need to get to the hospital."

Chapter Twenty-Three

My dad is fine.

He's asleep when I get there, his body looking small and frail in the hospital bed. Brookwood called an ambulance when he complained about chest pains. But once he got here, he said he felt fine, had no memory of his chest pains, and all of his tests showed no problems. They're keeping him overnight for observation, just in case.

I don't want to wake him, so I tell the doctor I'll be back first thing in the morning, then sink into a hard plastic chair in the waiting room.

The chair beside me squeaks. "Well, that's a relief, huh?"

I jump. "Nick! I forgot you were here!"

He raises his eyebrows. "The words I love to hear."

"I didn't mean . . . Ugh. You know. I was so caught up with Dad stuff that I forgot you came in here with me. Thank you, again, for driving me."

"Of course," he says. The two of us take a second to look around the waiting room, which is pretty deserted at this time of night.

"You know, I hate to brag, but I think we're the best-dressed people in this hospital," I say.

Nick smiles and hands me a package of Twix and a bottle of Coke. "I know this isn't a gourmet snack or anything, but I was working with what the vending machine gave me."

I tear open the package, then hesitate after I take a bite of Twix. Nick got this for me, without me asking. I know it's only candy, and I shouldn't be getting emotional over anything that comes out of a hospital vending machine, but it's been an emotional day.

I know everything else in my life is taking up one hundred percent of my time and attention (the fact that I'm in a hospital waiting room right now is a perfect example of that), but I let myself imagine for a moment what it would be like if Nick and I were together. In a relationship. Not a Netflix-and-chill situation like with Mikey Danger, or a no-strings, no-expectations thing like I've always had with everyone else, the kind of situation where I can never really drop my guard and relax. With Nick, I'm myself, all the time. I don't have to be responsible Chloe, caregiver Chloe, or therapist Chloe, because Nick doesn't need me to take care of him.

It's not that I don't have people I can count on. I do. I have Annie, and Tracey, and Uncle Don, and probably even Tobin if the emergency in question isn't time sensitive. But I've never wanted to depend on them, because I know what happens when you really let yourself rely on another person and then they disappear. You end up making your own fourth-grade Christmas concert costume at the last minute. It's easier to just make your own costume in the first place; that way the only person who can disappoint you is yourself.

I'm always the person in the waiting room, because I would never ask anyone to wait for me. But as I watch Nick, I realize that I could get used to having someone here, and I don't know if that's a good thing.

My eyes run over the angles of his face as he looks at his phone. The sharpness of his nose, the dark rumpled mess of his hair, the tantalizing scruff on his jaw.

Nick puts his phone down and looks at me. "Arc you choking?" he asks, leaning toward me.

I swallow. "No! Why did you think I was choking?"

He shakes his head. "Because you were staring at me without saying anything, and you looked terrified."

I force a smile on my face. "It's . . . been a long day."

Nick smiles. "You wanna go home?"

I nod, and fifteen minutes later, Nick drops me off. His truck waits in the driveway as I climb the stairs and unlock the door, and I wave to him as I step inside.

But then, as soon as he drives away, I open the door again and go right back down those stairs into the cold and wet night, then get into my car. There's someone I have to see.

Milo didn't answer any of my calls, so I pound on Mikey Danger's front door. There are a few drunk-looking college bros on the lawn of the duplex next door staring at me.

"Whoooooa. I wouldn't want that chick to be pissed at me," one of them says in what I think is supposed to be a whisper.

"You're right you wouldn't," I mutter, banging on the door again.

It swings open and Fred blinks at me a few times. "Uh, Chloe?"

He's wearing sweat pants and no shirt and he looks . . . well, he looks like a male model. "Oh, no," I say. "You were asleep?"

He shakes his head, waking up. "Yeah, but it's fine. Is everything okay?"

Fred is nothing but an innocent bystander in this situation, and I need to get to Milo. "Where's my brother?" I ask.

He gestures toward their room with his head. "When I got home from a shoot tonight, he was already in bed. I guess he fell asleep early."

I clench my jaw. The entire time I was

freaking out and visiting the hospital, Milo was sleeping like an overgrown baby who has zero responsibility?

"Excuse me," I say through my teeth as I step past Fred. "I need to go yell at my brother."

"I'll . . . wait here," I hear Fred say over my shoulder.

I swing the door open, grab a pillow off the floor, and throw it at Milo's sleeping form. When he doesn't wake up, I use my hands to jostle him.

"Hey. Hey!" I yell. He groans and rolls over, then startles when he sees it's me. He grabs his giant glasses off the floor and slides them onto his face. His mouth opens slightly and when he looks at me in confusion, I see him as tiny child Milo, the one who used to fall asleep on the couch in front of the television while watching cartoons. My heart softens a bit, but then I remember why I'm here.

"Dad's in the hospital," I say.

Milo sits up, scrabbling against the sheets. "What?"

I level a look at him. "I got out of the premiere and I had, like, a million missed calls from Brookwood and the hospital. Apparently he had chest pains and—"

"Is he okay?"

"He's fine. It's all fine. But what if it wasn't?"

Milo runs a hand over his face. "But it is."

"But what if it wasn't?" I ask again, my voice

rising. "You said you had this. You were on Dad duty tonight."

Milo throws his hands in the air. "I fell asleep! I fell asleep, okay? I'm sorry I made a mistake!"

I shake my head and point at him. "No. We're not at the apologizing point. Don't skip to that. You don't even know all the things you did wrong yet."

"Oh, I'm sure you're going to tell me," Milo mutters.

"Excuse me?" I ask, crossing my arms over my chest.

"Nothing. Just saying that you're really good at letting me know all the many ways I've failed you."

"That's pretty rich, seeing as you don't even know half of what I go through every day. It's hard taking care of Dad, Milo."

"I know."

"Actually, you don't know, because you aren't around. Because you split when things got tough and you left me here to handle it."

Milo rubs his hands over his face again. "I'm not like you, Chloe. It freaks me out, seeing Dad like that. I don't even know what to do, how to help. I can't handle it like you."

"What, do you think I have some sort of supernatural ability to handle things?" I explode. "Because, news flash, I don't. But I'm handling it because I have to, because I don't have a choice, because no one gave me one. You're gone, Mom's gone, I'm the only one who's here. The only one who cares."

"Mom and I care," Milo says, and I almost argue back before I realize what he said.

"What do you mean, Mom cares?" I ask, something clicking into place in my brain. "How would you know?"

"I talk to Mom sometimes," he mumbles, avoiding my eyes.

I freeze. Of course, I suspected this. Would Milo ask me about "forgiving" Mom so often if he didn't at least occasionally talk to her? But I thought it would be one of those things we never brought up, an open secret hanging between us.

My voice switches to syrupy sweet. "Oh, that's nice. And how's she doing? Feeling happy, after abandoning her entire family for a guy she met on the Internet?"

"Talk to her yourself if you want to know," Milo says, an edge in his voice that I don't think I deserve.

"Wow, no thanks! I would literally rather get trapped on a cruise ship with no running water. Also, if she's so hell-bent on talking to me, she could (a) go back in time and not ditch me, and (b) try to contact me herself."

"She's scared to talk to you because of . . ." Milo waves his hands at me. "This. You're terrifying."

Even though I'm angry, I feel a little proud. "If

she's afraid of me, that's her problem. She's the parent, I'm the kid."

"Only you're not a kid anymore, Chlo," Milo says, softening a bit. "You're an adult now, and our parents are getting older."

"Uh, yeah," I say. "I'm well aware."

"And I know you're mad at Mom. I am, too. Or I was, I don't know. But what do you have to lose from talking to her?"

"Where is she?" I ask.

Milo sighs. "She's here, in Columbus. They moved back."

I can only assume that "they" refers to her and her Internet boyfriend, but I can't even focus on that.

"Is *that* why you came back here?" I ask. "To hang with your deadbeat mom?"

"That's not the only reason."

My voice rises as the realization hits me. "Wow. *Wow.* I thought you came back because you had a change of heart, because you wanted to be around for Dad—"

"I do!" Milo starts to say, but I cut him off.

"I thought maybe you gave a shit about *me*. But that's not it at all. You came back for her. You came back for the woman who left us."

"Chloe." I look Milo in the eye and he's pleading with me, his face begging me to listen. This is the look I always cave for, the one that makes me give him whatever he wants.

But not anymore.

"I'm sorry, Chloe," he says. "I'll do better. But I never knew you needed my help—you never asked for my help."

"I thought the whole 'people should take care of their sick fathers' thing was kind of an unspoken rule. Forget it." I rub my temples. "I've done fine without you the past few years. I'll keep doing fine."

He rears back like I slapped him, but I don't wait around to hear what he has to say. I spin out of the room and through the kitchen, where Fred and Mikey Danger are sitting at the kitchen table, eating straight out of a pizza box.

"Oh, hey, Chloe," Mikey Danger says, toasting me with a piece of pizza.

"Is everything okay?" Fred asks with concern evident on his beautiful face. He probably heard me yelling at Milo; after all, the walls in this place are thin.

"Everything's fine," I say as I head out the door and into the night. "Everything's perfect. Everything's great."

I slam the door behind me, then notice that the drizzle has turned into pouring rain. I bolt toward my car. I'm soaking wet, my hair plastered to my face, my dress clinging to my body. I loved this dress when I put it on this morning, but now I want to set it on fire.

Once I'm in the safety of my car, I pull my

phone out of my purse and stare at it. I don't want to go home, to my silent, lonely apartment where I'll watch sitcoms late into the night instead of sleeping. I don't want to call Annie, because as bad as things were between us before, they're probably much worse now that I've ditched the premiere of her first movie. Everyone else I know is at the premiere, except for Tracey, who's on her anniversary trip with her wife.

Because everyone I know has someone. Someone to go home to, someone to call, someone to talk to, someone to *be there*.

Tears stream down my face as I look at my phone in my hand. I don't want to be here for a single second more, so I toss my phone in my purse and start the car.

Chapter Twenty-Four

Nick lives right above the coffee shop, but I've never been up there. The door beside the shop's door opens to a staircase that, presumably, leads to Nick's apartment. I stand outside it on the dark sidewalk and ring the doorbell once, and then again, and then again. I should've pulled a coat on over this revealing dress, or I should've picked a less revealing dress, but in my defense, I was trying to make my boobs look good, not protect myself from the elements. I look at my reflection in the window of the shop—between the crying and the rain, I look like a Muppet that's been put through the washing machine.

Another thing I should've done? Called Nick first, like a normal person, instead of showing up at his door. He probably isn't even here. He's probably hanging out with D-Money and the Shivanenator, or on a date with a cute girl from a dating app. I wrap my arms around myself and shiver as the darkened window of the coffee shop stares back at me.

I hear the thump of boots on stairs, and then his feet come into view through the window in the door. And then there he is, opening the door and stepping out onto the sidewalk, pulling me into his arms in one fluid gesture.

"What's wrong, honey?" he asks into my ear, and that's what does it, that little term of endearment that no one besides a TJ Maxx fitting room employee has ever, ever used to refer to me. My cries turn from regular-crying into outright sobs, and this is no Five-Minute Cry. This is a real cry, the kind that isn't going to stop after five minutes, or possibly ever. Nick's arms wrap around me and warm me more than any coat or blanket ever could, and he smells like Nick, like that old-person aftershave, and I want to stay here forever.

"Let's get you inside," Nick says, and I remember that, oh yeah, it's raining. I nod without saying anything and Nick guides me through the door, a hand on my lower back. I walk up the steep stairs, so tired that I can barely even think about how my ass is eye level with Nick's face.

"Oh," I say as we reach the top of the stairs and I walk through the open door into Nick's apartment. I don't know what I expected—I guess I imagined that Nick lived in a room full of flannel. Something about him made me assume there were, like, animal heads mounted on his wall, which doesn't really make sense considering that Nick doesn't hunt, but I always thought it would be uber-manly. And it's certainly not feminine—there are no dishes of potpourri or vases full of flowers or wooden signs that say *LIVE LAUGH LOVE* or anything. It's sparsely decorated, but everything looks clean and comfortable, the complete opposite of Mikey Danger's place. There's a huge, soft-looking gray sofa (not a futon!), and a real kitchen table unencumbered with piles of junk mail.

And through the half-open door, I can see into his bedroom, where a made bed sits in the darkness. I will not think about that right now.

"Your place is so clean," I say on an exhale.

"Again, you have the lowest standards possible."

"And it smells so good," I say, my arms wrapped around myself as Nick goes into the darkness of his room, then emerges with a stack of clothing.

"I'm reheating a lasagna I made yesterday," Nick says, handing me the clothes, then gesturing toward the bathroom. "Go put these on. You're soaking wet."

I'm too tired and sad to even make a sexual joke, which is really saying something. I head into the bathroom, which is also spotless, and peel my wet dress off my body, temporarily getting stuck. I pull on—oh, God, one of Nick's flannel shirts, plus a pair of the softest pants I've ever touched in my life. I put the shirt under my nose and sniff it, like a total weirdo, then catch sight of myself in the mirror. My braids have held up surprisingly well, but they're wet and deflated, and my eye makeup has migrated down to my cheeks. I grab some toilet paper and do my best to rectify the situation, but there's no escaping the truth: I'm in Nick's apartment, in Nick's clothes, and I look perhaps the worst I've ever looked in my life.

I exhale and make a face at myself in the mirror, then open the door and promptly trip over the trailing feet of Nick's pants.

"What the hell?" I ask as I almost run into Nick's coffee table (which, FYI, is *not* covered in half-empty Chinese food containers). "Why are you so tall? And what even are these pants? Are they made out of kitten fur?"

"I don't own pants made out of kittens. I don't think anyone owns pants made out of kittens. Those are my lounge pants," Nick says from his place on the couch, and then I notice that there's a plate of lasagna and a glass of something on the coffee table.

"*Lounge* pants?" I ask. "Specific pants for lounging?"

"What do you wear when you're relaxing?" Nick asks, looking confused.

I pause and think about it. "Well, I don't relax, but I suppose I just grab a pair of pajama pants off the floor. I don't have a wardrobe for *lounging*."

But this is making me think maybe I should.

Nick has his life so together; maybe I, too, would feel like a functional adult if I had an extremely soft pair of lounge pants to watch sitcoms in.

"Sit down and eat," he says, so I do.

"Nick," I groan with my mouth full. I smack him on the arm. "What's in this? Why are you so good at everything?"

Nick ignores my questions and asks, "So what's going on?"

I wonder how long I can keep eating this lasagna before I have to answer him. As it turns out, not very long.

"Well, Milo sucks," I say, putting my plate down. "He missed all the calls about Dad because he fell asleep."

Nick makes a face. "Oof."

I nod. "Oof is right. I kind of went off on him. Like, this is the one night I've actually gone out somewhere, the one night I've allowed myself to take a break and not worry about taking care of everyone else, and I can't even do that! I can't even have one night because I can't trust Milo to do anything. It's only me. It will always just be me. I'm all alone."

At this point, I realize I've been emphatically stabbing the lasagna with my fork, so I take a bite. "This is really good, by the way."

After chewing for a bit, I notice that Nick isn't saying anything, so I swallow and turn to look at him. He's staring at me with those big brown

301

eyes and it makes me feel a little dizzy, even though I'm sitting down. "Uh, what?" I ask.

"You're not alone, Chloe," he says, and even though he isn't touching me, I feel like he is. Or maybe like he should be. So I lean forward and put my head on his shoulder.

"Please give me the biggest hug in the world," I say into his neck, and he wraps me up in his big, long, Nick Velez arms and everything feels better.

"God, Chloe," he says. "You're shivering."

"Really? Huh. Probably from all the standing in the cold pouring rain I did earlier. Wearing that dress was probably not my greatest idea."

"No," Nick says, and even though I can't see his face I can hear him smiling. "Wearing that dress was a great idea."

I bite my lip to stop myself from smiling.

Then I remember what else Milo said and my smile disappears. "Oh, and did I mention that my absentee mother is back in town, and Milo's been hanging out with her, even though she's the worst?"

"I'm sorry," Nick says. "That sucks."

I snort. "Yes. Thank you for acknowledging that fact. It totally sucks."

"Come on," Nick says, standing up and pulling me to my feet. "We need to get you warmed up."

"Can't I sit here and watch old sitcoms?" I whine.

Nick gestures around his apartment. "No TV."

My mouth hangs open in disbelief. "But . . . but what do you *do?* How do you entertain yourself? Do you read bowling manuals?"

But Nick's walking into his room, toward that big bed, and I am powerless to stop myself from following him. If Nick were a cult leader, I'd be living on a commune and wearing a shapeless robe by now.

"Here." He pulls back the blankets and gestures toward it. "Get in."

I do exactly as he says, enjoying the feeling of having someone tell me what to do. It's nice to not be the one making decisions for once.

He tucks me in under my chin, then sits down on top of the blankets. "How are you feeling?"

I inhale the scent of his sheets, the scent of Nick. "Better. But I'm sorry I barged into your perfect apartment and bothered you."

He shakes his head. "You never bother me."

"I do, though. I bother you about all kinds of things. Mostly music-related things."

"Yeah, but." Nick meets my eyes. "I secretly love it."

"You're just saying that because my life is falling apart," I say. Then I scoot over. "Get in here with me. I'm cold and I need your body heat."

"Chloe," Nick groans.

"Come on. Didn't you hear me? My life is falling apart," I whine, and he exhales a laugh, then lifts up the blankets and slides in and there he is, his body fitting right next to mine, his legs pressed next to my legs.

"You think this is a good idea?" he asks, his voice low, his arms crossed like he's trying to avoid touching me.

"You help me fall asleep," I whisper. Our faces are so close that our noses are almost touching, and then I say the one thing I know to be true. "I feel comfortable with you."

"I'm wearing street clothes."

"Which is disgusting, but I'm willing to forgive it."

"How generous of you."

Neither of us says anything for a moment, and I listen to the sound of our breath as we stare at each other. "Thanks for taking care of me," I say. "And for coming with me to the premiere. And for . . . being there. All the time."

Nick reaches a hand up and brushes his fingers against the side of my face.

"Hey," I say before I can stop myself. "Whatever happened with the heart-printed-dress girl?"

Nick's fingers stop moving. "Who?"

"You know. The girl who came in and gave you her number. Did you guys go out? Did you—"

"No."

I exhale a sigh of relief right into Nick's face. "Really?"

"Really."

"And what about the apps?"

His face scrunches up in confused disgust. "The what?"

"You know." I shove his shoulder and leave my hand there. "The ones Shivan and Doug signed you up for."

Nick lets out a gruff chuckle. "Oh. Those. Yeah, I'm not doing that. They can make all the profiles they want, but I'm not going on a date with anyone."

"You . . . aren't?"

"Chloe," he says. "I don't want anybody else. I want you."

I stop breathing. My soul leaves my body.

"But here's what I need to know," he says. "What do *you* want?"

I swallow, hard. I am so tired, physically and mentally and emotionally. I'm tired of being the strong one, of giving up everything to take care of everyone else. I'm not even saying I want to stop doing that, but I want a break. I *need* a break. I *deserve* a break. I need one thing that's for me, to do one thing I want to do even if it doesn't make sense, even if it might cause problems later, even if it isn't a good idea.

"Nick," I say, and my voice comes out so low that it doesn't even sound like me. "I want you to kiss me right now."

I barely have the words out before Nick's

mouth is on mine, his hands pulling me into him. This isn't anything like our kiss in the shop; this isn't the kiss of two people who are confused and under the influence of a power outage. This is the kiss of two people who know exactly what they're doing and have all night to do it.

Nick grabs my ass, moving me in closer, and I slide my hands up under his shirt, then change my mind and reverse course, sliding my hand into his pants because, let's be real, that's what I've been daydreaming about for the better part of the year.

He takes in a sharp breath and I try to unbutton his pants to get better access. "This is why street clothes are a bad idea," I pant. "This is far too much clothing."

Nick moves his mouth to my neck and I groan; the groan only deepens when he slides his hand up my shirt—his shirt—and cups my breast, then rolls one nipple between his fingers.

"Are you trying to kill me?" I ask hoarsely, attempting to get his pants off. "Because if you don't take these off now I am going to expire, Nick."

He shifts on top of me, still kissing my neck. His persistent stubble tickles my ear as he says, "We don't have to rush, Chloe. We've got all night."

And suddenly, all thoughts of everything else—my family, the movie, my fight with Annie, my aimless life—float out of my brain, because there's only room for one name in there on repeat like a stuck record. *Nick Velez Nick Velez Nick Velez.*

I use all the strength I have to flip him over and get on top of him, because one night doesn't seem like so much time anymore, doesn't seem like it's enough time to do everything I want to do to him.

But Nick stops, puts his hands on my shoulders to stop me, too. "Hey," he says. "Are you sure? Do you want this? Because we can stop right now if you don't."

This might be a bad idea. It might be the worst idea in the history of the entire universe, but right now I don't care about a single thing except that Nick Velez is underneath me and I plan on staying in this bed all night.

"I want this," I say, and before the words are even out of my mouth, Nick rips off my shirt so hard that buttons ricochet across the room.

Chapter Twenty-Five

I open my eyes to darkness. Nick stirs, pulling me closer, and I let him, allowing myself a moment to feel comfortable and safe and held.

"Good morning," he mumbles, his breath warm in my ear and his voice gravelly. I am instantly turned on. *Everything* about Nick is a turn-on, like someone took all the individual things I find attractive and distilled them into one lethal person.

"Wow," I say, kissing his hand. "I can't believe we've been arguing and avoiding making out for so long when we could've been . . . you know, doing this."

Nick pulls me even closer, kissing my neck. "We can do this for the rest of our lives, Chloe. You just say the word."

My breath stops as my heart speeds up. The. Rest. Of. My. Life.

I try, as hard as I can, to imagine myself here for the rest of my life. At the coffee shop. In Columbus. In Nick's apartment. And no matter what I do, no matter how hard I squeeze my eyes shut, I can't see that vision. Eventually, my dad won't be here anymore, and even though I can't think that far ahead, I don't see myself staying here. I see myself somewhere else, somewhere far away starting a new life all by myself. Not caring for anyone else, or about anyone else. Being in charge of my feelings and my life only.

I lift Nick's arm and roll out of bed, pulling his flannel shirt over me quickly. He's so tall that it covers all the necessary parts; yes, he saw me naked in great detail last night, but it feels different now.

"Where are you going?" he asks, reaching for me. "I don't have to get up for . . ." He looks at his bedside clock with one eye closed. "Five entire minutes. We could do a lot in five minutes."

"That we could," I say. "But I'm going to hop in the shower. I stink, and people don't like to buy coffee from baristas who smell bad."

"I like your stink," Nick mutters into his pillow, but I head to the bathroom. I take the world's quickest shower, careful not to use all of his hot water. He has a fully stocked bathroom; he's not one of those men who uses a combination body wash/shampoo/conditioner on every part of his body. I shake my head, letting the water run over my face. Whatever. So he has body wash. As Nick often says, I have extremely low standards. So what if he has an array of hygiene products, a spotless-yet-comfortable apartment, and a talent for oral? So do lots of people. Probably. That doesn't mean I need to attach myself to him like a barnacle.

I dry off on what is hopefully a clean towel and use the emergency makeup I keep in my purse (because I may never know what the night will bring, but I do know I'll want lipstick and eyeliner in the morning).

I need to get out of here and into work, but the problem is that Nick will be at work, being all . . . Nick, and now that I know exactly what he can do with those hands, I won't be able to think about anything else. What a waste that he makes lattes all day when his talents lie elsewhere.

And I need to think about other things, unfortunately—the wedding my best friend is planning, the fight my best friend and I are in, the way my mom is apparently around, the fact that my dad is in the hospital, and, oh yeah, the unfortunate truth that I can't count on anyone but myself to do anything.

I exit the bathroom and find Nick's bed empty and neatly made. I hate that his Martha Stewart–level housekeeping skills only make me like him more.

"Eat this," Nick says as I walk into the kitchen, handing me a piece of toast with some kind of jam on it.

"What is it?" I ask, then take a bite without waiting for his answer. Sure, I may be experiencing morning-after awkwardness, but I have my priorities (food).

"Strawberry rhubarb jam," he says. "You like it?"

"Did you make this?" I ask with my mouth full.

"Yeah," he says, washing some dishes. "I got some rhubarb from the farmer's market."

Rhubarb? Farmer's market? "Wow, fuck you," I mutter.

"What?"

"This is good," I say brightly. "But I have to get to work."

He raises his eyebrows. "I know. We work at the same place."

"Yeah, but . . ." I gesture at the dress I put back on, which is dried out but stiff and smelly. "I realized I'm gonna have to go home and change. I can't roll into work looking like this."

"Is that not work appropriate?" Nick asks. "I think it looks good."

I shake my head. "You are such a dude. No, Nick, a going-out dress is not suitable for the morning shift. I'm gonna go home and throw on some normal clothing that shows a breakfast-pastry-appropriate level of cleavage."

"Hey," Nick says, then reaches for me with both hands and pulls me toward him. He kisses me and I melt into him, like I'm a chocolate bar and he's a radiator. He's so warm, and it takes everything in me not to pull this dress off once again and get back into bed.

I take solace in the fact that we couldn't do that even if we wanted to, because we both have to be at work. "Okay," I say into his mouth. "I really have to go."

He groans, the vibration reverberating through my body.

"My boss is gonna kill me if I'm late."

He snorts and finally lets me go.

I'm tired all day at work, but that's nothing new. Nick acts more or less normal, which is both reassuring and disheartening. I'm not sure what I expected . . . for him to announce to the shop that we boned? Either way, I try my best to focus on the fine art of coffee pouring but it's hard when I can feel his body heat radiating toward me, even when he's tucked away in his office.

When I get home, I sit down in front of my laptop at my kitchen table and check my school email.

"Wait," I mutter. "This can't be right."

I check my planner, then my online calendar. But it *is* right. I missed turning in an assignment today.

I slump in my chair. I've never missed turning in an assignment; I mean, that's kind of my whole thing. I'm Chloe Sanderson, and I get shit done. But one night of (okay, admittedly great) sex and I space out?

Clearly, I have to work harder.

. . .

But it's not just school I'm behind on. In my initial pom-math, I made a miscalculation, and now I don't have nearly enough poms. The amount I currently have would perhaps make a shin-height pom wall. Not impressive. I work so hard on catching up that I don't even visit my dad for the next couple of days.

When I finally do get to Brookwood, guilty and exhausted, Tracey greets me with a wave and a huge grin.

"So what's going on with Nick?" she asks, wiggling her eyebrows.

I lean over the desk and wave her off. "We slept together. Whatever."

She places a hand over her mouth to stop herself from shrieking. "Uh, excuse me? *Whatever?* You've been lusting after that dude for, like, ever, and now you're telling me that you jumped his bones and it was NBD?"

I rest my head on the counter. "I'm just really tired," I mutter.

Tracey reaches over and gently pushes my head up. "Pull yourself together, woman! Go see your dad, then go home and take a nap."

I sigh. The word *nap* provokes a Pavlovian response and I nearly start to drool. "That sounds great, but it's not gonna happen."

Tracey shrugs. "Well, your dad's pretty tired from that big family bingo thing we did earlier today."

I freeze. "Family bingo was today?"

"Yeah." Tracey glances at her computer, already back to work, uninterested in the fact that I'm having a personal crisis over here.

"But I was supposed to go to that," I say, my voice rising. "I must have . . . I must have forgotten. Did any volunteers play with him, at least?"

Tracey looks back at me, eyebrows raised. "Uh, no? Milo was here. I figured you asked him to fill in."

"Why didn't you remind me?" I ask her, my voice sharp.

Tracey sits back in her chair, then gestures around her. "No offense, but I do have a job, and it isn't as your personal assistant."

I shake my head quickly and rub my hands over my eyes. "You're right, you're right. I'm sorry. I'm being a bitch."

Tracey leans forward and smiles. "You're being a cranky baby. Go take a nap."

I nod. "Okay. I'm sorry again. I'll see you later."

As I walk down the hallway to my dad's room, I stare at my red flats moving slowly over the beige carpet. How have I dropped the ball on so many things lately? My dad. School. Wedding prep. I'm behind on everything, and why? Because I was spending so much time with Nick. Entire evenings I could've been working, could've been with my dad. Gone.

My phone buzzes and the screen shows a text from Nick. *Nick.* Pinpricks of sweat form at my temples and I toss the phone back in my purse. Not right now.

I knock on my dad's door, mentally trying to figure out how I'll possibly catch up on everything I have to do. One thing's for sure: I was right when I said I didn't have time for a relationship.

Chapter Twenty-Six

I show up for my shifts all week, providing our customers with the high level of Chloe Sanderson service to which they've become accustomed, but I avoid Nick like it's yet another job. I don't meet his eyes. I don't look at him when I can feel him staring at me. I definitely don't go into his office for any reason, lest I find him shirtless in there. It's pretty difficult, but as I remind myself, it's for the best.

"Hey," Nick says one night as we clean up. "Is everything okay with you? With your dad, and Milo?"

I shrug, wiping off a counter. "Um, as okay as it ever is. Which is to say, not okay at all, but that's normal."

He nods. "You seem a little off this week."

I bristle. "I'm sorry that handling a job, school, and the care of my sick father occasionally makes me into a less-than-pleasant person."

"That's not what I meant."

"Okay." I know it's not, and I know I'm not being fair. It's not Nick's fault I'm a screw-up who can't handle normal relationships because her life is so full of responsibilities. "Sorry. I'm being an asshole."

"Can I talk to you about something?" Nick asks. He leans against the counter until I'm forced to put down my cleaning rag and look at him.

"Talk away," I say, leaning away from him, wishing I'd never looked into those brown eyes.

He takes a deep breath, then says in a rush, "I think we should be partners."

I raise my eyebrows, then tilt my head, then squint at him, then make vague movements with my hands. Basically, I run the gamut of facial expressions and hand gestures before settling on one word: "What?"

"I think we should run the shop together. You and me."

"What?" I ask again. Apparently that's the only word I know now.

He shakes his head. "I don't want to be your boss, Chloe, not when you do more to keep this place running than I do. You're the one who makes the baked goods; you're the one people come in to see. You're the one who has the big ideas to make this place more successful, and most importantly, you're the one with business training. I'm floundering around over here, learning as I go, but you actually know things."

I start shaking my head as words start pouring out of my mouth. "Oh, no. No, Nick. I do not think that's a good idea."

"I know it seems like a lot of responsibility."

I snort. "Uh, yeah. And a lot of money, which, FYI, I don't have."

"I have money," Nick says simply.

I furrow my brow. "What?" I need to introduce some new words into my vocabulary, but this conversation is going some places I didn't expect.

"From when my dad died. He was pretty shitty at being a husband or a father, but he was great at making money, and I don't know if it was guilt or a tiny part of him that was actually a good person, but he left me a lot of that money." He squints at me. "Didn't you wonder how I keep this shop running?"

I stare at him.

"I mean, the rent in this neighborhood is astronomical and we don't sell that much coffee. We have *three* employees. But I can't keep it going on like this forever. We need to do something new, and you have ideas. You have *real* ideas, Chloe, for ways this place could be successful."

I can't lie; something in me stirs when he says that. I do have ideas, and not just about how to decorate the bathroom. I have big ideas, about shifting the business model to be more of a cute diner, one that, yes, serves coffee in the mornings but also has lunch and dinner, updated diner favorites. We'd use vintage-looking floral plates and mismatched teacups, serving recipes with names like Nick's Mom's Tortilla Soup.

I shake my head. No. This is not happening.

Nick keeps talking. "You can do this, Chloe. We can do this together. I know we can."

I surprise both of us by letting out a laugh, a sharp bark that rings through the empty shop. "There's absolutely no way I could take a risk like that."

Nick shakes his head. "I get it that you've never run a business before, but—"

"What am I supposed to tell my dad if it fails? 'Whoops, sorry about that, I gambled away all our money, have fun in whatever shithole we can afford now.'"

Nick leans forward and grabs my hand. "It's not a gamble, and you don't have to worry about money. I told you, what I don't have is ideas. Talent. I *have* money."

"Am I supposed to let you float me?" I ask, disgusted, as I pull my hand back. "What are you, my sugar daddy?"

Nick makes a face. "God. No."

I look down at my red flats. I so wish I could click my heels twice and send myself right back home, where this conversation wasn't happening. "It's not going to happen, Nick."

He throws up his hands, exasperated. "Why not? Give me one good reason, because I know you want your own place and this is a chance to do that—"

I raise my eyebrows. "You want one reason?

Let me give you a few. How about because I don't need you figuring out my life for me? I handle everything. I handle my family and I handle me. That's how it's always been, ever since I was a little kid, and that's not going to change. I don't want to be someone's charity case. I do things myself, because I can depend on me."

"You're not a charity case," Nick says in a low voice. "And haven't I proven by now that you can depend on me?"

I ignore him and keep going. "I have a family and they need me. My dad doesn't have anyone else, Nick. I can't count on my mom and Milo's doing God-knows-what, and I'm the only one who can make sure he's okay. And honestly? I don't want to be responsible for anyone, or anything, else. I can't take anything on while I'm taking care of him, and after . . . well, after, I don't want to be tied down."

"Tied down?" Nick exhales, then looks at me. He's finally starting to look a little angry, and the thought both scares and excites me. "So you're going to stay in stasis until your dad's gone?"

"I'm sorry my life is *so* boring for you," I say, letting the sarcasm drip off my voice. "Sorry I'm such a buzzkill, always taking care of my family and stuff."

"That's not what I meant," Nick says. "I'm just saying, I don't see why you can't do something you want, especially when someone wants to help you."

"Because I don't want this!" I shout, taking a step back. I gesture between us. "I don't want anything else to handle. I don't want anything else to take care of. I don't want another responsibility, and I sure as fuck don't want any help."

Nick laughs, and this time his smile is a small, bitter thing. "You don't want this?" he asks, mimicking my gesture. "Because that's not the impression I was under."

"It was a mistake," I say, meeting his eyes, daring myself not to look away. "*I* knew we shouldn't hook up, and *you* knew we shouldn't hook up, and we did and it was a bad idea. It was the movie that screwed everything up."

"That movie didn't change anything for me," Nick says, taking a step toward me. "It didn't change the way I feel."

I swallow hard and force myself to keep looking him in the eyes. "It was a mistake."

Nick stops moving and looks at me. Both of us stare at each other for a moment. "Okay," he says.

After a beat, I ask, "Okay . . . what?"

"Okay, you're right. It was a mistake."

I can't help remembering the last time we had almost this exact conversation in this exact place, after the first time Nick and I kissed, when

I told him we should pretend it never happened and I finally wore him down until he agreed with me.

Why do I do this, I wonder for a moment. *Why do I push every person who cares about me away until it's me, all alone, doing everything? What is* wrong *with me?*

But Nick agrees with me, and that's what I wanted. "It was a mistake." I stare at my feet. "So . . . what now?"

Out of the corner of my eye, I see Nick shrug. "It goes back to how it used to be. We're coworkers. We don't have to talk about anything or see each other outside of the shop."

"How is *that* going to work?"

"It'll be fine," Nick says, already back to work, already forgetting what happened. It's easy for him to turn this off; why is it so easy for him?

I nod and bite my lip. "Yeah. Well. See you tomorrow."

He lifts a hand in a wave without looking at me, the way he would to any coworker he didn't care much about.

I grab my stuff out of the back and head out without saying another word or looking at him again. It's not raining on my short walk home tonight; in fact, it's unseasonably warm, the kind of spring evening that would typically fill me with joy. I stop and look at some flowers pushing their way up through the soil in someone's front yard, and I'm seized with the desire to reach over and pull them out.

I keep walking. Nick's right; it will be fine. I got exactly what I wanted.

So why do I feel like crying?

Chapter Twenty-Seven

The next week passes in a blur. Nick isn't cold or cruel, but he treats me like anyone else. I didn't realize how much of our conversations before consisted of what Annie would refer to as playful banter; now, we talk solely about coffee. He hasn't brought up the idea of being partners in the business again. And why would he? I said no, and I meant it.

When I'm not working, I'm making poms and pies. I've figured out a way to read my business textbooks while rolling out a piecrust, which is pretty impressive, although I'm not sure it's leading to much more productivity since I'm very slow at both. But I have lots of pies frozen for the wedding, enough that I've taken over Don's regular freezer and the freezer in the basement where he typically keeps taquitos. I've made and frozen the dough for the pies that need to be fresh, so I feel somewhat prepared for the dessert portion of this wedding.

Which is good, because we have less than a week to go.

The rest of the wedding, however . . . well, I wish that Annie and I were on better terms. We're not antagonistic toward each other, but things have been chilly since our fight. After a lifetime of getting along, I never imagined we'd have our biggest disagreement ever right before her wedding.

And then there's the pom wall. When I volunteered to do this, I may have underestimated the time involved in making so many poms. One pom? No big deal. But do you know how many poms you need for an entire wall that can serve as a photo backdrop? So. Many. Poms. Martha Stewart herself would faint. I've already given myself multiple paper cuts, and I'm running out of Band-Aids over here. I tried to recruit Don and Tyler to help me, but it turns out they couldn't concentrate on folding tissue paper while rewatching the entirety of *Game of Thrones* for the millionth time (seriously, they tried, but they made some wonky-ass poms).

So I guess it's just me. As usual.

It's 9 P.M. on Monday night, five days before the wedding, and I'm sitting on my apartment floor surrounded by tissue paper in every shade of pink you can imagine. It would be easier if I were doing this over at Don's, where at least I'd have more space for this pom explosion, but Annie's home tonight and I don't want her to see how distraught I am. Plus I have another pie in the oven, and I need to keep an eye on it.

The poms aren't hard—the tutorial from some

325

bridal site promises they're an "easy and quick way to add a pop of color!" and, honestly, they're right. But they're not easy and quick when you're making a metric shit-ton.

I concentrate on folding the tissue paper, tying it off, and fluffing it up. Then I smell something. Something burning.

"Oh no!" I yelp, standing up and crushing one of the poms with my left foot. I run toward the oven and open the door, then wave away the smoke that billows out. This whiskey apple pie is definitely not going to work for the wedding, unless Annie wants to go with the charred look.

I pull the pie out of the oven as the smoke alarm goes off. I grab a chair and reach up to the ceiling, slamming the button with my open palm until it stops chirping. It finally quiets, but I lose my balance, and after a wobble I fall off the chair, right onto the pile of poms.

This should be funny. In other circumstances, it would be. Here I am, lying on top of the destroyed poms that took me hours to make, after injuring myself by falling off a chair, and my apartment smells like burnt piecrust. It's a laugh riot.

Except that it's not, because I'm tired and frustrated and hungry and thinking about Nick Velez and the way he's barely even looked at me in the last week.

I sit up, look around, and wonder, for a moment, if I can scrape the burnt part off the pie (no, because the entire thing is a burnt part). I wonder if the poms are salvageable (the majority of them, yes). And then I wonder if I could actually ask someone for help.

I know Nick is mad at me, but I also know that if I show up in a crisis, he'll help me. He'll have to, because that's the kind of person he is. He's Nick Velez.

So I pack up the rest of my tissue paper and head on over.

Again, I didn't call or text—I didn't want to give Nick the opportunity to pre-reject me, and I figure he'll let me in if he sees me out here on the street in the dark.

I ring the doorbell and nothing happens. I wait a few moments, then ring it again. And again.

Finally, I hear the soft creak of bare feet padding on old wooden stairs, and then Nick's legs come into view. Nick's bare legs, because he's wearing boxers and a T-shirt.

He has good calves, but I'll keep that thought to myself.

He swings open the door and squints at me. "Chloe?"

"Were you asleep?" I ask, incredulous.

He rubs his eyes. "Yes."

"But it's so early! It's not even ten P.M.!"

Nick gives me a look. "You know what time I wake up. What's wrong?"

"What?" The harshness of his voice almost makes me step back.

"I mean." He gestures outside, toward the dark sky and the sidewalk and me. "Something must be wrong if you woke me up, right? Is your dad okay?"

I swallow. "Yeah. I mean, he's fine. It's . . . I . . ."

My self-assuredness drains out of me as Nick looks at me expectantly.

"I'm having kind of a freak-out," I whisper.

Nick rubs his hands over his face. "A freak-out? What does that mean?"

I shift from foot to foot. "Well, the wedding's coming up, and I have so much to do, and I burned a pie and then I fell off a ladder and crushed a bunch of poms and I—"

Nick holds out a hand. "No."

I stop talking. "No what?"

He shakes his head, looking at his feet. "No, I can't help you."

"But I'm . . ." I attempt to take the whine out of my voice. "I'm having a personal crisis."

"Chloe." Nick looks up and meets my eyes. "When *aren't* you having a personal crisis?"

I swallow again, hard. "I . . . I thought you would help me."

"Because I always do, right? Because you can

treat me however you want and I'll always be here?"

My mouth goes dry. "What do you mean, treat you however I want?"

Nick crosses his arms. "You've been ignoring me for a week."

"It's not my fault I don't want a relationship," I say, my voice shaking. "I was honest with you about that. You knew I was screwed-up and busy and—"

Nick shakes his head. "You weren't exactly honest, though, were you, Chloe? I knew this would happen. I knew it would, but you kept doing your thing until I broke down and thought maybe you were serious. Maybe you actually wanted to take a chance on this, to have a real relationship."

Someone walks by with a golden retriever, and neither of us says anything until they're out of earshot.

"But you're doing what you always do," Nick whispers, even though no one's around anymore to hear. "You're showing up only when you need my help."

"I don't just show up when I need your help!" I almost shout. "We're friends. Friends help each other."

"This." Nick points between us. "This is not how friends act. I can't keep being your unpaid, on-call therapist."

"Well, I wouldn't have sex with my therapist. That would be a serious ethical breach on their part."

"Cool," Nick mutters. "Keep making everything into a joke, like you always do."

"We *are* friends, Nick."

"I don't want to be your friend."

"Why not?" I ask, tears springing to my eyes.

"Because I'm in love with you!" he shouts. "Isn't it obvious?"

I drop the bag of pom supplies, then kneel and start picking things up. Some of the tissue paper has come out of the stuffed-full bag and now it's on the ground, soaking in rainwater, getting completely ruined. It's fine. Anything to avoid standing up and facing Nick again.

The stillness of the night expands around us, the only sound the gentle swish of a car driving slowly by.

He groans. "Let's forget this entire conversation ever happened, okay? Forget anything either of us said."

I stand up, nodding, inspecting my bag. "Yep. Okay."

"Hey." Nick leans in, forcing me to meet his eyes. "This doesn't change anything about work. I would never do that. You have a job here as long as you want one. But I can't keep doing the rest of this anymore, okay?"

I nod.

His voice softens. "Please don't keep doing this to me, Chloe."

"Okay, um." I gather my bags under my arms. "I need to . . . be somewhere. Now. Bye."

I start off down the sidewalk and Nick calls after me, his voice resigned, like he can't help himself. "Do you need help?"

God, even when he hates me, he can't stop himself from helping me. He's too perfect.

I lift one hand in a wave without looking back, then almost drop my bag. "I'm good. See you at work."

I speed-walk around the corner, tears rolling down my face. *What the hell?* My tears were neatly contained for years, but this week I'm a geyser. What is wrong with me?

And what the hell did I do to Nick? It was pretty clear, from both his words and his expression, that I hurt him. Deeply. Someone who only wanted to hclp mc and all I did was take advantage of him, use him, play with his emotions like this was all a game for me. He said he loved me, and I . . .

Well.

I care about him, so much. Obviously. But I don't have room in my sad, broken heart to love anybody. Nick deserves better than a girl who treats him like this, who weasels her way into his heart only to blow the whole thing up. He deserves better than someone whose entire life is already dedicated to other people. He deserves better than me.

What was initially a pom-and-pie crisis has now evolved into a full-blown entire-life crisis, and I guess I have Nick to thank for teaching me a valuable lesson, one I maybe should've learned a long time ago. It isn't fair to expect people to put up with my bullshit, to welcome me with open arms when I treat them like garbage. I may have to stay up for the next forty-eight hours to get everything done, but that's my problem, not anyone else's.

I walk past house after house, each one probably home to a family that loves and helps each other. A group of people who can count on each other, not just one woman who has to shoulder everything all by herself. They're all sleeping peacefully in their beds, not even realizing how good they have it, while I clomp down the sidewalk, sad, alone, carrying a bag of tissue paper decorations.

I finally reach home and I'm about to walk down the driveway to the carriage house when I hear a tiny voice say, "Um . . . hello?"

I jump and drop my bags, then squint in the darkness. "Annie?"

She stands in the small front yard, behind the wrought iron fence, holding . . . a leash.

"Do you have a dog?" I ask, crouching to pick up my bags.

"What are you doing?" she asks me.

"You go first."

In the darkness I see her shrug. "Uncle Don and Tyler got a dog. They went to the Columbus Humane Society 'just to look,' but you know how that goes, and now . . ."

"Now they have a dog."

Annie picks the dog up, and even in the dark I can see it eyeing me warily. "She's some sort of terrier mix, I think? All I know about her is that she loves barking, peeing, and dog treats."

"Wow." I take a step closer, the gate between us. "Don got a dog and I didn't even know."

"You should come over more often," Annie says gently.

"I'm busy." The words come automatically.

"Speaking of which . . ." She points with her free hand at my bag. "What are you doing?"

"Nothing," I say, attempting to shift the bag and then almost dropping it again. "I'm gonna go into my apartment and—"

"Chloe," Annie says in a voice so full of understanding and warmth that I almost want to cry. "Just come inside."

Chapter Twenty-Eight

Annie sits me down on the floral sofa and wraps me up in a crocheted blanket.

"I should be taking care of you," I complain. "You're the one who's getting married in five days."

"But you're the one who's shivering," Annie says. "It's chilly outside! Why were you wandering around without a coat?"

"I didn't even notice."

Annie plops down beside me on the couch and we sit facing each other, our legs pulled up and tucked under us. "Chloe. What's going on?"

I sigh. "Do you want the long version or the short version?"

She rolls her eyes. "You know I want the longest of long versions, with copious tangents."

I explain to her what happened with Nick. She widens her eyes when I tell her we slept together but doesn't say anything (although I can tell that it's hard for her). I tell her about what happened after the premiere with my dad, how I haven't spoken to Milo since, and how awful work has been. I tell her about how Nick wants us to be partners at the shop and she finally interrupts me.

"You would be so good at that." She reaches out and puts a hand on my knee. "You know you would."

"I'm also pretty good at making decorative poms," I say, pointing to the bag on the floor. "That doesn't mean I need to make a career out of them."

"I told you, you don't have to do that, okay?"

"But I want to!" I say, my voice rising. The dog lifts her head up from her place on the floor and gives me a curious look. "Wait. What's the dog's name?"

"Leia."

"Huh. I would've assumed Don and Tyler would go for more of a *Star Wars* deep cut."

"Don said she looks like a Leia, and don't change the subject." Annie prods me with her foot. "What's so wrong with being partners with Nick?"

I shake my head quickly. "I'm not like you, Annie. I'm not like Don."

"Thank goodness," Annie says. "I love him, but I can only handle one Don."

"I mean . . . it's not that easy for me, having a relationship. I'm not the kind of person who can just be with someone. *Depend* on someone."

Annie wrinkles her nose. "Do you think it's easy for the rest of us?"

"Well . . . yeah."

She laughs. "Um, do you remember the profound

335

personal crisis I went through when Drew wanted to date me? I mean, I told him *no*. I thought it would never work out because he's, you know, famous. I didn't think I could be in a relationship with him."

"Because you were living in your own rom-com."

"Don got together with Tyler when he was in his midfifties, and it's his first-ever relationship. Not that he would get into the details with me, but I'm sure it wasn't easy for him to handle such a big shift."

I nod. "Yeah, but you guys are . . . you know. Normal people."

Annie lowers her voice. "Neither Don nor I are even remotely normal."

"You know what I mean."

"Actually, I don't."

"My life is a *mess,* Annie. I'm taking care of my dad and I'm not even doing that good a job. I should be happy Milo is in town, but instead I blew up at him and now we aren't speaking. Everyone I know is rolling into their thirties with relationships and businesses and dream jobs and I'm working at a coffee shop while struggling to even get my bachelor's degree. I'm exhausted and I'm making myself sick and I'm not going to subject Nick to this. I wanted to sleep with him more than anything, and trust me, I would do it again . . . but that's not fair, because I'm not his problem. I shouldn't make my life anyone's problem."

"Chloe!" Annie looks at me incredulously. "Is that what you assume other people think of you?"

"Um." I think for a minute. "Yes?"

Annie shakes her head. "You've been baking pies for me for weeks. You're driving yourself bonkers making tissue paper poms for my wedding. You're helping me with my problems."

"Those aren't real problems, though," I say. "No offense."

Annie holds up her hands. "Talk to me when you've dipped a toe in the wedding industrial complex. You lose perspective on what's a real problem."

"I will never. But I *like* helping you. I like doing these things, because that's what I do. I take care of things for other people. I don't ask people to do things for me."

"Why not?" Annie asks, and I pause. I think about it for a moment, then lean back against the couch arm.

"Maybe," she says cautiously, "do you think if you ask people for anything, they won't love you anymore?"

"What are you, a therapist?" I mumble.

"I want to know what's going on with you. You know that, right? But you ignore my texts and you change the subject whenever I ask about your life. I mean, I had to text your brother to make sure nothing was seriously wrong."

"Please don't do that again."

She holds up her hands. "It was a onetime thing. But you were there for me when I was going through hard stuff. You've been there *every* time I've gone through hard stuff—remember how you psyched me up to go confess my love for Drew?"

I nod. "Some of my best BFF work."

She looks right into my eyes, and I don't know if it's the power of her guileless gaze or what, but I can't look away.

"Can you please just let me be there for you the way you've always been there for me?" she whispers, her eyes wide.

I bite the inside of my cheek. I will not cry right now, not when Annie's wedding is coming up and she has enough to worry about. I will calmly say what I mean, no tears involved. "I didn't have anyone to help me when I was a kid."

Annie nods. "I know."

"And I don't mean to make my problems sound bigger than yours, because I know your dad died when you were little . . ."

"It's not a competition."

"My mom abandoned all responsibility for my problems, and I took over. I handled my problems, my dad's problems, Milo's problems. I did both of our science projects, I ironed my dad's work shirts, I made dinner for all of us. It was all me, all the time, because I couldn't count on anyone else to do it. When I asked Milo to do something, it didn't get done. And I would never ask Dad to do it, not when I saw how he handled Mom leaving. It's always been me."

Annie nods.

"And I—" My voice breaks and I pause, then keep going. "I guess part of me wonders, do I handle all my own problems because this is the way I've always done things? Or do I handle my own problems because . . . well, because I'm afraid that people only love me because I do things for them?"

"Chloe." Annie leans across the couch and tackles me in a hug. Leia freaks out, hopping around us and barking. "That is not why we love you."

"What else do I have to offer, though?" I ask, wiping snot off my nose.

Annie laughs into my shoulder. "So much, you dummy. You're funny and you're kind and you always smell like vanilla."

"Why be friends with me when a scented candle could do the trick?"

"And," Annie continues. "I love you. We love you. We want to help you, Chloe." She leans back, her hands on my shoulders, and looks me in the eyes. "Let us help you."

"But I'm used to being the helper," I say. "I'm

used to being the one who gets shit done. I don't want to be a burden."

"You are not a burden," she says firmly. "Do you feel like I'm a burden when you're baking all those pies? Do you feel like your dad's a burden when you're taking care of him? Do you feel like Nick's a burden when you're staying late to clean up?"

I snort. "Of course not."

"Well, then, trust me," Annie says, looking smug. "You're not a burden to anyone. Not even a little bit. Now." She claps her hands. "Let's make some poms!"

"You can't make the poms!"

"I'm going to help you," Annie points out. "And you *did* say you were going to do a better job of letting people help you."

"I didn't say that, but okay, I'll let people help me more. But not with this. It's your wedding; you can't be making your own poms."

Annie waves me off. "This looks fun, and you know I'm crafty."

"No one has ever called you crafty."

Annie picks up the remote and scrolls through Netflix before settling on *While You Were Sleeping*.

"No. I am not going to sit through this movie again."

"It's my wedding!" Annie uses my own words against me. "I get to choose the entertainment."

Together, we coast through making the poms. Annie's *much* better at pom-making than Don and Tyler were, and after a couple of hours, we have more than enough poms for our wall.

"Turns out this is way easier when I'm not doing it by myself and attempting to bake a pie at the same time," I say.

"Who knew?" Annie holds up her latest pom to admire it. "So what are you going to do about Nick?"

"Oh, no," I say. "I do *not* want to talk about that."

Annie puts the pom down and gives me a stern look, and with an uncharacteristic no-nonsense tone in her voice, she says, "Well, you showed up in the driveway cold and crying, so tough shit. You have to tell me about it."

"Geez," I mutter. "The film industry has turned you into a real potty-mouth."

She spins a finger at me. "Start talking."

"I don't know, Annie. That's the whole problem. I . . . well, I . . ."

"You love him," she says simply.

"Dial it down."

"You like him."

"I'm not a child."

She thinks for a moment. "You could see yourself falling in love with him someday. Is that right?"

I know that's not how to describe the way I feel

about Nick, that I've been lying to myself about it for weeks, months, maybe even years. My first impulse is to keep it to myself, to keep this as another personal issue that I don't want to burden Annie with. But maybe she's right. Maybe I should try to let someone in.

"The truth," I say quietly, focusing on the pom in my lap, "is that, despite everything I've told Nick, I have some very strong feelings for him."

Annie smiles, but it isn't smug. "Do you think you should, I don't know . . . tell him?"

I grimace. "That's literally the worst idea ever. What I did to him, the things I said . . . You didn't see his face tonight, Annie. Even without trying, I think I broke his heart. I'm not making him deal with more of this." I gesture at myself and make a face.

Annie shakes her head. "I agree with you that you shouldn't play around with Nick's emotions. You know the kind of music that man listens to; he's prone to big feelings. But that doesn't mean you should write this off just because you made a mistake. He knows you, Chloe. He knows everything about you, and he loves you. He wants to deal with this." She mimics my gesture.

"Why are you being so nice to me?" I ask. "We're supposed to be in a fight."

Annie laughs. "We're not very good at fighting."

I sigh. "No. We're not. I'm sorry I got so upset about the movie."

Annie shakes her head, her curls bobbing. "No, I'm sorry that I didn't even consider how you felt about the movie. Honestly, it was kind of screwed up to write a movie about your life."

"But this was your big break," I say, reaching down to pet Leia's head as she sniffs my feet. "I wasn't going to tell you not to do it."

"Yeah, but." Annie bites her lip. "I wish we could've talked about it. You didn't have to pretend like everything was fine to make me happy."

"Well." I shrug. "That's kind of my thing."

"I know what you need to do," Annie says with sudden confidence.

I eye her skeptically.

"A grand gesture," she says, and all of a sudden I remember us sitting in her old room, our roles reversed, as I tried to help her get Drew back after they had a fight and he jetted off to New York. She wanted to live out her rom-com dream, and I encouraged her to follow him to the airport and then to New York City to declare her love for him in what turned out to be an on-air segment of a morning show.

I could kick Past Chloe for how naïve she was.

"No, no, no." I shake my head exaggeratedly, like Annie is a small child and I'm explaining why she shouldn't stick her finger in an electrical socket. "Grand gestures are great for you, Annie. But those things only happen in movies, and they're clichés. Tropes. Not real life."

"All I'm saying is, there was a grand gesture in my real life, and it worked out pretty great for me."

I scowl. "Yeah, but you *wanted* your life to be a romantic comedy. That's the difference: I don't."

Annie tilts her head and looks at me. "Maybe you need to accept that your life *is* a rom-com, whether you want it to be or not."

"No thanks," I mutter. "But maybe you're right about the whole 'letting people help me' thing. Thanks for helping me with these poms."

Annie smiles, then looks at the floor and groans. "Leia pooped on the floor again."

Finally, we've found one thing I actually don't want to help with.

Chapter Twenty-Nine

The next day, I stop by Dad's to pick him up for a follow-up appointment at the doctor's. Since I've been so busy with wedding prep, I haven't been by his place as often as usual, and of course I'm feeling guilty.

As I lift my hand to knock on Dad's door, I hear voices on the other side and frown. Dad doesn't have a lot of other visitors, although he does pal around with some of the other residents here (not the ones he accuses of breaking his TV). But this voice sounds young. It sounds like . . .

I open the door. "Milo?"

He waves and offers up a smile. "Hey. Dad and I were watching . . . uh, what were we watching?"

Dad snorts. "We're watching the best television show ever made, *M*A*S*H*."

"We're watching *M*A*S*H*," Milo says, giving me a wide-eyed look. "I don't know what's happening and everyone has a weird name, but the theme song is tight."

"This is an American classic," my dad grumbles, and I squeeze in beside Milo on the love seat, thinking about how Nick and I sat here together not too long ago. The three of us sit in almost-silence, and I'm grateful once again for the healing balm of television. Sure, we may have our differences, and my dad may have his bad days, but classic television is a surefire way to spend a little bit of bonding time without talking to one another.

We don't have long before we have to leave, so I make sure he has plenty of reading material (I don't know how much he retains, but every week he picks up a few paperbacks from the library truck) and crossword puzzles, then check to see that his fridge is fully stocked.

"I'm just gonna go talk to Milo for a minute in the hallway, but I'll be right back to take you to your appointment," I tell him as another episode of *M*A*S*H* starts.

He stands up and gives me a big hug and a kiss on the head. "It's so good to see you kids together," he says, his arms around me. "I'm glad you're still best friends."

I meet Milo's eyes over Dad's shoulder, and he looks away.

"Be right back," I tell Dad as Milo gives him a goodbye hug, knowing he'll probably forget about the appointment by the time our conversation is over.

I shut his door and wait until we're a respectable distance down the hallway before I turn to Milo. "What the hell are you doing here?"

"Visiting Dad," he says defensively, then gives

me puppy-dog eyes that would rival Leia's. "I knew you wouldn't respond if I texted, but if I showed up here, you'd have to talk to me."

I sigh. "You were right."

"I'm sorry," he says as we move out of the way for an employee helping a woman with a walker.

"You promised you'd be there," I say, my jaw set. "You promised you'd be the one on Dad duty, so I could have one night. Just one! And you couldn't even do that."

Milo opens his mouth to talk but I don't give him the chance.

"And don't think you can do the thing you do and that I'll fall for it like always," I say. "I know you're so charming and everyone loves you, but that's not enough for me anymore. I'm not letting you take advantage of me and avoid Dad because that's how things have always been. I'm over it now. You need to step up."

Milo places a hand over his heart. "Wow. Okay. So, there were some real compliments hidden in that dragging. Bless you."

"Not the point, Milo."

Milo grabs my shoulders and looks me in the eye. "I *am* sorry. Not just for that night. For everything. For leaving. For making you deal with all of it. I shouldn't have done that."

"You shouldn't have."

"I was being a real piece of garbage, okay? But I didn't grow up as fast as you did, Chloe.

347

Maybe it's because you were always there to be a mom for me, but I kept thinking you'd handle everything, because you always have. And I know that was crappy. I talked to Fred about it, and he helped me realize that you're my family, and I need to take responsibility, too."

"Fred is an angel with a body that won't quit, and I hope he never leaves you," I say.

Milo points to the ceiling. "From your lips to God's ears, babe."

"Thanks for the apology. Really. But it means nothing until—"

"I'm moving back," Milo says.

"What?" I screech so loud that a resident sticks her head out of her door and gives us a dirty look. I wave at her and direct Milo toward the double doors that lead into the courtyard.

"For real?" I ask once we're seated on the wicker furniture overlooking a birdbath and a small garden. "Don't get my hopes up if this isn't for real."

"We signed a lease yesterday," Milo says. "Fred said he told you about how he's been wanting to get out of the city anyway, so it's perfect timing. We're renting a house that's far away from drunk college students and, while I will be forever indebted to Mikey Danger for his kindness, I'm happy to report that he will not be joining us."

I can't help myself; I lean forward and hug Milo. "So this is real? You're really back?"

"Fred and I are buying furniture now, and I'm pretty sure he found the perfect spot for a puzzle table."

"A house isn't a home without one," I say, pulling back from our hug.

Milo smiles at me. "This is real. I'm here for Dad, and I'm here for you."

I close my eyes for a moment and let those words sink in. *I'm here for you.* It's hard, but I let myself believe them, let myself accept that I might not be the only one handling Dad's bad days. Milo will be here. It's like Annie said: maybe I need to let people in.

"Um," Milo says, and I open my eyes. He looks at me warily. "Are we having an impromptu meditation session?"

"Nope." I smile. "I'm glad you're here. Do you need a ride?"

"Actually." Milo stands up and grins. "I drove here."

My mouth falls open.

He holds out his hands in a giant shrug. "I know, I know. It's like, 'Who does he think he is? A self-sufficient adult?'"

"But you don't have a car."

"I borrowed Mikey's delivery car," Milo mutters. "My point still stands."

"You obtained a temporary vehicle." I pat him on the shoulder. "This is progress."

"Don't condescend to me." Milo points a

finger at me. "Things are changing. This is the new Milo. The one who can handle himself, the one who . . ." He pats the pockets of his denim jacket. "Oh, shit. I think I left the keys in Dad's room."

I snort-laugh as he runs inside. Sure, it's great that things are changing, but it's also kind of nice that some things will stay the same.

When Milo leaves, I head back to Dad's room. I knock on the door, then walk in to find him sitting in his recliner, a crossword puzzle book on his lap.

"Well, hi there, sweetheart," he says, pushing himself off the recliner with some effort. "I didn't know you were coming over!"

I don't tell him that I reminded him about this appointment last night and this morning and put it on his calendar. I know it won't help him.

"I'm here to take you to the doctor for your follow-up appointment," I say. "Are you ready?"

He shuffles toward his closet. "Just let me get my coat."

I check the clock on his wall. I left us plenty of time, but my unexpected Milo encounter means we're probably going to be late. "Hurry up, okay?"

"Yeah, yeah, yeah," he says, his voice muffled as he searches through his closet. I can't help but smile because, for this moment at least, he sounds the way he used to—full of good-natured annoyance when I tell him what to do.

"So how are things going with Dave?" he asks, then shuffles back toward me, attempting to button a shirt that looks almost exactly like the one he had on before.

"Let me." I reach out and start buttoning his shirt for him, biting my lip. It's not like I thought he'd remember what happened when Nick was here. But it still hurts to know that I couldn't possibly talk to him about everything with Nick, even if I wanted to have one of those traditional movie-worthy father-daughter heart-to-hearts. This is yet another thing his disease took from us, and it sucks.

"Dave and I aren't together anymore," I say, focusing on his buttons.

"I just want you to be happy, Chloe," he says, and, again, I feel my heart start to crumble into tiny little pieces.

"I am happy, Dad," I say quietly.

"Dave's the guy for you," Dad says. "I can tell."

"You think?" I ask, buttoning the last button.

Dad waves a hand. "You can always tell. Like with your mother, I knew things weren't right from the beginning."

I raise my eyebrows. "You did?"

"Yeah, yeah." He shrugs. "You wanna be with somebody you can't stop thinking about.

Somebody who takes care of you, even when you're being a real asshole. Somebody who makes sure you know that you're the only person they want."

Nick's words, *I don't want anybody else. I only want you,* play in my mind but I push them away.

"A person shouldn't make you feel like they always have one foot out the door," Dad says. "That's how your mother always is."

"Was," I mutter. I've always avoided talking about Mom with Dad, worried it would upset him too much, but he's talking about her with less emotion than he uses to discuss characters on TV.

"But you and Dave, I can tell you have something good."

I'm not sure who Dad is talking about—actual, spiky-haired Dave from high school or Nick—but this feels so much like a real father-daughter talk that I just go with it. "Yeah?"

Dad nods. "The way you two looked at each other—you'd have to be an idiot not to tell."

"Dad," I say gently. "I don't think things with Dave are going to work out. I have a lot going on right now and it's not really the right time for me."

Dad snorts and waves me off. "It's never the right time. But when you're in love with someone, what can you do? Let me give you some advice, Chloe: life can really put you through the shitter. If it tosses something good your way once in a while, don't think twice about grabbing it."

I frown, my heartbeat quickening.

He looks me straight in the eyes then, his own eyes clear and full of conviction, seeming so much like the Dad I used to watch sitcoms with in our living room. "Not everyone's your mother, sweetheart. Not everyone's gonna leave you."

My heart is now pounding so loud that I can feel it all over my body, a thump-thump-thump in my fingers and toes. Was that what I was really afraid of with Nick? Is this like what Annie said, that I'm afraid no one will want me if I'm not helping them? Was I just afraid that he would leave me once he got to know the real me, the me who isn't cheerful and confident one hundred percent of the time?

I knew I liked Nick. I knew I cared about him. I knew I missed him when he wasn't around, thought about him all day, wanted to share everything that happened with him. I knew he was the first person I thought about in the morning and the last person I thought about at night. I knew that I wanted to spend every second of my life in his arms. And what is that if not bone-deep, soul-swallowing, mind-blowing love?

Holy shit. I'm in love with Nick.

I bark out a short laugh and Dad laughs back, neither of us in on the other's joke, but it doesn't matter.

"Thanks, Dad," I say, wrapping his body in a hug.

He hugs me back. And while I know that we've been having two different conversations, and he doesn't even know what he's helped me realize, it doesn't matter. Because we had our father-daughter heart-to-heart. He helped me, like a dad does, even if he'll never know it.

"Thanks for coming over, sweetheart," he says, shuffling back toward his chair.

"No, Dad, we're going to the doctor, remember? Come on."

"I spend my entire life at the doctor," he grumbles, but he follows me out the door.

After his uneventful appointment, I drop him off at Brookwood and walk back out to my car. As I dig in my purse for my keys, my hand comes across a piece of paper I somehow missed before.

It's a phone number, followed by a few words in Milo's handwriting, which I recognize because it looks the same as it did when we were writing and illustrating largely plagiarized versions of Disney stories in first grade and passing them off as original works of fiction by The Talented Sanderson Twins (we thought being a twin-author team would add a certain cachet).

Mom's number. She'd love to hear from you.

I groan. I know what Annie would say about this, if I told her. She'd say my romantic comedy arc has led me toward personal growth; I'm accepting help from her and Milo, owning up to the fact that I can't do everything myself, receiving the love that was around me all along. Now, I just need to forgive my mom.

One catch, Annie, I say in my internal monologue. *I don't want to forgive her. She sucks.*

I know, I know, I know. I'm an adult now. I'm almost thirty. I should be over this, all easy-breezy like, "Her? You mean the woman who abandoned us and left me alone to care for our family when I was a child myself? Oh, honey, I barely remember!"

Well, that's not real. The truth is that I remember everything, and it majorly screwed me up. A kind of screwed-up-ness that has stayed with me my whole life, the kind that has sabotaged relationships and led me to push people away. The kind of screwed up that made me think it was normal to avoid Nick, a person who has only ever been good to me and who I'm definitely falling in love with.

Mom walked away from us. And now, apparently, she's older and wiser and wishes she hadn't scooted out of our lives without so much as a goodbye.

My mom may have made a mistake that she's going to spend the rest of her life regretting, but I don't want regrets, and I can avoid her mistakes. I want to stay close to the people who love me, instead of abandoning them when it gets uncomfortable.

I'm in love with Nick, and I won't spend the rest of my life wishing that I let him love me back. Although she's on my semipermanent shit list, I have to give my mom credit for showing me the road *not* to take.

I get in my car, turn on the Doobies, and compose a text, deleting as many words as I add until I come up with something satisfactory.

> It's Chloe. Milo told me you're around, and he told me you're sorry. Honestly, I'm not sure how to feel. I don't want to talk right now, but maybe someday we can.

I press send and exhale, a heavy weight lifting off my chest as that text flies into space (or wherever texts go; I don't know, I'm a baker/ businesswoman, not a scientist). I'm allowed to forgive my mom and stop carrying so much hatred toward her, but that doesn't mean I have to forget what she did or pretend that everything's okay.

Maybe that's not a perfect, tied-up-in-a-bow rom-com ending, but it has to be enough.

But speaking of rom-coms . . .

If I'm going to convince Nick that I'm head-over-sparkly-flats in love with him, then I've gotta go big. This isn't the kind of problem that a simple apology can fix. I need to show him that I mean what I say, that I've changed, that I understand how wrong I was.

I need a grand gesture.

I tap out a text to Annie. If I'm going to re-create a rom-com scene, I'll go to the master.

Chapter Thirty

The night before the wedding, Annie and I stay up late to finish the millions of little details that even a small wedding requires. We fall asleep in her old room, her on the twin bed and me on the trundle bed that pulls out underneath it. It's sort of like being in high school again, except this time one of us is marrying a movie star and the other one of us is about to barf at the thought of being publicly rejected by the man she's finally admitted she loves.

But, you know, no big deal.

After a few hours of stress-nightmare-filled sleep (for me, anyway), we round up all of our stuff and get ready to drive the couple of blocks over to the wedding space. Since it's a pretty huge loft, we're having both the ceremony and the reception there. As soon as Annie and Drew say their vows, the bridal party will get pictures taken while everyone else gets to eat appetizers. While we're gone, Tyler and the D&D guys (minus Don, who's going to be in the pictures) will pull out some folded tables and rearrange the chairs from the ceremony, then decorate the tables with simple bouquets and battery-operated twinkle lights. Everyone will drink cocktails from the bartender (Nick), and then the wedding party will be back and it will be time for dinner. And dancing. And toasts. And me embarrassing myself.

The shop is closed today, on account of all the employees and most of the patrons will be at the wedding, so we get ready in Nick's office. It's almost painful to think of him sitting at that desk, all the times I've insulted him and poked at him until he was forced to banter back. I run my fingers over the keyboard, imagining that his fingers have touched it.

"Hey, creep, stop lovingly caressing Nick's keyboard," Annie says, then puts a hand on her face. "Sorry. Wedding stress is turning me into a bitch."

I laugh. "If this is your idea of being a bitch, then I think you're all good."

Since Annie didn't do the traditional wedding party thing, it's just me back here. Tyler's popped in a few times to give us updates from Don, and she'll let us know when we need to walk a few buildings down the sidewalk. I did Annie's makeup (impeccably, I might add . . . thanks, YouTube tutorials from talented thirteen-year-olds!) and she looks stunning in her dress. It has lace sleeves to her elbows and an extremely low neckline, which manages to not be overly distracting on her because she has no boobs (we've often joked that I got all the boobs in our friendship). The dress cuts in right at her tiny waist (it's so early in her pregnancy that she's not even showing yet), then flares out into a relaxed but glamorous skirt. Basically, she looks like if Kate Middleton and Meghan Markle combined their styles, then made it even more romantic. Her curly hair is pinned into a loose updo, and my style mirrors hers. A few artfully natural waves spring free, and the rest of my hair is twisted up.

And while I know that all eyes will be on Annie . . . I love my dress. If I wanted to get married, I'd get married in this dress. The sparkliness, the fluttery sleeves, the blush pink color that makes me feel ultra-feminine.

"You look so pretty," Annie says, and I look up to see her staring at me, her eyes welling with tears.

"No, no, no!" I shout, reaching into my bra for a tissue and then lunging at her. I hold a tissue under each eye, then whisper, "No tears. We are *not* messing up your eyeliner."

She laughs. "I'm emotional. A wedding *and* pregnancy hormones . . . it's too much for me to take."

Sensing that she's stable, I remove the tissues. "Also, I'm the one who should be telling you you're beautiful. And you are. Annie, you're always gorgeous but today you're something else."

She beams. "You think Drew is gonna like it?"

I snort. "Um, good luck getting through the ceremony without him whisking you off to a closet somewhere to do it."

She frowns. "Not *exactly* the vibe I was going for, but I'll take it."

I pull out a compact and touch up my own lipstick.

"So . . . is everything in place for the grand gesture?"

I make a face at my reflection and close the compact. "We're not talking about me right now. But actually . . . are you sure you're okay with me hijacking your wedding to tell Nick I love him?"

Annie's mouth drops open. "I'm sorry, have we met? This is my *dream*. Performing a grand gesture at my wedding is the greatest gift you could possibly give me."

"Good, because I didn't get you a real gift."

"Please. You baked a million pies and helped me with everything. That's a gift."

My phone buzzes with a text from Milo. It's a selfie of him, Fred, and my dad at Dad's place.

We've watched two episodes of *Three's Company*. I actually . . . love this show?

I snort-laugh and think for a moment about how glad I am that Milo's making the effort to help out now. But on the other hand, it means that all the worry I would normally direct toward my dad is now flowing in only one direction: my upcoming grand declaration of love.

But then Annie grabs my hand and whispers, "I wish they were here."

She doesn't have to tell me who she means. Her parents. The hopeless romantics whose love story was better than any rom-com.

"They are, Annie," I say softly. "I feel like they're here, don't you?"

She presses her lips together and nods, batting her eyelashes quickly like she's trying not to cry, and before I can grab one of my emergency tissues, Tyler knocks and pokes her head in. "We're ready for you guys. Dungeon Master Rick looks like he's getting impatient."

Annie sighs. "Well, I chose Dungeon Master Rick as my officiant because I knew he'd run this wedding with the same ruthless efficiency he displays in a D&D campaign."

"I understand about half of that sentence," I say, following Tyler out of the office. "But let's go."

We walk down the sidewalk, Annie carefully maneuvering in her heels, cars honking at us. Annie waves and smiles, and it starts to feel real. This is her wedding, the day she's been dreaming about forever. And a part of me, a part I don't like to admit exists, feels a bit sad. Not because I'm dreaming of *my* fairy-tale wedding, but because this is where our paths irrevocably separate. Up until now, even when she's been out of town for work, we've been the same: girls from Ohio, girls who grew up being each other's person, girls who shared everything, girls who technically lived on the same property, if in different houses.

And now, that's changing. It's not like she's been staying regularly in her old bedroom anyway, but at least I knew there was a chance she'd be there. Once she's married? Probably not. As she's told me before, Drew barely fits in that twin bed (and something tells me she's not going to banish him to the trundle).

But even with the pinprick of sadness, most of me is happy for her. She got what she always wanted—the job, the guy, the baby, the whole dream. How many people can say that?

We walk up the creaky, uneven stairs to the loft and see Uncle Don in the stairwell. He looks nervous, probably because he has to walk Annie down the aisle and he hates people looking at him (that's why he tends to wear a Chewbacca costume when he goes to conventions—it covers his entire body).

Tyler opens the door to the loft and peeks in, then looks back at us. "Okay," she says, meeting all of our eyes and imparting this information as if she's a football coach and we're about to get a chance to make the winning play (or something like that . . . I don't watch a lot of football, clearly). "I'm gonna stand right here, and you guys watch me through the window in the door. Chloe, when I'm ready for you I'll hold up a finger." She holds up a finger in case I've forgotten what fingers look like. "And you'll walk up the aisle. Go slow, and smile."

I beam at her to demonstrate that I do, in fact, know how to smile. Beside me, Annie shakes with suppressed laughter.

"And once Chloe's in place and your song starts, Annie and Don, I'll signal you." She holds her finger up again. It's kind of sweet how seriously she's taking this, and for a moment I think about how nice it is that Don found someone who fits into their small family so well, someone who loves them both so much.

Then I focus on what she's saying. In mere moments, Annie will walk up that aisle and this will be it—her wedding. My heart starts racing and Annie and I look at each other at the same time. Her eyes are full of fear.

"What if I trip, Chloe?" she says in a rush. "What if I trip and then Drew realizes he could never marry such a klutz?"

I put my own nerves on the back burner. I have to take control of this situation, for Annie.

"Annie." I place my hands on her shoulders. "Drew loves you, and you love him. There's nothing you could do during this ceremony that would make him love you any less. And even if you did fall . . . well, you guys met when you tripped onto him. That's a nice, full-circle moment, right?"

She exhales and closes her eyes. "I guess."

"And I'll be holding on to you," Uncle Don says, putting an arm around her. "I won't let you fall."

I bite my lip, afraid that I might start crying and ruin my makeup. Annie may be so unlucky in some ways, but how lucky she is that she has Uncle Don—how lucky we all are that we have each other, the three of us living on the same property all these years. How will we survive it when everything changes? When Annie's really gone? I mean, I can't live in that carriage house forever. Eventually, none of us will live together. Will we still feel like a family? Will we still need each other?

Through the window, we see Tyler hold up a finger.

"It's go time," I say, and Uncle Don leans over to give me a hug. And then it's me and Annie, staring at each other one last time before she walks down the aisle.

"I love you," she says, her voice shaky. "You're my best friend."

And even though I know today is all about her and Drew, and even though I'm thinking about all the things I want to say to Nick, for now, I'm reminded that romance isn't the only great love story of our lives. Sometimes the love we have with our lifelong friends, the ones we can depend on through changes and fights and joys and heartbreaks—sometimes those are the greatest love stories we have.

"I love you," I whisper as I squeeze her hand. And then Tyler's no longer holding up a finger but full-on waving a hand at me, so I step through the door and walk down the aisle.

I know Nick is out there in one of those folding chairs, looking at me and probably hating me, but I don't let myself think about it right now. I keep a smile on my face. I walk slowly. Drew smiles at me and I give him a wink, then take my place on the opposite side of the aisle, directly across from his very tiny brother.

And then the music changes. Harry Nilsson's version of "Somewhere over the Rainbow" starts to play, because of course Annie wanted to walk down the aisle to the song from the end of *You've Got Mail*. There are more than a few sniffles as she and Don slowly make their way toward us, and when I turn to look at Drew, he wipes his eyes, too.

"Here," I say, handing him one of my bra tissues while all eyes are on Annie.

Annie smiles shyly, taking slow steps toward us, and I make the mistake of looking out into the crowd. I see the rest of Don's D&D friends, Gary (and his wife!), Tobin (who's definitely wearing a T-shirt under a blazer, bless him) . . . and Nick. Looking right at me.

My heart stops. My mouth dries. I'm frozen in place (which is fine, because I'm not supposed to move right now). His eyes are creating some sort of magnetic force field and I'm unable to escape.

"Oh shit," I mutter, because I'm in it, big-time. No matter what Nick says or does when I tell him I love him, this is it for me. There isn't another person on earth who could make me feel the way he does.

Dungeon Master Rick gives me a dirty look, so I attempt to cover up my profanity with a prolonged sniffle, pulling another tissue out of my bra to wipe my nose.

By then, Annie and Don have completed their long walk down the aisle. Uncle Don gives Drew a hug, and Dungeon Master Rick doesn't do the whole "who gives this woman away" speech, probably because Annie told him not to.

The rest of the ceremony passes in a blur. I think someone reads an E. E. Cummings poem, or some song lyrics, or that one Bible verse about love. I manage to mostly pay attention—I take Annie's bouquet when it's time for her to hold hands with Drew and say their vows—but I don't know what anyone says. My heart's back to beating one name, over and over. *Nick Velez Nick Velez Nick Velez.*

I jolt into the present when Dungeon Master Rick pronounces Drew and Annie married, and they kiss, and we clap, and I link arms with Drew's brother, who doesn't come up to my shoulders, even with the "growth spurt" Annie claims he had.

The second we make our way up the aisle, the D&D guys spring into action, moving chairs and putting out tables as people mill around and "This Will Be (An Everlasting Love)" starts playing (Annie showed me her playlist, and it is *entirely* songs from her favorite rom-coms). The photographer leads us outside to take some photos on the brick-lined streets and in Schiller Park, near the newly green buds on the trees and the finally blooming tulips. I can't resist one more look over my shoulder, but Nick is lost somewhere in the small crowd, presumably already getting his bartender on.

I'll have to talk to him later. *Oh, God.* I'm going to talk to him later.

Chapter Thirty-One

After stopping by The Book Loft courtyard, where Annie insists on taking a picture with Drew because apparently they once shared a romantic moment in the store (it's *extremely* Annie to have a romantic moment in a bookstore), we end up in Schiller Park. The photographer shuffles us into every imaginable combination for pictures. Drew and Annie and his family, Drew and Annie and Uncle Don, Annie and me, Drew and Louis, Drew and Annie and me and Louis, looking like the most mismatched double date in the universe.

"Hey," Annie whispers to me as Drew and his family take another photo together. "How are you feeling?"

"Nauseated. Full of doubt. Like I want to melt into the pavement."

Annie frowns. "This is your public declaration of love. You should be feeling urgent! Determined! Passionate!"

I exhale. "Annie, we're gonna have to settle for queasy, okay? What if Nick is like, 'Ew, no'? What if he's mad? What if he doesn't even like me anymore?"

Annie waves me off, like this is all preposterous. "That's not the way this works. Have you ever seen a romantic comedy where a person who is true of heart makes a declaration of love and the other person denies it?"

"My life isn't a movie!" I shout, and Drew's family turns to look at us. I wave and purse my lips, then turn back to Annie. "You didn't script this, Annie. It might not work."

"Come on. This is true love we're talking about. Weren't you listening during our wedding readings?"

"No."

She rolls her eyes and smiles. "Love never fails, Chlo."

I swallow hard. "I don't know if I believe that."

She squeezes my arm. "That's okay. I believe in it enough for the both of us."

And even though I'm so nervous that I'm seriously considering puking on some daffodils in front of Drew's entire family, I trust her.

We return to the wedding, where the D&D guys have done a great job setting everything up. The floral centerpieces are surrounded by tons of battery-operated candles (Annie's seen enough rom-coms to know the mishaps that lit candles can cause), which flicker romantically in the almost-dark.

In a word, it's beautiful.

I sit down next to Annie and Drew at the head table; Louis is on Drew's other side. Everyone else mills around, some people at their seats, most people standing up and eating pigs in a blanket (the traditional Midwestern appetizer) while sipping drinks. My eyes scan the crowd until I see him; at the back of the room, behind a table, pouring a drink for some elderly woman I've never seen who must be one of Drew's relatives. I'm overwhelmingly jealous of this octogenarian who gets to touch his hand for even a brief second as he gives her a drink.

"Chloe."

I look to my left and see Annie staring at me with concern. "You are, like, vibrating."

I take a deep breath. "Yeah, well. I don't handle nerves well. This is why I stay in my comfort zone, okay?"

Annie knocks back a cup of Sprite and then smiles at me. "Fuck your comfort zone."

I recoil. "Excuse me? Who are you?"

"I'm a woman who just got married, and right now I need you to give me the greatest gift I could possibly receive: a grand gesture."

Drew leans across Annie and looks me straight in the eye. "This is Annie's wedding day. You need to give the woman what she wants."

"You told him?" I whisper-hiss at Annie.

She shakes her head, eyes wide. "Of course not! I swear."

Drew rolls his eyes. "Give me a break, Chloe. Everyone in this room, and anyone who's ever been into Nick's, can tell that a cloud of sexual tension surrounds you and Velez at all times. Annie didn't have to tell me you slept together; I figured it out."

Annie and I stare at each other, mouths open.

"What are you, some kind of relationship expert?" I ask when I've recovered. Annie lifts her cup of Sprite to her mouth, shaking her head in amazement.

"In case you forgot, I'm married to the greatest rom-com writer of our generation." He holds up her hand and points to her ring. "I think I can tell when a grand gesture is about to happen."

Annie snort-laughs so hard that she spits Sprite all over her plate.

The telltale clink of wedding silverware on wineglass cuts through the air, and everyone cranes their heads around to see who it is.

Uncle Don stands up beside his table, and Annie whispers, "Is he . . . giving a toast?"

Giving any sort of toast would be very unlike Don; giving an unplanned, undiscussed toast is even more out of character. But as soon as the crowd quiets down and most people find their seats, he starts talking.

"Thank you all so much for coming today. I know many of you have traveled from far away to be here, and we appreciate it. I wanted to take a moment to say how much I love my Annie. I may not be her parent, and I may not have any right to say this, but I'm so proud of the woman she's become."

"Oh, God," Annie says, her eyes filling with tears. I yank another tissue out of my bra and hand it to her. At this point, my tissue stash is going to be deflated before we even get to the first dances.

"But I also want to express how grateful I am to Annie, because even though I'm the older and supposedly wiser one, she's taught me so much through the years. After watching so many of those movies she loves, and seeing the way she lives her life, I've learned that when you love someone, you've gotta tell them. So, Tyler . . ."

Uncle Don gets down on one knee and everyone in the room gasps.

"I've loved you since the second we met online, when you were just WookieeLover001. And as I've gotten to know you, that love has only grown. Will you do me the honor of being my wife?"

Tyler's hands cover her face, but her rapid nods communicate a clear yes, and everyone cheers as she stands up and Uncle Don easily lifts her into a hug (she's about the size of a pixie and he's, well, Chewbacca-sized).

Beside me, Annie lets loose a full-on sob at this display of love, her mascara running down her cheeks. Oh well. I tried, and at least photos are already done. Maybe some brides would be mad that a proposal stole their spotlight, but not Annie.

"This . . . is the best . . . thing . . . that's ever happened to me," she chokes out through her sobs.

"Um." I meet eyes with Drew, who has his arm around her. "Didn't you just get married?"

She waves me off. "Oh, besides that."

"Also." I gesture to Drew to turn the other way, and he rolls his eyes and starts a conversation with Louis. "What in the ever-loving hell am I supposed to do now? Don stole my grand gesture thunder in a major way."

Annie blinks a few times. "Oh. Yeah. Maybe you could propose, too?" she suggests brightly.

I smack her arm. "Get real. I don't want to get married; I want to have sex with Nick every day for the rest of our lives until both of us die in our nineties after having simultaneous orgasms."

"The two things can coexist, you know," Annie says, then blows her nose.

"No thanks," I say, scanning the crowd again as a caterer places a plate in front of me. I say thank you, not even noticing what's on it. I don't remember what I selected: Chicken? Fish? Sautéed car tires? Who cares? Gary's about to announce the toasts.

An air horn sound comes from the DJ booth

374

and everyone shrieks. "You know what that sound means, folks!" Gary shouts into the microphone.

"We don't, Gary. None of us know what that means," Annie says, even though Gary can't hear her over the sound effects he's playing. "Remind me why I chose him for our DJ again?"

I place a hand on her arm. "Because you love him and because if Gary doesn't have a task, he gets anxious. And because he knows how to use the equipment from when he was a morning radio DJ in the '90s."

Annie nods. "Right. Okay. Well, as long as I had a reason."

"It's time for toasts!" Gary finally says after playing a few Austin Powers catchphrases. "First up, we have the brother of the groom and best man, Louis Daaaanfooooorth!"

Gary plays a sound effect of a crowd clapping, and the rest of us clap along.

"So, uh . . ." Louis stands up and, hands shaking, pulls a piece of paper out of his pocket. "When Drew first told me about Annie, I was like, 'Wait, who? Didn't you used to date a really hot actress?' "

Annie slowly turns to me and I shrug.

"But then I got to know Annie and, honestly, she's pretty cool. She makes Drew happy, and he's less of an asshole to me when she's around. So I guess she taught me that being hot isn't the most important thing in a relationship. Thanks, Annie."

He sits down, and everyone slowly starts to clap.

"Uh, you're welcome. I guess?" Annie says as Drew leans over to kiss her, laughing.

Another air horn noise startles everyone and provokes a few shrieks. "Gary!" Annie yells, giving him the universal *cut it out* gesture. "Cool it with the sound effects."

"But I want to make the most of all this!" Gary shouts back, gesturing toward his equipment. Annie shakes her head and he finally nods, chastised.

"Okay, everyone," he says, his voice more somber. "Up next we have the one, the only, the maid of honor . . . Chloe Sanderson."

I can tell it physically pains him not to introduce me with a sound effect. I stand up, feeling as nervous as Louis looked, and scan the crowd. Nick is back there, behind the makeshift bar, but I can't focus on him or I'll lose my confidence. I swallow hard.

"Uh, hey, everybody. Annie wanted me to say thanks to all of you for being here, and to so many of you for helping out with the decorations, and the . . . um . . . drinks, and the DJ-ing."

Gary salutes me.

"I think it goes without saying that Annie is the best friend in the entire world. She's the most loyal, the most trustworthy, the kind of person you can call at any time of the night and she'll come running to help you. And, kind of like Uncle Don said, Annie's taught me a lot. Because she's been through her share of hard times, but she never lost faith. You know, I always made fun of her . . . well, her full-blown *obsession* with romantic comedies."

Everyone laughs.

"I thought they were unrealistic and silly because true love always fixed everything at the end, and that's not how real life works. Falling in love doesn't mean you don't have problems anymore. But after watching, like, five million of them, I thought about it. And the thing is, even in the rom-coms Annie loves, love *doesn't* always fix everything. Sometimes things still suck. Sometimes the characters are dealing with insurmountable challenges, but by the end of the movie, they have a person to share those challenges with. They have someone to help them get through it."

I swallow and look out at the tables full of people, at all the eyes on me.

"But the main thing that Annie and romantic comedies taught me is that when you mess up, you shouldn't give up. Instead, sometimes it takes a grand gesture to really show someone how much you care. And listen, I know we've already had a proposal tonight, and generally it's frowned upon to make these surprise proclamations at someone else's wedding, but I think we all know Annie loves it, so . . . ."

I look down at Annie, who has moved onto Drew's lap. Both of them give me a thumbs-up.

I take a deep breath. "So, Nick Velez, I'm in love with you. It's cheesy and clichéd and straight out of a movie, but you make me happy. The terrible parts of my life are never going to be less terrible, but when you're around, everything is better. I can handle things when you're with me. I was wrong when I said I didn't want to take a risk on a business or a relationship, because life, if you're living it right, is nothing but a series of ridiculous risks that may pay off or may go down in flames. But if you're not trying, if you're not leaving your comfort zone . . . well, then you're not really living, are you? I was scared before, and I'm not scared anymore . . . or I guess I still am, but I don't care. So this is me, saying 'screw you' to my comfort zone, and asking you to please, please love me back."

I've been avoiding looking at Nick this entire time, but finally, finally, I let my eyes meet his magnetic grip, expecting to see him smiling or laughing or even asking me to get over there and kiss him.

But he's just . . . staring. His face is blank, and this is a Nick Velez expression I can't read. And if I don't know what it is, it must be bad. It must be too late.

Gary plays the air horn noise again and Annie hisses, "Not now, Gary!"

"Okay, um . . . that's it," I say, then drop the microphone and run out, the murmurs of all of Annie and Drew's loved ones swirling around me.

I go down the narrow stairs so fast that I almost trip and fall on my dress, then burst out onto the street. "Shit, shit, shit," I say, leaning against a lamppost and pressing my hands into my eyes. What a colossally bad idea. Why did I let Annie talk me into thinking this would work, just because it works in the movies? Now I've ruined her wedding and the only thing people will remember is that the maid of honor humiliated herself.

"Chloe."

I turn around as Nick steps out of the building, the door swinging shut behind him.

"Are you crying?" he asks, closing the distance between us with a few of his long-legged steps.

"I'm sorry," I say through my tears, aware that this isn't how I wanted to look right after I confessed my love to Nick. I know my makeup is all over my face and I'm pretty sure I'm covered in snot. This isn't a cute movie cry; this is an ugly cry, and now I have to do it in front of the man I love while he tells me he doesn't love me anymore, because I'm too much of a mess to deserve this kind of love.

"I shouldn't have—I didn't—you were—" I try and fail to start about seventeen different sentences.

Nick grabs me by the shoulders, yanking me toward him. His mouth finds mine and he kisses me hard, his hands pinning me to him as I wrap my arms around his back. This isn't a kiss like our first one, that urgent, secret, power-outage kiss. Nor is it a kiss like the night we slept together, a long, lazy, passionate kiss. This is something else. This kiss is a promise, a vow, an oath stronger than anything legally binding that says that Nick Velez is mine, forever and ever amen.

"Oh," I say, stepping back. "That . . . wasn't what I expected."

Nick runs a hand through his hair, that gesture that is still as unbelievably sexy as the first time I saw it. "Me neither. It's just . . . in there . . . I was surprised. I didn't think . . ." He trails off.

"Nick," I say, looking him in his dark brown eyes. "I'm so sorry I took you for granted, and that I told you we made a mistake. It wasn't a mistake. I am so in love with you. I want to do it all with you—life, the café, everything. I mean." I gulp. "If you want to."

He wraps his arms around me again. "I have *always* been in love with you, from the very beginning. Come on. You knew that."

I shake my head and bite my lip. "Nope. Didn't know that."

"Well, now you know," he says, his voice low as he rests his forehead against mine. "Before I met you, I thought I was fine with my life the way it was. When you started working at the shop, I didn't understand anything about you. Your outfits, your music, the way you always tried to get me to smile."

I frown. "Please tell me where this is going."

He squeezes my shoulders. "But then I realized I was looking forward to seeing you. I was counting on the way you made all the gray days into something colorful, and I didn't *want* gray anymore. I fell in love with you, Chloe. And the offer still stands. The café, I mean. And us. All of it."

I inhale and let the air out shakily. "Yes. Yes. Yes. That's all I want, me and you, doing everything together."

Nick smiles, and he's so close to my face that he blurs into an abstract Nick Velez painting. "Good."

"Also, that is, like, by far the most you've ever said at one time. I didn't even know you were capable of that. Are you winded?"

"Don't get used to it," he mutters, looking embarrassed.

"Oh!" I step back and look at him with renewed intensity. "But you should know. I don't want to get married and I do *not* want children. I'm not harboring any secret maternal urges, and I'm about to turn thirty but my biological clock is remarkably silent, so I don't think it's gonna happen. Are you okay with that?"

Nick laughs. "Chloe. Yes."

"And I don't know if I want to stay here forever. I love Columbus, but I can't say I'm gonna stay anywhere for the rest of my life."

"Hey." Nick pulls me to him again. "Shut up, okay?"

"Wow. Your crude language is ruining my grand gesture."

Nick tries and fails to suppress a smile. "Stop it. Stop coming up with bullshit reasons for me to push you away."

I nod, my breath shaky.

"I want you anywhere, Chloe. I'll go where you go. You can be yourself, you can do what you want, and I'm always going to be with you. You can stop trying to manage my expectations or figure out my life for me, okay? Because the only thing I need to be happy is you."

I close my eyes and exhale, feeling like the biggest burden has suddenly been lifted off my shoulders. I've never felt this light before, not in my whole life. I've never felt like I can *be,* just as I am, and still be loved.

I nod, then grab his hand and start pulling him down the sidewalk.

"Where are you going?" he asks. "Don't you want to go back inside? We're missing the wedding."

I turn around, holding his hand. "I have this long-standing fantasy of us having sex on your office desk. It's extremely detailed and I'd love to reenact it now, while the shop is empty."

Nick stares at me.

"Are you . . . going to say no?"

Nick smiles, the smile that means he's mine forever, and says, "I'm never going to say no to anything you ask me, not for the rest of my life."

Chapter Thirty-Two

I'm attempting to fix my hair in the reflection in Nick's computer (turns out bridal hairstyles are *not* meant for vigorous desk-sex) when we hear banging on the windows.

"What the hell?" Nick mutters, pulling his pants back on.

"I know for a fact the *Closed* sign is up," I say as both of us step out of the office.

Doug and Shivan pound their fists on the windows, pausing occasionally to cup their hands on the glass and peer in.

"Hey!" Doug's voice is muffled through the glass. "I see you in there!"

Nick unlocks the door and they tumble in. "Dude, we've been texting you and asking if you want to go . . . Wait." Doug looks back and forth between us. "Did you just have sex?"

Shivan studies us and points at Nick. "Yes. That is the face of a man who just had sex."

"Hell yeah, dudes!" Doug gives us both high fives. "Sorry to interrupt, but, uh . . . did everything go okay?"

I shake my head. "Not doing a sexual post-mortem with you, bro. Not gonna happen."

Doug frowns.

"Hey," I say, eager to change the subject. "You guys wanna crash a wedding?"

"Yes," Shivan says immediately. "Is there an open bar?"

"I'm supposed to be bartending and I'm currently here, so . . ." Nick trails off.

"So it's extremely open, is what he's saying," I finish.

"Look at you two." Doug leans back and crosses his arms. "Finishing each other's sentences. I called it when you came to bowling."

Nick sighs. "You did not."

Doug looks to Shivan. "Did I or did I not say, 'This chick is his soul mate'?"

Shivan nods. "But to be fair, you say a lot of stuff. You also thought Burger King was a good idea for breakfast, and we both ended up puking."

Doug leans toward me. "He's never looked at anyone the way he looks at you. It was obvious. He got pretty lucky with you."

Nick and I look at each other, and for a second, it's like Doug and Shivan aren't even here. "No," I say, smiling at him. "I think we both got pretty lucky."

The music reverberates through the stairwell as we climb the creaky stairs. I squeeze Nick's hand and he squeezes mine back and then we open the door and step through.

Pete Townsend's "Let My Love Open the Door" is playing, which is yacht rock adjacent so I'm here for it. Gary waves to us from his spot in the DJ booth, then gives us a thumbs-up when he sees that we're holding hands. Doug and Shivan immediately spot the bar and head there.

Everyone has a plastic cup in hand—people seem to have ransacked the bar in Nick's absence, and judging by the dancing we're seeing, they poured with a heavy hand.

"Chloe!"

Annie rushes toward me and envelops me in a hug. Nick leans in and says, "I'm gonna go check out the damage at the bar and try to keep the guys in check," and the feeling of his stupid-sexy beard against my cheek and his whisper in my ear is enough to make me want to go right back to his office.

But I wouldn't want to miss this. Annie releases me from her hug, then leans back and stares at me. "You just had sex!" she says, her jaw dropping.

"Keep it down." I look around us, making sure no one's paying attention.

"You have SEX HAIR!" Annie shouts. "Did you and Nick just HAVE SEX?"

"Shut up, drunkie," I say, grabbing her by the arms.

"I'm pregnant," she reminds me. "I'm not

drunk. I'm so, so tired and so, so happy and honestly, kinda loopy. Get back to the sex hair."

"Yes, we had sex. In his office."

"Wow." Annie breathes. "Very . . . business-like."

I shake my head. "Whatever. The point is . . . it worked. The grand gesture worked!"

Annie beams. "You bet it did. Romantic comedies are the source of all wisdom and they will never let you down. The sooner you accept that, the better. Oh! The pies are amazing!"

"They are?"

"I think you did it," she said. "You finally made the perfect pie."

"I don't really trust your assessment right now," I say, but even though I haven't tried any of the pies yet, I think she may be right. Maybe the perfect pie is the one that's served at the perfect time, with the perfect people.

She grabs my hand and attempts to spin me around, but since she's so much shorter than me I end up having to duck under her arm and do a partial backbend.

"It's wonderful!" she says. "This is the perfect wedding. Let's do it again sometime!"

"You need a nap," I say.

The song ends and a slow song starts playing. "Annie," I say.

She smiles at me.

"Is this 'When I Fall in Love,' from *Sleepless*

in Seattle?" I don't even know why I'm asking; I've seen that movie so many times that I have everything, including the soundtrack, memorized.

She nods. "I told you; the entire wedding is nothing but songs from rom-coms."

I sigh and smile. "I love you."

"I love you, too." She hugs me, and then Drew grabs her for a dance.

I feel a hand on my shoulder and turn around to see Nick. "So, uh . . . you wanna dance?" he asks. "Are you into dancing? I don't even know."

I place my arms on his shoulders. "I'm into anything if it's with you."

"What the hell is this music?" Nick asks as we spin slowly.

"Even at a wedding, Nick Velez has to criticize the music."

"I'm not criticizing, I'm saying—"

I lean forward and kiss him.

"You can't do that every time you want me to stop talking about terrible music," he says.

"Actually." I smile. "I bet I can."

He groans. "I bet you can, too."

I look around us, at Annie with her head on Drew's chest, her eyes closed. At Uncle Don and Tyler, staring at each other, in their own private world. At Louis, talking to Tobin, probably about skateboarding. At Gary dancing with his wife, Martha, behind the DJ booth. At Shivan and Doug, who've taken over the bar. At everyone living their lives, taking chances, getting hurt, and waking up the next day to start all over again. How beautiful it is that no matter how badly things are screwed up, we can always keep dreaming, keep wishing, keep hoping that things will get better.

"What are you thinking about?" Nick asks.

"Wondering if there are any more pigs in a blanket left," I tell him.

He pulls me closer and I rest my head on his shoulder.

"I'll make you whatever you want when we get home tonight," he says.

And sure, maybe if my life were really a romantic comedy, it wouldn't have ended with me and Nick discussing a tiny hot-dog-based appetizer. But real life is so much better than a movie anyway.

Epilogue

"Order up!"

Nick slides a bowl through the window between the kitchen and the front counter. That window was one of the first changes we made when we converted Nick's into the Butterfly Café.

I grab the bowl of chicken tortilla soup and carry it through the café, weaving between tables and barely avoiding crashing into the two-year-old who toddles into my path.

"Nora Marie!" Annie hisses, grabbing her arm. "You almost tripped Aunt Chloe."

Nora (named after Annie's heroes, Nora Ephron and her mother) frowns and points at me. "Chicken nuggets."

I bend down, holding on to the bowl of soup. "I'm sorry to be the one to break this to you, Nora, but we don't serve chicken nuggets and we never will. How about fried avocado?"

She stares at me without saying anything.

"Sorry," Annie says with a smile. Even when she's annoyed at her child, she looks overjoyed to be with her. "Come on, baby, let's go sit down. Mommy's feet are swollen."

She eases her very pregnant self into a chair with Drew's help—maneuvering her around is kind of a two-person job at this point in her pregnancy. They're back in town because their second child, a boy, is due any day now and she wants to have him here so Don and I can be around for the first few weeks of his life. Not to brag, but I was a pretty great labor coach during Nora's birth, which might be a calling for me if this restaurant thing doesn't work out.

Annie's kept up her writing career while being almost constantly pregnant, a feat that amazes me. But then again, it doesn't *surprise* me. This is what she's wanted her entire life, after all: the career in movies, the babies, the sweet and sensitive husband.

I leave them to their chaos and place the bowl of soup down in front of Gary. "Chicken tortilla soup. Need anything else?"

Gary looks up at me and smiles sweetly. "Yes. Have you considered the suggestion I placed in the suggestion box last week?"

"Okay, well, for the millionth time, that's the tip jar, not a suggestion box. And I keep telling you, we're never going to allow your ferrets in here, Gary. We would get shut down."

Gary shrugs. "I had to try."

I can't help smiling as I make my way into the kitchen. "Hey," I say, bumping my hip into Nick's as he assembles a salad.

"Don't start," he mutters, throwing on some feta cheese. "This is sexual harassment."

"Don't tell the boss," I say. "Oh wait. I'm the boss."

"Did you see that Annie's here?" he asks, finishing the salad and wiping his hands on his apron before turning to look at me.

"Yeah, I talked to them for a minute. I'm happy for Annie, but just seeing her is the single most effective form of birth control."

"Good," Nick says, leaning toward me. "Because I have no desire to share you with anyone else."

I wrap my arms around his neck as he grabs my hips and pulls me into him, giving me one of those patented Nick Velez kisses, the kind that makes me forget I'm in a cramped café kitchen.

That is, until Tobin clears his throat.

We break apart from each other and turn to see him standing at the grill, staring at us, disgust written all over his face. "Not okay, dudes," he says.

Now that we've expanded what we offer and increased our business, we've hired several new employees, making Tobin a senior member of the staff, and apparently all this authority has gone to his head.

"You guys have to stop that," he mutters as smoke billows behind him. "It's unsanitary as hell."

"Tobin!" I shout. "Flip that burger! It's burning!"

He turns back to the grill and flips it with nonchalance even as smoke wafts in his face.

"Remind me again why we put Tobin on the grill?" I ask Nick in a low voice.

"Because," Nick says. "This way at least he doesn't drop the plates."

He hands me the salad. "Order up, boss. Oh, wait, don't forget the pie."

I give him another quick kiss before heading back out into the café. But as I step through the door, I stop for a moment to take it all in. The brightly painted chairs. The floral artwork on the walls. The Christopher Cross playing over the speakers. The spicy, appetizing smell in the air. The tables full of loyal customers and friends who feel like family.

Even though I dreamed about opening a bakery for years, not a restaurant, it turns out this is even better than what I imagined. I get to feed people every day, get to take care of them, but in a way that serves me. And although I did end up finally earning my degree, I didn't even need it to open the Butterfly; it turns out that all I really needed was my years of experience and the willingness to take a chance on myself and believe that I had a good idea. And now, all of this is mine.

Well, it's not *just* mine, and that makes it so much better. It belongs to me and Nick, because

I have someone to help me now. Someone to support me, someone to show up in the waiting room, someone to take care of me when I'm sick. Someone to be there.

I don't have to handle things by myself anymore. Now, I have Milo and Fred here to check on Dad, to spend time with him, to attend bingo night. And when I visit him, Nick comes, too, and he never ever flinches at how painful it is, how much it sucks that Dad's forgetting so much and changing every day. Sometimes, I even have a longer-than-five-minutes cry in the car with Nick, and he doesn't have to say anything to make it better, because nothing ever could. He's just there, and that's enough.

"Hey." Nick opens the door. "You doing okay out here?"

I turn and smile at him.

"You're doing the thing again," he says. "Where you stare at me and smile."

"Hmmm, am I?" I spin around and walk through my café.

As I place the salad and slice of pie on Annie and Drew's table and Nora pelts me with a fistful of crayons, I look over my shoulder. Nick is still standing there, staring at me, smiling, just like I knew he would be.

And as I smile back, I can't think of any place I'd rather be.

Acknowledgments

As usual, I find myself deeply afraid that I'll forget to thank someone who had a crucial role in shaping this book, so please accept this as a blanket thank-you to everyone I've ever met, but especially the following people.

I'm so lucky to have Stephen Barbara as my agent. Thank you for being a voice of reason and helping my books find their perfect homes.

I'm still pinching myself that I get to work with Cindy Hwang, editor extraordinaire, who always knows exactly how to make my books better (and who, instead of asking me to avoid writing about bodily fluids so much, actually offers suggestions on how to make said discussions even more disgusting).

I'm grateful every day for the Berkley team, including Diana Franco, Tara O'Connor, Angela Kim, Jessica Brock, Fareeda Bullert, Brittanie Black, Elisha Katz, and all the people I haven't met who work so hard on my books. I appreciate everything you do.

Infinite thank-yous to Farjana Yasmin for designing yet another beautiful, perfect, eye-catching cover. I can't even believe I'm lucky enough to have it on my book.

One of the biggest joys of the past year has been

visiting independent bookstores both near and far. Thank you to the stores that have hosted me, and thank you to the stores I haven't yet visited but who have championed my books, put them on display, and hand sold them to customers. I already loved bookstores as a reader, but as a writer I can truly see how much care and love you put into your jobs. Special thanks to Joseph-Beth Booksellers for the support and also the life-size Tom Hanks.

I wrote and revised a large part of this book at Columbus Metropolitan Library branches, and I'm incredibly grateful to have an extraordinary library system in my city.

Giant, heart-shaped thank-you GIFs to the bookstagrammers and bloggers who post about my books. It is such a joy to hear from you.

Thank you to librarians everywhere for supporting my books and also books in general.

The biggest possible thank-you to Lauren Dlugosz Rochford and Emily Adrian for reading early drafts of this book, giving me invaluable feedback, and pointing out when I used the same word fifteen times on one page (a slight exaggeration, but only slight).

Thank you to Tess Malone for taking the time to read this book, even though it was on a computer, and giving me such immensely helpful feedback.

As always, thank you to my weird, wonderful

family, especially to Mama Winfrey, the one who takes care of everyone else.

To my readers: I'm so glad you read my books, recommend them to others, and buy copies for your moms/sisters/grandmas/etc. I very literally couldn't do this without you and I'm grateful that you care about these characters.

Thank you to Hollis for taking time off work whenever I need to get on a plane and visit a bookstore or go to the library and stare at a computer. People frequently ask how I get work done as a stay-at-home parent, and here's how: I have a supportive partner who shows up and values my career.

To Harry, who always wants to look for my books when we visit the library: I love your curiosity, your imagination, and the fact that you're downstairs screaming as I write this. You make everything better.

And to anyone out there who cares for anyone else—a child or a parent, for family or for work, in any capacity—thank you for doing such hard, important, and undervalued work.

Kerry Winfrey writes romantic comedies for adults and teens. She is the author of *Love and Other Alien Experiences*, *Things Jolie Needs to Do Before She Bites It*, and *Waiting for Tom Hanks*. When she's not writing, she's likely baking yet another pie or watching far too many romantic comedies. She lives with her husband, son, and dog in the middle of Ohio.

Connect Online
Twitter: @KerryAnn
Instagram: @KerryWinfrey
AYearOfRomComs.tumblr.com

Center Point Large Print
600 Brooks Road / PO Box 1
Thorndike, ME 04986-0001 USA

(207) 568-3717

US & Canada:
1 800 929-9108
www.centerpointlargeprint.com